unmistakable

USA TODAY BESTSELLING AUTHOR

KARA KENDRICK

Read UNEXPECTED - the Prequel for FREE.
https://karakendrick.com/unexpected/

BLURB

I've been crushing on my best friend's twin brother forever.

Parker Montgomery is the hottest playboy in Seaglass Beach. Hell, maybe the entire state of Florida. His panty-melting charm is the stuff of legends. And I've seen that dazzling smile shatter the resolve of more than one Southern belle. I doubt there's a woman alive who can resist him.

Including me.

He's never so much as glanced my way, so I've all but given up hope on anything ever happening between us.

Until a hurricane blows through, knocking out a good portion of my tiny duplex, and **suddenly I'm Parker's new roommate.** For the first time, things between us are heating up. The closer we get, the more I see beyond his pretty face and player ways.

But I'm not sure I should trust the biggest heartbreaker in town, even if he is hot as sin and deeper than his reputation suggests.

My feelings for Parker are unmistakable—but should I risk falling in love with a man who could become the biggest mistake of my life?

1

PARKER

"Parks? Did you order the extra tables and chairs for the inn's anniversary dinner this weekend?" My twin sister, Poppy, scrunches her nose up at me.

I smack my head. "Shit. I knew I forgot something."

"Parks!" Poppy scowls and I chuck her in the arm, grinning.

"Just kidding. Of course I did. I mean, I called Seaglass Celebrations and asked Liv to order them. But same diff."

"You're such a jerk." She smiles over her shoulder at me, though, so I know we're all good. It's how we roll, me and Poppy. She's the responsible one, with to-do lists and planners and shit, and I'm the screw up, always forgetting my lunch. I've grown up a bit since grade school—I do run my own contracting business—but no one around here gives me any credit.

It's fine. Keeps expectations low.

"We're two days out. Liv should be swinging by soon to drop the bar supplies. You can help her unload, right?"

Wiping the tiki bar down with a rag, I nod. "Sure. I'm

training the extra bartender tonight, but I should be able to get away for a while. Relax, Poppy—the party's going to be great. It always is."

She huffs out a breath, her honey-colored hair feathering with her exhale. "I hope so. It's such a big event for the inn. And now that Mom and Dad are gone . . ." Her voice trails off and a heaviness fills the salty air between us, the sounds of the ocean waves filling the silence.

I take a deep breath, swallowing hard over the lump in my throat. Our parents died in a car crash three years ago, but sometimes the loss still feels fresh, raw.

Like today.

Our mom loved throwing this party every year, honoring the history of the Seaglass Inn and partying with her friends and the community. We continue the tradition due to resident demand, but none of our hearts are in it like before.

"It's okay, Poppy. We'll make Mom and Dad proud." I reach over the bar, locking eyes with my sister, and squeeze her arm.

She swipes a tear away and I pretend not to see, ducking down to check the liquor supply.

Damn. I hate seeing anyone cry, but especially Poppy. I'm a good-time guy, preferring to swim in the shallow end of the pool. I leave the deep stuff to my older brothers, Roman and King. They're far more stoic than me and mentally equipped for this type of thing.

"Hey, I've gotta run over to the restaurant and snag another bottle of vodka before we open. You good?" I cut my eyes at her, willing her to say 'yes.'

She nods, so I jet, moving as fast as I can away from that convo.

Buzz, buzz.

I pull my cell out of my pocket, read the text.

Britney: Hey sexy. You working tonight?

Which one is Britney? The blonde from Tinder? Or is she the brunette waitress from Hot Wings?

Not that it matters either way. But I like to stay sharp.

Parker: Yes ma'am. You?

Nice punt. Maybe she'll drop me a hint.

Britney: Office is closed, silly. Watching the weather tonight.

That rules out the brunette. Britney must be the Tinder blonde.

Parker: Sounds exciting

Britney: LOL. You're so funny!

I'm not. This chick must really want to get laid.

Parker: Are you a weather junkie?

Britney: Haha, you're hilarious! No. But everyone's watching the storm in Puerto Rico. It looks like it'll turn into a cat 1. Might hit us.

Parker: Oh damn. Seriously?

Britney: Yeah. Might not come our way,
but I like to be ready

Parker: Smart

I click on my weather app and sure enough, rain's fore-casted for the next few days. Poppy's gonna flip out. We have a weather back-up plan, but the party's always way better outside, under the stars on the beach.

An alert pops up on my phone, a bright yellow banner beaming in the dusky light.

Oh hell. Tinder Britney is correct. We're under a hurricane watch, effective immediately.

My cell buzzes again, but this time it's a call from Poppy.

"Parker! You almost back? I have to run and catch up with the kitchen staff, give them a debrief on the menu."

"Um, Pops . . . have you checked the weather lately?" I try to keep my voice calm and even, knowing she's about to freak out.

"No, I've been slammed all day. Why? Don't tell me it's supposed to rain Friday night?" A slight note of hysteria ticks her voice up a notch.

"It's a little worse than that. In fact, we can definitely count on rain."

"Worse? Define worse."

"Seaglass Beach is under a hurricane watch."

"Noooooo!" Several loud thuds follow and I picture Poppy slamming her tiny fist down on the tiki bar.

"Calm down. We'll be fine. You know we hardly ever

get hit. The storm'll probably spin out to the Atlantic and fizzle."

"Or turn and hit us directly," Poppy groans. "Plus, people won't show up because—hurricane prep. Should we cancel now?"

"Nah. Too many perishable goods. Let's wait and see what the next twenty-four hours bring."

"I'm calling Liv right now."

A large drop of rain splashes onto my neck, then another, as thunder rolls in the distance.

Not a great sign, but I don't mention it as I disconnect from my near-hysterical sister and duck into the main building of the inn.

Buzz, buzz.

"Hey, King, what's up?" I answer, ambling through the airy lobby toward the supply closet, my flip-flops slapping against the shiny tile floor.

"Have you seen the forecast?" My oldest brother's deep voice rumbles down the line.

"Just saw it."

"I won't be able to come into town tonight. I need to tackle things at the ranch, in case the storm turns. We still having the party?"

Knots tighten in my stomach, a cold slither of dread creeping down my spine. If King's worried, we should all worry because he's as steady as they come.

"Party's on for now. I told Poppy we have too much food to waste. But if the forecast gets worse, we'll obviously cancel. You need help out at the ranch?" I ask, thumbing through my keys in search of the one for the supply closet.

"Roman's coming. You and Poppy stay and handle the inn and the party."

"Will do."

"And tell Poppy not to freak. We're gonna be fine."

King disconnects without saying goodbye and I shove my phone into my pocket, scrubbing a hand over the back of my neck. A hurricane is never a welcome development when you live at the beach, let alone on the weekend of our biggest event of the year.

My pocket buzzes again.

> Britney: Wanna come over and hang after work? Hunker down in case of hurricane?

> Parker: No can do. I have to help my family secure the inn. Stay safe!

> Britney: You too hun. Xoxo

"Hey, Parker."

A familiar voice trills behind me, and I jump, swiveling around and running straight into Liv, my sister's best friend and the event planner.

"Hey, Fizz, what's up?" I shoot her a grin and she rolls her eyes at me and her nickname, stemming from the time I gave her Pop Rocks at our house and she almost choked when they started popping and fizzing. She's never living that down.

She smooths her dark ponytail over her shoulder. "The winds are up, that's what. Is this party still on?" She bites down on her full bottom lip and I try hard not to stare. Under normal circumstances, Liv has the exact kind of mouth I'd love to kiss. But alas, these are not normal circumstances.

She's my sister's best friend—since the second grade—and we live in a small-ass beach town.

Forget it, Parker. Move the fuck on.

I run my fingers through my hair and nod. "As far as I know. Is it raining hard now?"

"What do you think?" Liv gestures at her soggy T-shirt, large patches of dampness blooming on her ample chest, and I half-grimace, half-chuckle.

"Yes?"

"Mm-hmm. Correct. And that might be an understatement. At this rate, I expect the Weather Channel to send a camera crew our way any second. I think there's zero percent chance this storm is missing us. At the very least, we're in for heavy winds and rain. Think Poppy would be open to postponing? I know it's a big night for y'all."

"Liv!" Poppy races into the lobby, slipping and sliding across the slick white tile, her arms waving frantically in the air. "Did you just dare to utter the word 'postpone'?"

Liv bites down harder on her lip and I bury my hand in my shorts to hide my growing stiffy. Luckily, neither of them is paying any attention to me anyway.

"I'm sorry, Poppy, but I think it's for the best. They're already calling for a warning and we may even get evacuated."

"Dammit!" Poppy stomps her flip-flop, folding her arms across her chest. "Now what?" She turns and looks at me, then Liv.

"Hurricane party?" I suggest. "We have a shit ton of food. And alcohol."

"Can you ever be serious?" Poppy shoots me an icy

glare, but Liv cuts her eyes at me, the corners of her lips tipping up into a smile.

"I side with Parker on this, babe. We need to get rid of this food somehow. Let's freeze what we can, donate as much of the perishables to the shelter as possible, then come up with an evacuation plan."

"Evacuate?" Poppy's voice rises another octave as all three of our cell phones shriek at the same time.

"Yeah, evacuate." I stare down at the words every beach resident dreads. "That storm is officially a hurricane and it's headed right at us."

2

LIV

I SPEND THE NEXT HOUR HELPING POPPY FIGURE OUT what to do with all the food, schlepping perishable items out to my van and loading them up for the shelter. Parker disappears to begin the inn's official evacuation protocol, which is a good thing. I need to focus on salvaging as many of the party supplies as possible, and honestly, I can't think straight when he's around.

It's not entirely his fault, but the man is distracting with a capital 'D.' Between his lopsided grin, that surfer hair swooping down over his deep blue eyes, and his easy, laidback charm, I can barely form a cohesive sentence around him, let alone an entire Plan B. Couple that with the fluttery feeling I get every time I'm close to him, and I'm a freaking disaster. Plus, I really don't need grief from Poppy about my stupid—and futile—crush on her twin brother.

Yeah, Parker Montgomery is my favorite lost cause and has been for oh, going on fifteen or so years. Give or take a few.

"Liv? What do you want to do with the flower arrange-ments?" Poppy stabs at the checklist on her clipboard and I rocket back down to Earth.

"I'll call the florist and see if I can reschedule the order. Maybe they'll take pity on us." I slide the last tray of shrimp cocktail into the back of the van. "The tables, chairs, and linens should be fine. Same with decorations. I'll cancel the band and the lighting crew."

"And the extra bartenders and waitstaff?" Poppy winds a strand of hair around her finger, her tell-tale anxiety sign.

"Yep. I've got you."

"Thanks a bunch, Liv. You're the best." She leans in and squeezes me in a tight hug and an all-too-familiar pang of guilt hits me in the gut.

I really should stop lusting after her brother.

Mentally adding that to my list of confessions, I slam my van door. "Alright, I'm off while there's a break in the weather."

"After you make the delivery you're coming back, right?" Her voice is tight, worry lines creasing her normally smooth brow.

"Yes, Pops, I'll come back. We can ride out the storm together. I'd rather not be alone in my tiny house anyway. Are you and Parker staying here, even if we get a formal evacuation notice?"

Poppy shrugs. "I don't know. I guess if it's a cat three or worse, we'll evacuate. We don't like leaving the inn unsu-pervised, though."

"I know," I say, patting her arm. "Call me if anything changes. If not, I'll plan on coming back."

"Will do."

A warm blast of wind whips around us, vortexes of sand swirling across the asphalt.

"I better go. See you soon." Shooting Poppy a quick wave, I hop into the driver's seat of the van, then inch my way down the dark drive, away from the Seaglass Inn.

Fiddling with the radio, I tune in to the local weather station.

"This storm does not look good for Seaglass Beach and surrounding areas. Anyone living within five miles of the beach should make plans to evacuate and seek shelter due to the strong likelihood of a dangerous storm surge."

Wonderful. That would be me. And Poppy and Parker and pretty much everyone else we know.

Seaglass Beach is a quaint town sitting on the northeast coast of Florida, bordering the Atlantic Ocean. Historically, we've been lucky in the hurricane department— mostly our sand dunes wash away and we're in a constant battle to renourish them. But for the most part, our little piece of paradise is sheltered by the Florida topography and a very fortunate dip in the coastline. Sure, we get lots of rain and wind, but usually the storms turn and head west or beeline to Orlando or spin out and wallop the poor people of coastal Georgia.

Eventually, though, our luck's bound to run out. For the town's sake, I can only hope now isn't the time and this storm stays weak.

Beep. Beep. Beep. "This is a message from the Emergency Broadcast System. Seaglass Beach is officially under a Hurricane Evacuation Order. Secure your residence and seek shelter as soon as possible. Damaging wind gusts in excess of ninety-five miles per hour have been reported and are expected to intensify overnight. Additionally, residents can expect dangerous storm surges. Stay tuned for more information."

I grip the steering wheel, sweat beading my brow as I crawl down A1A. Traffic had already picked up while I was at the inn, sun-soaked family vacations cut short due to the impending storm. Every pump is taken at the gas station and a line's beginning to form; my type-A-plus personality is paying off because I filled up this morning in anticipation of the party.

Ring, ring. Ring, ring. My cell phone trills and I fumble around in the passenger seat, sliding my thumb across the screen.

"Olivia? You okay? I just saw the news." My mother's worried voice fills my ears and a wave of homesickness rolls over me.

"I'm fine, Mom," I say, pinning the phone to my ear with my shoulder. "The weather isn't even that bad."

"Yet," my mom warns, her tone ominous. "Hurricanes. I hate them. I'm so glad I moved to Maryland. I wish you would move up here."

"I know, Mom." I sigh, my stomach twisting into a giant pretzel. *No way am I moving to Maryland with my mother and stepdad. No freaking way.* "But I have a good job down here."

"Pshaw, Olivia. You can plan parties anywhere."

"Events, Mom. I plan events."

"Parties, events, what's the difference? Anyway, Sam cleared out the back bedroom. You can catch the next flight out and be here by midnight."

The last place I want to sleep is the back bedroom of my mom and Sam's house, formally known as "the cats' playroom." Cats, as in plural. A vision of a cat curling up on my face, tickling my nose with his tail, while another swats at my feet with his sharp little claws pops into my head and I stifle a groan.

"The airport's probably closed, Mom. And if I somehow *did* manage to score a seat on a flight, it'd cost a million dollars."

"Another reason to get a better job in a bigger city. It's what I've been saying for years. And wouldn't be a huge inconvenience, since you're still single," my mom clucks.

How did this conversation move me from homesick to annoyed in less than five minutes? That's gotta be a freaking record.

"Thank you for the career advice. Listen, I have to go. I'm packing my bags and spending the next day or two with the Montgomerys."

"Of course you are," my mom says, sounding a touch irritated. "They've always been your home away from home. Tell Poppy and everyone to stay safe. Charge your cell and keep me posted, young lady!"

"Will do, Mom. Love you." I disconnect and toss the phone down onto the seat. I'm not sure why I expected my relationship with my mom to get better over time, but I kind of did.

Wrong.

Dead fucking wrong.

Ever since she started dating Sam, things between us are more strained than ever. It doesn't help that my brother is the golden child—a successful lawyer, no less—and lives three miles away from Mommy. The perpetual kiss-ass, he picked up and moved law firms to be closer to her.

#annoying.

But it's fine. My mom's correct—I have the Montgomerys, and that's always been enough for me.

Well, almost enough.

I'd be lying if I said I don't fantasize about actually *being a Montgomery*, if you know what I mean.

Mrs. Parker Montgomery. Then I'd be Poppy's sister for real *and* I wouldn't have to hear my mom harp about me being single.

Honestly, all my life goals unlocked.

But, le sigh—it'll never happen.

Parker's made that pretty freaking clear over the last decade or so, as he works his way through every single eligible female in the county.

Except me.

Never me.

It's like I'd been earmarked for the friendzone from day one.

Intellectually, I get it—he's just not into me.

But tell that to my stupid, hopeful heart. Every time he shoots me his dazzling smile, or touches my arm, my pulse races a little faster and that tiny sprout of hope pops back up.

I'm gonna end up dying alone because no one can compare to Parker freaking Montgomery.

I ease the van into the parking lot of the homeless shelter and my cell buzzes again. Mentally preparing a comeback for my mother, I lean over and snag the phone.

> Parker: We have plenty of wine and snacks. Bring batteries if you have them. See you back at the inn.

Cue the stupid heart pounding.

Liv: I'll bring what I have. Need anything else?

Parker: Don't forget your cell phone charger.

Liv: I have a portable charger I can bring too

Parker: Good thinking. Be careful, winds are picking up

Liv: I will be

Parker: See you soon

I impulse-text **XOXOXO**, then delete it immediately. *Get a grip, Liv. It's a hurricane, not the end of the world. Don't blow your cover now.*

Ignoring his text, I unlock the van and begin unloading.

3

———

PARKER

I stare down at the three whirling dots for one minute, two. Then they disappear. Pop back up, then disappear again. But no new text from Liv.

I hope she's okay.

It's unlike her to not finish a text.

Maybe she's busy. And also, why do you care? You can't go there anyway. Besides, she's practically your sister, you perv.

But she's not, I reason, scrolling mindlessly through my contacts.

Ashlee, Britney, Cameron, Kayla, Mary Beth, Sylvie. All perfectly nice, willing, beautiful females.

And I've had fun with each of them.

Sure, none of them lasted long—two, three weeks, max —but I sometimes still chat, grab drinks, maybe dinner with each of them.

But nothing long-term. Ever.

Because I'm not that kind of guy.

I'm Mr. Right Now, not Mr. Right. Life is short and my attention span's shorter.

Except when it comes to Liv.

"Parker?"

I jump, moving so fast I probably have whiplash.

"Yeah? What's up?" I run a hand through my hair. Cool, nonchalant. Not like a guy comparing his hook-up list to his twin's best friend and coming up all kinds of short.

"How many guests do we have left?" Poppy leans over the desk, tapping at the keyboard and pulling up the reservation system.

"Only three families. I spoke with the Crabtrees in Room 104. They're checking out in the morning. Same with the Butlers and the Johnsons. Cancellation emails went out to anyone with a reservation next week. We need to field calls, but everyone's pretty much clearing out."

Poppy sighs. "I can't believe this. Having to cancel and reschedule the anniversary party is a huge pain in the ass. Not to mention all the revenue we're losing on the hotel."

"We'll recover, Pops. Don't worry about it."

"Don't worry about it? How can I not? This is a huge financial hit, Parker, and it's high season. But you never take anything seriously." She levels her most serious gaze at me, squaring her shoulders.

"Not true."

Cocking her head, she raises one brow high and I hold my hands up in surrender.

"Fine. Kind of true. Maybe. But I'm still certain everything will work out."

"I hope you're right, baby brother."

I throw my arm around her neck, rubbing her hair with my knuckle.

"You know I am. And you're older by two minutes. Hardly constitutes baby status."

She giggles, relaxing in my grip, and I'm happy to see sunny Poppy re-emerge.

She quickly turns her attention back to the evacuation tasks though. "Have you set the pool filters to automatic? Secured the gates? What about the hurricane shutters?"

"Yes, yes, and we can handle the shutters in the morning when Roman comes back. It's too much for the two of us, especially in the dark."

"Good point. What about your job sites? Don't you need to take care of those?"

"Luckily, we only have one job at the moment—the Bennett house—and I already texted Smith. He's handling it, so I can focus here."

"Is he staying?"

"No, he's heading to Atlanta to see Elise."

Poppy's face breaks into a wide smile and she sighs, a dreamy look in her eyes. "Ah, true love. They're so cute together. You think he's going to marry her?"

"Full stop there, Pops. They've only been dating a few months. And she just finalized her divorce. I think you can hold off on the wedding plans for a while."

"Did somebody say wedding?"

Heat floods my body and mingles with relief at the sound of the familiar voice, knowing Liv's safe. But I keep my eyes glued to the computer screen, pretending I don't notice her.

As if.

Every part of me notices her. Her flawless olive skin, the dark hair curling in tendrils around her heart-shaped face, her cute button nose.

"We were talking about Smith and Elise. And how I think they should get married," Poppy says.

"They are super cute together. If Smith pops the question, let me know. I love planning weddings."

My chest constricts and now I'm desperate to change the subject. "Everything okay at your house?" I finally take my eyes off the computer screen, forcing myself to act normal.

"Seems to be. I packed my bag, then booked it outta there. It looked like Mr. Waycroft evacuated already."

"Most likely. Your neighbor's eighty years old, Liv," Poppy says.

"True. But he's a spry eighty."

"His family probably came and scooped him. It's not safe for him to be home alone in a storm."

"Yeah. Plus, he has a cat," Liv says. "Do you two need any more help?"

"No, I think we're good for now. Let's go to the kitchen and get something to eat. Then we should decide where we're going to bunk for the night." Poppy links arms with Liv, then grabs me by the forearm. "You too. We need to stick together—the power could go out any second."

As if on cue, the wind howls, rattling the windows, and Poppy scrunches up her nose.

"I do not like the sound of that," she says, peering nervously out at the dark.

"We'll be fine, Poppy," I say, patting her arm. "We should find the flashlights, though. Just in case."

The three of us cut through the empty lobby, making our way over to the dining room. Without guests milling about, the inn is eerily quiet, as if the place is deserted. Even though no one's dining, all the tables are set for dinner service, the overhead lighting bright.

"It's so weird, being in here without guests," Poppy

whispers. She's practically tiptoeing over the carpet to the kitchen doors.

"It's a little strange," Liv says, matching Poppy's whisper. They clutch each other's arms and I can't help myself, reaching my hand out and grabbing at both of them.

"Ahhh!" Poppy screams. Liv jumps about a foot into the air, then they both swivel around, pounding my chest and arms.

"Sorry, sorry," I say, throwing my arms up for protection. "It was just too easy, ladies."

"You owe us, Parker." Poppy glares at me and I chuckle.

"Fine. I'll make you both a drink. Come on—let's get everything we need now. If the storm gets bad, I don't want to be fumbling around in the dark."

I fill up a cooler with beverages while Poppy and Liv concentrate on the food situation, packing sandwiches, chips, desserts, and anything else they can cobble together.

"Don't forget snacks," I call out across the stainless steel counter.

"We'd never, Parks," Poppy says, winking. "We have pretzels, nuts, our signature snack mix, cookies, and some fruit. Will that hold you over, you think?"

I bite my lower lip, thinking. "Probably. Hopefully we'll be able to make it down here for breakfast."

"Good point," Liv chimes in, throwing bagels into the bag. "Just in case."

"A girl after my own heart," I say, teasing, as her face flushes a soft pink.

"Ahem." Poppy clears her throat, the sound echoing loudly in the cavernous kitchen, breaking our banter. "I think we should go to Villa Three. It's a two-bedroom with a full kitchen. And it's the farthest from the beach."

"Agreed," I say, swallowing hard, my throat now dry as the reality of the situation sets in. "That'll give us the most space."

I duck back into the fridge, pretending to survey the remaining contents, and give myself a chance to chill out.

It's no big deal. You've spent the night with plenty of women.

But none of them were Liv.

And having Poppy right there to scrutinize my every move is less than ideal. Maybe I should sleep somewhere else?

"Do y'all want me to stay here in the lobby, hold down the fort?" I ask, backing out of the fridge.

"What? No!" Poppy cries. "What if the lights go out? Or we need you? I don't want you to be here in the main building."

"Definitely not," Liv says, shaking her head.

"Okay. Bad idea. Let's go then, before the weather gets worse."

It's gonna be a long night.

I can only hope the storm passes quickly. Then everything can go back to normal.

4

—————

LIV

Under typical circumstances, spending the night with Poppy and Parker would be weird.

But we're about to get slammed by a hurricane, so nothing about this situation is typical.

Besides, I'll bunk with Poppy, and Parker can have his own room.

It's fine. Everything's fine.

"Oh shoot," Poppy murmurs as we stand outside the door of Villa Three. Lights gleam from the edges of the window and my stomach sinks. "I forgot the Butlers upgraded. We'll have to go over to Villa Two."

"The one bedroom?" Parker asks, shoving a hand in his pocket.

"Uh-huh. Unfortunately. Sorry, Parks."

He shrugs, the fabric of his polo stretching across his broad shoulders. "No biggie. The couch folds out."

"Thanks for taking one for the team," Poppy says, "You're the real MVP."

"If the storm gets worse, maybe y'all should head out to the ranch. I can hold things down here." Parker's face tenses, his words punctuated by a low rumble of thunder. Rain begins to splatter around us and we start running toward Villa Two, trying to dodge puddles along the way.

"I can't leave you here alone," Poppy cries, her voice getting swallowed up by the whipping wind. Palm trees bend and I wonder how high these winds will actually get.

"I'm not leaving either," I shout. "Unless we all go."

"Let's get in, dry off, and watch the weather," Parker suggests as Poppy finds the master key, unlocking the door.

We all tumble into the villa, and Poppy flicks on the lights. Instantly, the room glows and calm washes over me. We'll be safe here, at least for the night.

Shutting and locking the door behind us, Parker crosses to the fridge and begins unloading the cooler. "I promised you ladies a drink. What'll it be?"

"A vodka soda," Poppy chirps from the bathroom. "It's been a day."

"Wine," I say, shifting from foot to foot.

Why am I so nervous all of a sudden?

"White, right?" Parker asks, pulling a bottle of chardonnay from his stash.

"Yes."

Of course he knows what you like, Liv. He's a bartender, for goodness sake. Stop reading things into the situation.

My stupid, hopeful heart has a bad habit of doing that.

"Here." Poppy reappears, shoving a fluffy white towel into my hand, and I gratefully take it. "I'm going to change out of my wet clothes."

"Good idea," I say, kicking off my soggy sneakers.

"Actually, do you mind if I take a quick shower?" Poppy swipes at the water droplets beading her arms.

"Not at all. Go." I wave her off and she hurries back to the bathroom, leaving me and Parker alone.

I lean against the counter, suddenly lightheaded. My mind's blank and my mouth's so dry, it's like I swallowed cotton balls.

Buzz, buzz.

Parker's cell vibrates loudly, lighting up his pocket. My eyes travel down to the glowing rectangle, but he makes no move to answer it. Eventually, it stops ringing.

Buzz, buzz.

His shorts pulsate again and I press against the counter, trying to seem calmer and cooler than I feel.

Buzz, buzz.

Another call.

The back of Parker's neck flushes deep red, but he still doesn't reach for his phone.

"Aren't you going to answer that?" I ask, folding my arms over my chest.

"No. It's probably nothing." He waves his hand through the air, brushing the calls off.

"Nothing? That's three calls in a row. What if it's your brothers out at the ranch? What if they need help?"

"Fine. I'll check." He stops making drinks, whipping his cell out of his pocket and scrolling.

I watch his face, curiosity gnawing at my insides.

"Nope. Nothing important." He shoves his phone back into his pocket, locks his deep blue eyes on mine.

"Huh. Usually if someone calls me three times in a row it's an emergency." I press my lips together, my tone neutral.

"Trust me—it's not."

"Your latest conquest?" I quip, a sharp stab of jealousy piercing my chest.

A flash of something—Remorse? Guilt?—crosses his face, and I instantly regret my words. He turns his back on me, going back to making drinks, and my face flames.

Why couldn't I just keep my stupid mouth shut for once?

"Sorry—none of my business." I chew at the corner of my lip to keep from saying anything else stupid, wishing I could eat my words, a real-life Ms. Pac Man.

He hands me a glass of wine with one ice cube, just how I like it, and I take a sip, grateful for the distraction. Parker's uncharacteristically quiet and a long silence stretches between us, the rain thudding loudly against the glass. He swallows, his Adam's apple bobbing in his neck, and I vaguely wonder if bunking with Sam's three cats would have been a better option.

"You have those drink yet, Parks? I'm parched." Poppy flounces out of the bathroom in her pajamas, oblivious to whatever weirdness just transpired between me and her brother.

"One sec." Parker breaks his gaze, turning his back to me, and I slink off to the bathroom to take my shower.

WHY DID I SAY THAT? *STUPID, STUPID, STUPID.* I HAVE NO claim on Parker and he can be as big of a man whore as he wants to be.

But honestly, every time I see him flirt with another hot blonde, a little piece of me dies inside.

Geesh, my mother is right. I should move to Maryland. Far, far away from Parker and his flirtcapades. Because I'm not sure how much longer my heart can handle this special brand of torture.

Shutting off the water, I step out of the shower and towel off.

I'm going to go out there and pretend everything is fine. The old fake-it-till-you-make-it approach. Besides, I've been doing this duck and weave with Parker forever. I can certainly handle a few nights under the same roof.

Right?

I throw on my very unsexy *Friends* T-shirt and a pair of grey sleep shorts, take a deep breath, and saunter out of the bedroom.

"Liv! Hurricane Clementine's heading right at us!" Poppy shrieks.

"No!"

"Yep." Parker nods, pressing a fresh glass of chilled wine into my hand. Our fingers brush and my breath catches in my throat.

"Thank you," I murmur and he nods.

All is forgiven. Another thing I love about Parker—he never holds a grudge.

I suppose that's what makes him a great booty call.

Stop.

I push that thought out of my mind as Poppy settles on the sofa, legs crossed beneath her, her wide eyes fixed on the television.

"Hurricane Clementine has turned north, with wind gusts up to eighty miles per hour. The storm is now officially a Category One and is expected to make landfall north of Daytona Beach mid-day tomorrow." A local meteorologist points at the map behind him, highlighting the stretch of coastline in question.

"Ohmygosh," Poppy says. "Not good."

"Glad we cancelled the party." Parker perches on the couch armrest—notably, as far away from me as he can get in this small space.

"Residents of Daytona are being asked to evacuate, as well as surrounding areas, including Palm Coast, Crescent Beach, Vilano Beach, Seaglass Beach, and St. Augustine Beach. Local shelters are open—don't delay." The meteorologist delivers the news none of us want to hear.

"Now what?" Poppy twirls a damp strand of hair around her finger, round and round.

"We stay the course for tonight," Parker says, taking a sip of his drink. "And tomorrow we reassess. Hopefully it won't be raining too hard because we have to get the shutters up ASAP."

Poppy nods. "After that do we evacuate out to the ranch?"

The wind howls, the roof creaking from the blast of air, and Poppy grabs for Parker's hand.

"It'll be fine. Let's wait until the morning to make any more decisions." Parker eases the remote away from Poppy. "Until then, let's take our minds off this." He lowers the volume on the television until the meteorologist is barely audible.

"How? What are you thinking?" I ask, tucking my leg up under me.

"Throwback Thursday." Parker grins, a devilish glint in his eyes.

"Huh?" Poppy raises her eyebrows. "What are you talking about?"

"Taking it way back, all the way to middle school. Truth or Dare," Parker says, looking first at Poppy, then at me. "Liv, you go first."

5

———

PARKER

Liv blushes fuchsia. "You want to play Truth or Dare? Like we did in middle school?"

"I didn't bring board games. And we need to conserve our cell phone batteries."

"Oh-kay," Liv stammers, the blush creeping up the side of her neck. "Truth, I guess."

"You never have been one for dares," I say, teasing, and she smacks my arm.

"What? It's true."

"So? I don't like living on the edge. Is that such a bad thing?"

"No, it's fine. Just stating facts," I say, sipping my drink. "We'll go clockwise. That means Poppy asks you a question."

Poppy rests her head on the couch cushion, tipping her eyes up to the ceiling. "Let's see . . . not much I don't know about Olivia here. How 'bout—" She pauses, passing her glass from one hand to the other. "Biggest celeb crush?"

"Softball question, Poppy," I say, chiding her.

"We can ease in, Parks."

"Fine. Biggest celeb crush, Liv. Go."

Liv twists her mouth up, thinking. "I don't know. Mark Wahlberg?"

"Oh, good one!" Poppy rubs her hands together. "You're right—he's hot."

"Really? You think?" I narrow my eyes at the girls.

"Uh, yeah, Parks. We think. He has an eight-pack. Super hot." Poppy fans herself and Liv giggles.

So far, I'm not loving this game.

"Your turn, Parker. Truth or dare?" Poppy asks.

Without hesitating I answer. "Dare."

"Why am I not surprised?" Liv rolls her eyes as I set my glass down on the table.

"C'mon, hit me. Give me the toughest dare you can think of."

Liv groans. "I don't know, Parker."

"You can think of something, Fizz."

"Fine." She taps her finger on the side of her cheek, like she did back in school when she concentrated hard during a test. "Do your best impression of me."

Chuckling, I stand up and pretend to smooth my hair down over my shoulder, then clear my throat to hit a higher pitch and talk into my pinky finger. "Yes, I can absolutely deliver one thousand tulips from the Netherlands to you by tomorrow. Are they out of season? Definitely! But I'll get them to you. And set them up myself. You need them by eight a.m.? That's a toughie, but I got you!"

Poppy claps her hand over her mouth, giggling hysterically, and Liv shakes her head, although the corners of her mouth tip up in a half-smile.

Emboldened, I continue: "I'm getting another call. Talk

later." I hold out my palm, pretending to click over on my imaginary cell. "Oh hey, Poppy! Yeah, I'd love to get drinks, but I'm swamped. Fine, one glass of wine at Seaglass Sips. See you in thirty."

I disconnect my fake phone, then act like it buzzes with a text message. Squinting at my hand, I narrow my eyes. "No. Too short." Swipe left. "Too tall." Swipe left. "Definitely no." Swipe left. "I don't date professional athletes." Swipe left. "Too far away." Swipe left. "Too close to home." Swipe left.

Liv throws a pillow at me, hitting me square in the chest. "Not true, Parker. I'm not *that* picky. And I would never promise one thousand tulips out of season."

Poppy's laughing so hard, tears roll down her cheeks. "Liv—you have to admit, that was a spot-on impression." She doubles over on the couch, clutching her stomach.

"No, it wasn't." Liv frowns. "Sometimes I say 'yes' to dates."

"Like when?" Poppy swipes a tear from her face. "I can't remember the last time you had a date."

"Rude." Liv crosses her arms over her chest. "I've been busy with my career, that's all."

"It's okay, we still love you." Poppy encircles Liv in a hug, and a sharp pang shoots through my chest. I wish I could reach out and hug Liv, but that would never fly. Especially with my sister.

"My turn!" Poppy claps her hands, moving the spotlight to her. "And I'm going Truth, too."

"Of course you are," I mutter, wondering what the hell I can ask her that I don't already know. Even though we're almost thirty years old, Poppy and I are still stupid-close.

"Poppy—love or money. You can marry your true love or win five million dollars. What'll it be?"

"No contest. Love. Hands down," Poppy answers, her voice bold and confident.

"Not even a little hesitation? Five mill is a lot of coin," I say, pressing.

"Nope. None. Because if I'm alone, what am I going to do with all that money anyway?"

"Spend it on your favorite twin?" I tease.

Poppy laughs. "Sure. But no—I'm still going with love."

"Really?" I ask, stroking my chin.

"Wouldn't you pick love, Parks?" Poppy asks, staring at me.

I shrug. "I dunno. I could do a lot with five million dollars."

"Do you even want to get married, Parker?" Liv asks and I freeze as both of them eye me.

"Um—" I stall. "Maybe? I guess? I want to eventually, I suppose."

"But then you'd be committed to one woman. Not really your style, right?" Poppy playfully hits my bicep and my gut clenches. *How had a fun little game of Truth or Dare turned into 'Grill Parker' night?*

"Right," I say, sucking in a breath. "You know me. Just here for the good times. Liv, your turn." I change the subject as quickly as I possibly can, wiping my sweaty palms on my shorts.

"Truth," Liv says and I groan.

"Come on—are y'all gonna pick Truth all night?"

"Yes." Liv nods her head.

"Probably," Poppy agrees.

"Y'all are boring." Rattling the ice in my glass, I take a long sip of my drink.

"Sorry we're not all former frat boys," Liv teases.

"Anyway, back to the game." Poppy turns her wide eyes on Liv. "Biggest regret."

"Wow, Pops—that's a real downer of a question." I scrub a hand over the back of my neck, secretly glad I don't have to answer as I stare into the grass-green eyes of mine.

Liv blinks, dropping her gaze to her hands. A clap of thunder shakes the windows, and Poppy hugs her knees to her chest. For a moment, we sit in silence while the storm rages outside, each lost in our own thoughts.

Finally, Liv lifts her head, making direct eye contact with me. "I don't have a ton of regrets." Her voice is barely above a whisper. "But if I had to pick one, I guess it would be holding back."

"What do you mean?" Poppy asks, her brows squished together. "Like, with a person? In your job? With your mom?"

Liv toys with a stray piece of thread dangling from her T-shirt, two bright spots of pink staining her cheeks. "In my personal life."

"Who? Who are you holding back from?" Poppy leans in close, ready for the gossip, but Liv sits back, her lips a tight line.

"That's all I'm saying."

"What?" Poppy's hands fly into the air. "Liv! You're holding out on me, I can feel it."

"Real intuitive, Poppy. She literally just told you that." I knock my sister's bare foot with my flip-flop.

"This game is terrible. I'm going to bed." Poppy stands and stretches, yawning. "You two can play without me."

Poppy retreats to the bedroom, leaving me and Liv alone together. I stretch my legs out, relaxing my upper body against the edge of the couch. My muscles twitch, and a flush of warmth surges through me. Deep down, I know I should bail too, but the opportunity to be this close to Liv—alone—isn't something I can easily pass up.

"I guess it's my turn to ask you a question then." Liv smooths her shirt down. "Truth or dare?"

"Truth," I say, without even thinking.

Shit. Why did I say that?

The last thing I need is to show my hand right now. Maybe she'll go easy on me.

Boom! Another loud clap of thunder, and Liv jumps, startled. The lights flicker off and on for a second, before returning to full brightness.

"Shit, I thought we were going to lose power there for a second." I rake a hand through my hair, my mouth dry.

Sitting with Liv in the dark would be too much.

Liv exhales. "Me too. And Truth, really? I thought that was 'boring'?"

She air quotes the word, and my own lecture bites me in the ass.

"Mixing it up a bit."

She leans back. "Okay, Parker—here's my question: why are you still single? Surely after dating everyone in Seaglass Beach, someone would stick. What gives?"

I screw my mouth up, racking my brain as to what to say. How can I tell her no one stacks up to her, but I'm not allowed to go there?

Shrugging my shoulders, I take a sip of vodka, crunch the ice. "Nah. Not yet. It's going to take someone really special to get me to commit."

"What are you looking for? Because you've dated every female I know, besides me and Poppy."

I swallow hard over the Texas-sized lump in my throat, casting my eyes down to the shiny white tile floor. "I don't know," I lie.

"Well, that's your problem then," Liv says, dusting her hands together, like she's solved the problem of world peace. "You need a checklist. Then you'll know when you find her."

"Easy as that, huh?" I tip my head to the side, bemused.

"Yes, I think so."

"Do you have a list? Because last time I checked, you're still single as well."

"I'm good at giving advice, not taking it."

"Ah, I see."

We lock eyes and I hold her gaze for one beat, two, until she finally looks away.

"It's getting late. I should go to bed. Big day tomorrow." She makes a show of stretching and yawning and I can't help staring at her. Her skin, her mouth, those perfect tits.

She really is beautiful.

FML.

"Right. Same. Me too."

"Night, Parker."

"Night, Fizz."

I watch her saunter to the bedroom, only breathing once the door closes behind her.

Hurricane Clementine better pass real quick because

I'm not sure how long I can withstand being in close quarters with Liv.

Even worse, I can't even take care of business on a fucking fold-out couch.

6

————

LIV

Lying in bed next to a snoring Poppy, I obsess over all the things I said tonight—and the things I left unsaid.

Why did I mention holding back out there? Now Poppy's going to hound me on specifics, and what am I going to say? Oh, I'm holding back from making a move on your twin brother—and have been for the last decade?

I can never admit that to her, even though she's my bestie.

Even thinking about Parker in that way feels like a colossal betrayal.

But how can I not? He's the hottest man in Seaglass Beach. Of course I like him.

Everyone likes him.

From the clerk at Town Hall to the entire local Delta Delta Delta sorority, Parker charms every female he meets. When he turns his dazzling, lopsided grin on you, it's all you can do to keep your clothes on.

Honestly, I've seen more than one coed offer her bikini top (or bottom) to him at the tiki bar, along with her digits.

He's beyond gorgeous and funny and sweet—the entire package. Any girl would be lucky to have him.

And you have absolutely no chance with him. Ever. He's made that abundantly clear over the years, so I should take his impression of me to heart and move the fuck on with someone else.

My chest physically aches at the thought.

But I think it might be the only way to bury my Parker obsession once and for all.

Get out there and date.

Someone. Anyone.

It's not like I haven't dated, not exactly. A year or so ago, I connected with a realtor up in St. Simon's and we went on a few (lackluster) dates. But that's as far as it went. Nothing serious.

And as my mother is so fond of reminding me, I'm not getting any younger. How long am I going to live next door to Mr. Waycroft and his cat, sharing a wall so thin I can actually hear the can opener sawing open the Nine Lives every night at six p.m.?

Gawd, my life is pathetic.

Definitely time to make some changes, starting with dating. Surely there are a few eligible men left in Seaglass Beach unrelated to Poppy.

Or a Capelli. I can't date any of them, either, on account of the feud between the Montgomerys and Capellis.

Not that I would anyway. Jagger's a swaggering asshole, and his brothers, Cash and Damon, aren't much better.

Maybe I should get back on the dating app. Come up with a checklist, like I suggested to Parker, and put myself back out there.

All of this sounds fine theoretically, in my head, but I'm not sure I can execute in real life.

Parker stole my heart the second we met. Moving on means leaving a piece of me behind.

Worse, it feels final.

I scrunch my eyes shut tight against the twin terrors of being single forever or falling out of love with Parker Montgomery as the winds of Hurricane Clementine pick up speed outside our villa.

"RISE AND SHINE, SLEEPYHEAD." POPPY SHAKES MY shoulder, rousing me from a dreamless sleep.

"What time is it?" I ask, rolling over and glancing out the window. The sky's a dark slate color, but at least it's not raining.

"Eight. Would you mind helping us with the shutters? Parker called our maintenance crew in as well, but we could use as many hands as we can get."

"Give me five minutes."

I hop out of bed and hurry to get ready, brushing my teeth and scraping my hair back into a ponytail, then throw on workout clothes and sneakers.

"Poppy, you want coffee?" I shout in the direction of the bathroom.

"Yes, please!"

I amble out of the bedroom, a tiny stab of disappointment hitting me in the chest. Parker's already gone, the couch folded back up and the pillows fluffed.

Of course he snuck out early. It's his M.O.

Shoving away that thought, I pour myself and Poppy two steaming mugs of coffee—presumably brewed by Parker—and scroll through my weather alerts while I wait.

Hurricane Clementine remains a Category One, but picks up speed

I click into the alert, gleaning the important details. Gusts up to eighty-five miles per hour, strong likelihood of a storm surge, hitting Seaglass Beach later today.

"Poppy, you better hurry up. The weather reports have Clementine landing here today."

"What? I thought tomorrow."

"Not anymore. Clementine made landfall sooner than expected and she's still picking up speed. Come on . . ."

Abandoning coffee, Poppy dashes out of the bathroom, shrugging into her teal raincoat.

"Don't you have a raincoat?" she asks, eyeing my outfit.

"It's not raining."

"Yet. It may start and we have a lot of work to do."

"Fine." I jog back to the bedroom and grab my raincoat, even though it's hot and not that cute.

"Okay, let's go."

Poppy locks the door behind us and we hustle over to the main building of the inn, a strong wind whipping our faces.

"And this is before the storm hits." Poppy shouts to be heard over the sharp gust.

Cold dread nestles in the pit of my stomach. Even though I've lived in Florida most of my life, hurricanes still freak me out. They're messy, unpredictable.

"There's the crew." Poppy gestures at the team of workers lining the front of the inn. They're lifting dark grey hurricane shutters up and securing them over each window. I spot Parker, his long arms outstretched as he wields a cordless power drill. His biceps flex, corded muscle straining the cotton of his T-shirt, and my stomach swoops.

I do love a man brandishing tools. There's something so sexy, so primal about it.

A hot flush creeps up my neck and I avoid looking at Poppy, certain my cheeks are hot pink.

"Hey ladies." Parker waves at us from his perch on the ladder and I wave back, glad he's too far away to see my blush.

"Parks, what do you want us to do?" Poppy shouts.

"Make sure all the guests checked out. Then supervise. We need every window boarded, sooner rather than later."

"What? I'm not even getting to use any power tools?" I ask, disappointment leaking into my voice.

Parker cocks an eyebrow at me. "Really, Fizz? You want to use tools?"

I nod. "Sure. I can do it. And y'all need help."

He mulls this over for a second. "Fine. You can help me."

"I don't need a chaperone, Parker. I know how to use a drill."

"You gonna keep arguing or are you gonna help?" He stares down at me over his broad shoulder.

I give a huge, showy huff, but mutter, "Help."

"Okay, then." Parker finishes securing the shutter, then climbs down the ladder. "Here's some screws—" He hands me a rectangular box of screws and I shove them into my coat pocket. "Enrique, me and Liv will take the rest of these—" he gestures to the row of lobby windows—"You and Skip take the back."

Enrique shoots Parker a thumbs up, then they grab as many shutters as they can carry and head around the building.

"Have you ever hung hurricane shutters before, Fizz?"

"I rent a duplex, Parker. No, I haven't."

"The hardest part is balancing on the ladder. You can screw the bottoms first, then I'll go up the ladder and drill the tops. We should be able to knock these out in thirty minutes working together."

I nod, trying hard to focus on the task at hand, not the dark flecks of navy in his aquamarine eyes or the way his shirt clings to his muscular chest.

"Ready?"

Parker hands me the drill and holds the shutter in place while I notch the screw, then drill the wood into place.

"Nice work, Fizz. C'mon, do this side." I move to the spot where Parker's standing, sliding in front of him. He lifts his arms in a wide V, holding the shutter flush against the building, his arms caging my head. He's so close I feel his warm breath on my ear, smell the fresh scent of his bodywash rolling off his skin. If I shimmy my rear back a fraction of an inch, I'll rub against his toned torso.

Instead, I drill the shutter and add impure thoughts to my growing list of confessions.

"Perfect." Parker reaches down, grabbing the drill from me, then swings easily up onto the ladder. "Hold the right side as much as you can, okay?"

I watch as he scales the building, drilling first the left, then the right side of the shutter in half the time it took me to finish only one side. Then he climbs down, grabs the next shutter, and we repeat. We work for the next thirty minutes, the wind blowing sand in from the beach, pelting us. I'm grateful that at least it's not rain, although that would probably be less painful. I try to focus on keeping the ladder still and steady for Parker, even if I can't help myself from staring at his very fine ass.

Finally, we secure the last lobby shutter and Parker climbs down the ladder. "Nice job, Fizz. You can be my assistant anytime."

"Only assistant?" I tease, smacking his strong forearm.

"That's a promotion, babe. I don't even let most people assist." He winks at me and my heart flip-flops in my chest.

Why does he always have to be so damn cute? If he were more of an asshole, this whole moving-on thing would be a lot easier.

"You two done here?" Poppy sneaks up behind us, startling me.

I flush, guilty, even though she can't possibly know what I'm thinking.

"Yeah. What about you? Everyone cleared out?"

Poppy nods. "Yes, all gone."

"I think you girls should head out to the ranch. It'll be safer there, with Roman and King." Parker's brow furrows as Poppy bristles next to me.

"No way am I leaving you here alone." Poppy folds her arm across her chest, digging in.

"Can't we all go?" I ask, eyeing the angry sea behind us. The surf's already higher than I've ever seen it, licking at the strip of sand separating the hotel from the ocean. If there's a storm surge, power will definitely go out and potable water might become an issue.

Parker runs a hand through his hair, staring out at the

Atlantic. "I suppose we could. Since everyone's gone. You two head out now, I'll follow later."

"No. No way," Poppy says, shaking her head. "I know you, Parker Collin Montgomery. You'll pretend you're coming and then try to be a hero and stay back. I'm leaving when you do."

Large drops of rain start to fall, and my stomach knots even tighter. "What else do we need to do before we can get out of here?" I ask.

"Finish setting up the sandbags. Y'all can't help with that—they're too heavy. Me and the crew will do it. Poppy, you and Liv pull in any remaining outdoor furniture and store it. And check the back-up generator, make sure it's on."

"Got it. And Parks?"

"Yeah?"

Poppy pulls her hood up, securing it tighter around her face. "Hurry up."

TWO HOURS LATER, WE'RE SAFE AND SOUND IN THE COZY kitchen of the Montgomery ranch. All rustic wood and wrought iron, the family ranch is the exact opposite of the white tile and teak vibe of the Seaglass Inn.

Even though the ranch is only thirty minutes away from town, out here we're nestled deep in the old Florida countryside. Wind and rain swirl outside, but we're far from the storm surge evacuation zone, and for the first time since hearing about Hurricane Clementine, my muscles relax.

The rest of the Montgomerys aren't so chill, though. King sits at the head of the table, a full bottle of whiskey in front of him. Roman's pacing the kitchen, Parker's staring at the live footage of the hotel, and Poppy's humming nervously.

King stands, returning to the table with five shot glasses. He lines them up in a neat row, pouring amber liquid into each one, and passes them around.

"Thanks," I murmur, accepting the shot from Poppy.

The siblings raise their glasses, a varied level of worry etching each of their faces. King seems the most concerned, followed by Roman, then Parker, then Poppy.

At the moment, I'm happy I don't own the Seaglass Inn.

Hell, I don't even own a goldfish.

"Bottoms up." King tips his glass, and we all follow suit, taking the shot.

The liquid burns my throat going down, and a rush of heat spreads through my chest and belly. I'm not much of a liquor drinker, so I'm sure I'll be feeling this in a few minutes.

The mood is somber as torrents of rain pelt the cabin. Poppy clears her throat, plastering a smile on her face.

"Anybody have hot gossip?" She glances from King to Roman to Parker. King remains stoic, Roman shakes his head 'no,' and Parker scrolls through his phone.

"No? Nothing?" Poppy thrums the table with her fingers, tapping in tune with the rain.

"The Ellis – Scarborough wedding got called off," I offer, trying to help ease the tension.

"Wow, I'm surprised. I thought Mary-Kate was crazy about Pete," Poppy says.

"I thought so too. Her parents paid all these non-refundable deposits—the flowers, cake, catering, venue."

"What happened, then?" Poppy leans in, ready for the tea.

"Well, this is all speculation—"

"Go on . . ." Poppy scoots even closer to me.

"Supposedly, Pete found Mary-Kate over at Cash Capelli's house."

"No!" Poppy gasps, her mouth forming a perfectly round 'O.'

"That doesn't even make sense. Why would anyone in their right mind leave Pete Scarborough for a Capelli?" Roman says, scowling. "C'mon."

"Yeah, especially Cash. He's a total fuckwit," Parker chimes in, glancing up from his phone. "Dude can't even hold down a real job. Has to stick to the family business of I don't know what. What do they do?"

"They pretend they're in real estate and land development," Roman says, his frown lines deepening in disgust. "But they should stick to what they know—slumming around with low-lifes, drug deals. That sorta thing."

"Harsh," I say, even if a part of me believes this to be true. I do have vivid memories of Jagger offering me weed back in the seventh grade.

"Tell me it's not accurate," Roman challenges.

I shrug. "Can't verify that."

"Exactly."

The radio on the table squawks and we fall silent, ready for the latest update on Clementine.

"Residents of Seaglass Beach have been asked to evacuate the area. At this point, all bridges are closed due to high winds and dangerous storm surge conditions. Record rainfall has been recorded in the area, and river levels are high. Power outages have been reported. The storm is expected to make landfall within the next few hours. Stay tuned for regular updates."

No one speaks, and I can feel the anxiety thrumming through the room. All talk of Cash Capelli's forgotten. Parker stares at his phone, watching the live feed from the inn.

"No surge yet. Everything looks fine," he says. The brothers exhale in relief, and Poppy perks up.

"Can we talk about dinner now? I'm starving. Parker didn't even bother feeding his hurricane prep crew today." She shoots her twin a glare and Roman chuckles.

"Might as well eat. Nothing left to do now but sit and wait," King says in a grave voice.

7

———

PARKER

I spend the rest of the day alternating between staring at my cell or staring at Liv. Both raise my heart rate, but for very different reasons.

Forget it, Parker. You 1000 percent cannot go there.

No matter how adorable she is when she nibbles on her bottom lip. Or tucks a loose strand of hair behind her ear or talks to herself as she works through a problem.

No. I have to do the right thing—be a good brother and completely ignore Liv's cuteness.

Instead, I focus on the inn. After all, it is my family's legacy. But after an hour of riveting viewing of grainy black-and-white images on my tiny phone screen, I'm beyond bored. It's worse than watching paint dry, and I've had some experience in that department.

"This sucks," I mutter, tossing my phone down onto the leather couch cushion. "I'm over Hurricane Clementine already."

"Parks, the storm didn't even hit yet." Poppy glances up from the worn paperback she's reading. King's gone out to the stables to feed the horses and Rome's up in his room watching TV. Liv's still at the kitchen table, typing away on her laptop.

"I know," I groan, raking a hand through my hair. "Let's do something. I can't just sit here and stress." Nerves thrum through me, and I'm antsy, my legs twitchy.

Standing, I grab Poppy's arm, dragging her out of the wingback chair in the corner.

"What? What do you want to do? Another round of Truth or Dare?" she teases.

"I don't think so. Not in the mood for Truth or Truth at the moment."

"Rude," Liv chimes in from the table, frowning.

"We could do a jigsaw puzzle." Poppy motions at the built-in entertainment cabinet filled with puzzles and board games.

"Boring." I yawn, wide and dramatic.

"You're such a jerk." She punches my arm. "Monopoly?"

"Nah."

"Oh! I have an idea—let's go up to the attic and see if we can find some vintage stuff to showcase at the inn." Her eyes brighten at the task and I notice Liv perk up as well.

"Still not all that exciting, but okay," I say. "Better than sitting around down here doing nothing. Let's go."

The three of us troop upstairs, and I pull the attic ladder down from the ceiling. "Ladies first."

Poppy doesn't hesitate, gripping the rungs of the ladder, slowly making her way up. Liv follows and I take a moment to admire the view, watching Liv's round, firm ass climb the ladder. Finally, I scale up behind them.

As soon as I pop my head into the attic, a blast of warm air hits me, along with the strong, earthy smell of cedar.

The room is dark and Poppy clicks on a flashlight, the yellow beam flickering over the walls. She spots the chain for the lone lightbulb and pulls it, a diffuse white ring of light appearing on the wooden floorboards. Most of the room still sits in shadows, save for the small patch of space directly below the bulb.

"Open the shade, Parks." Poppy points at the window and I make my way over, careful not to trip over any boxes.

Raising the shade only helps a fraction because it's now dusk, plus heavy storm clouds block any existing moonlight. I shiver, the hairs on the back of my neck rising. Honestly, the attic still creeps me out a little, but I'm not going to let that on to the girls.

"What should we look for?" Liv's eyes scan the neatly stacked and labeled boxes appreciatively. Our mother was very organized, unlike me or Poppy. King and Roman are more like her, but none of us are as extreme in our methods.

"I don't know," Poppy says, her voice low. "Anything that looks old?"

"Wow. Tons of guidance there. Thanks," I say, glancing around the crowded attic. "Who knew we had this much shit?"

Liv chuckles, but Poppy gasps. "Parker! It's not shit. It's family heirlooms. Show some respect."

"Uh-huh. You call Roman's baseball card collection an heirloom?" I shove a plastic bin into her arms.

"Well, no. Not exactly, but I'm sure there are nuggets here. We just have to find them."

"Good luck. Mom was super tidy; if we had anything valuable, we'd know it by now."

"Maybe she ran out of time, Parker," Poppy says, her voice fading.

My gut clenches, a shooting pain searing my chest, and I shove a hand deep into my pocket.

"Maybe this isn't such a good idea," Liv says, squeezing Poppy's arm. "I'm up for another game of Truth or Truth."

Poppy shrugs Liv off and forges ahead. "No, let's keep searching. I want to refresh our lobby and having something vintage on display would be super cool."

Poppy crouches on the ground and begins rooting through the nearest box. Clearly, she's not giving up on the concept.

Sighing, I join the search.

Thirty minutes later, I'm sweaty, dusty, and over the whole damn idea. All I managed to find was baby albums and cheap trophies from my Little League days. Liv finds Roman's elementary school report cards—why our mother kept them, I have no idea—and the ashes of our first dog, Bandit. Poppy has yet to report any treasures, but is methodically working her way around the room.

"Eureka! I've got something good!" Poppy squeals. Her body's hidden by an old mannequin dress form my mom used for sewing, her arms waving madly in the corner. "And it's so cool!"

"Oh, I want to see!" Liv hurries over, stepping gingerly to avoid trampling the contents of the boxes Poppy's already unearthed.

"It's a wedding dress, I think. But not Mom's. Maybe Gran's?" Poppy holds up a lacy cream-colored gown.

"That dress is tiny." Liv circles the garment, reaching out and touching the lace. "I think it would fit you, though, Poppy."

"Hah! Not a chance," she scoffs.

"Yes, definitely." Liv lifts the dress to Poppy, holding it up against her frame. "A perfect fit."

"Too bad I'm not getting married anytime soon. But it'll be an awesome piece in the lobby display case. Do you know anyone who does dress restoration?"

"Of course. I can get you a name and a number."

"Great."

"We good here?" I ask. "Because I'm hot and thirsty."

"Sure. Let's tidy up, though. Mom always told us to leave things neater than we found them." Poppy recites one of our mother's favorite expressions and another wave of grief hits me.

I have to get out of here. Too many memories.

Shoveling shit back into plastic bins, I rush to escape the stuffy confines of the attic and ghosts from the past. Trading cards, jerseys, photos, all crammed back into their neat compartments, filed away for safekeeping.

"Y'all ready?" I look over at Poppy and Liv, eager to get the hell out of here.

"Yep. I have the dress. Let's go." Poppy carefully folds the dress, then climbs down the ladder, and Liv follows. I start my descent, then notice I forgot to pull the shade.

"I have to close the shade. Be down in a sec."

Hopping back up into the dark space, I hustle over to the window and start to lower the shade. A stray moonbeam shines through the dusty glass and a cardboard box catches my eye.

Poppy and Parker – Middle School

What the fuck's in that box? It's way smaller than the others, closer in size to a shoebox than a moving box, and the label isn't a fancy printed one from Mom's label maker. Rather, it's Poppy's scrawling middle school handwriting in black Sharpie.

Curiosity grips me and I bend over, picking up the box and carefully unsealing the masking tape. Inside is a hodge-podge of worthless middle school trinkets—a concert ticket stub, Poppy's recital program the year she danced in 'The Nutcracker,' scratch-and-sniff stickers—don't ask me why we bothered saving those.

Buried beneath all of this is a hot pink spiral notebook decorated with yellowing tiny surfer stickers. I open the journal, instantly recognizing Poppy's loopy handwriting. Scrawled across the first lined page is the welcoming title: **POPPY'S PRIVATE DIARY. KEEP OUT.**

I snicker, remembering how many times I did not keep out, instead diving in and reading all of the thoughts she thought were such deep, dark secrets. In reality, all of Seaglass Beach Middle knew every one of them because Poppy is an open book, always has been.

Flipping through the notebook, I skim through the mind of young Poppy. So innocent and sweet.

And then I come to the page. Signed by Poppy and Parker Montgomery on April 8 at 3:45 p.m.

The Pact

We, the Montgomery twins of Seaglass Beach, vow on this day to enter into an agreement called THE PACT. Each of us has chosen one person in this whole wide world we are absolutely forbidden to date or have any type of romance with—ever. We

*do hereby solemnly swear. Cross our hearts and
hope to die.
I, Parker Montgomery, promise to never go out
with Olivia Drayton.
I, Poppy Montgomery, promise to never go out with
Brant Starling.
Forever and ever. Amen.
Signed,
Parker Collin Montgomery
Poppy Florence Montgomery*

Holy shit.

Here it is, in actual sixth grade handwriting. I can't
believe Poppy kept the journal all these years.

I never should have agreed to such a stupid pact. But
how was I supposed to know—at eleven—that Liv would
turn out to be the one woman in the world I adore? Who
makes my heart pound when she smiles in my direction,
who brightens my day with her laugh?

Corny as fuck, I know, but no other woman's even
come close.

Maybe if I burn the stupid thing, the Pact becomes
defunct? And then Poppy won't hate me and I can finally
pursue Liv.

"Parks, you okay up there?" Poppy's voice startles me
out of my magical daydream.

"Yeah, all good," I shout. "Be right down."

Rolling the journal up newspaper-style, I shove it deep
into my pocket and seal the box, lower the shade, and head
back downstairs.

After this fun-filled trip down memory lane, I could use a hot shower and an ice-cold beer.

8

LIV

Overnight, Hurricane Clementine rolls through and we . . .

Sleep. Through. It.

Well, sort of. I toss and turn, what with all of Poppy's snoring. But we never lose power at the ranch, even with the whipping winds and the heavy rain.

All that build-up and the storm's kind of a sleeper. Another overhyped natural disaster.

I probably could have stayed home.

"How's the inn?" I ask Parker, taking a seat across from him at the kitchen table.

"Everything looks fine on the monitor, but I want to head out soon, get eyes on the property."

"Makes sense." I stir sugar into my coffee mug, staring down at the dark espresso in lieu of his deep blue eyes.

"Have you heard anything about your place?" he asks. "Or your office?"

"No update on my house. But Diane texted me and said

Seaglass Celebrations is closed for the time being. Storm clean-up. The office is okay, but all events are cancelled."

"Oh. Well, at least you have a long weekend, right?" His blond hair flops over his forehead, and he brushes it casually to the side. Morning sunlight streams through the picture window, catching the golden highlights in his surfer hair—I'd kill for highlights like that—and my stomach gets all fluttery.

I need to get out of here. Being this close to Parker for so long is torture.

"When are you leaving? Think I can get a ride?" The words pop out of my mouth.

Why is my brain not connected to the rest of my body when I'm with Parker?

"Sure, no problem. Be ready in twenty?" He eyes my pajamas, and a fiery tingle spreads through me.

"I can do it, thanks. I'll go pack up." I hurry and retreat back to the bedroom, running straight into Poppy.

"Whoa! Where are you going this morning in such a rush? And what's going on with the storm?" She cranes her neck, peering around my shoulder at the yard. "It's sunny outside. Are we in the eye now?"

"It's over, Pops. You slept through it," Parker says, chuckling.

"What? It's over?"

"Yep. You snored right through the entire thing."

"How's the inn?" She hurries around me and snatches Parker's cell from his hand. "Anything damaged?"

"Here." Parker taps on the phone screen, pulling up the live feed from the Seaglass Inn. Poppy's head bobs up and down, her face breaking into a wide smile.

"I think it's okay!"

"Me too, Pops. But I'm going to head out in a few to check on everything."

"I'm coming too. We may need to get the crew back in and I can start rebooking guests. We're back in business!" She pumps her fist in the air.

"Don't celebrate too soon." King's deep voice thunders behind us. "Parker's right—y'all should go check on things before you start taking reservations. Heard on the news that things are worse in town."

"Fine," Poppy says, twirling her hair. "We were heading out in a second, anyway. Unless you need us here."

"Nope. Y'all go. Rome's helping out at the barn, then we'll head your way. Call if you need anything."

"Thanks, bro." Parker pats King on the back, drops his coffee mug into the sink. "Thanks for letting us crash here."

"Any time. Glad everyone's safe." King's expression is flat; only his navy gaze gives away any emotion.

"Love you." Poppy spontaneously hugs King and he stiffens, awkwardly patting her arm.

"Thanks, King," I say.

He grunts at all of us and the conversation is closed.

"This bus is leaving in fifteen minutes. Hustle, ladies." Parker loops his finger in the air and Poppy and I kick into high gear.

"Got it, boss!" Poppy teases, grabbing me by the hand and dragging me to the bedroom. "We'll be ready!"

Thirty-three minutes later, Parker and I sit in his SUV, waiting on Poppy.

"For fuck's sake. We were here one night, how much

stuff can she have?" He leans on the horn, sounding a long, impatient bleep.

"Parker—how long have you known Poppy? She's a lot of things, but speedy isn't one of them."

"True. I'm not known for my punctuality, either, but c'mon. I told her to hustle."

Poppy sticks her head out, holds up a finger. "One more sec!"

Five minutes later, she breezes out and climbs into the passenger seat. "You can't hurry greatness, Parks."

"Pfft. Finally." Parker's SUV rumbles to life and we head back towards town.

The ride's silent, except for the country station playing on the radio. Luke Bryan's warbling about July fireworks and falling in love, and I can't help but sneak a peek up at Parker. His high, chiseled cheekbones, that square jaw. I don't even know how many hours I've spent wondering how it would feel to press up against his strong body, nuzzle against his warm chest, his arms wrapped around me. Holding me close, like he never wants to let me go.

Too bad it'll never, ever happen.

He's never looked my direction, not even one freaking time.

Buzz, buzz.

A message notification from someone named Amber pops up on the infotainment screen. Parker keeps driving, ignoring the message.

Buzz, buzz.

Another message from Amber.

Buzz, buzz.

Then a third.

Geez, Amber sure is persistent.

"Want me to read you the messages, Parks?" Poppy says with a cheeky grin.

"Nah. It can wait."

"You sure? I bet it's entertaining."

He doesn't answer, keeping his eyes on the road. A Kenny Chesney song comes on and I try to ignore the sharp stabs of jealousy knifing me in the chest.

Buzz, buzz.

"Oh look. Another one, but not from Amber. This one's from Kimbra. Can I read it? Please?" Poppy begs, giving Parker her best puppy dog eyes.

"No, Poppy. Forget it." He turns up the radio, drowning out her pleas, and I bury my nose—and my hurt feelings—in work emails for the rest of the drive.

"WANT ME TO DROP YOU OFF FIRST, FIZZ?" PARKER ASKS, locking eyes with me in the rearview.

"No, it's fine. My van's still at the Seaglass anyway."

"Okey-doke." He makes the turn toward the Seaglass, and I peer out the window, taking stock. Tree limbs are down, littering the side of A1A, and large puddles of rainwater cover parts of the sidewalk. A few street signs hang crooked, and a power line droops dangerously low. Traffic is light because it's still pretty early, despite Poppy's slow-crawl departure from the ranch.

Anxiety creeps in as we get closer to the Seaglass Inn.

What will we find? Standing water isn't a great sign, and we're still blocks from the beach.

Parker makes a right, then another right, and now we're less than five minutes away from the inn. There's more junk in the road—downed palm fronds, trash, debris—but other than that, everything looks normal.

I hold my breath as we pull into the circular drive of the Seaglass, parking in front of the lobby. Every shutter's intact, although piles of white sand glitter on the grass, twinkling in the bright sun.

"Nothing a good raking can't fix," Parker says, taking inventory. "Windows seem fine."

Poppy nods, her face pensive. "Let's walk around."

Parker cuts the ignition and we climb out of the SUV. A warm, salty breeze hits my face and I inhale.

"Beach first." Poppy points to the walkway leading to the beach and we head out. "We can check out the Bungalows, then the Villas."

The three of us amble down the path, no one speaking. I'm tense, and I don't have any ownership over the property —I can only imagine how Parker and Poppy feel right now.

"I don't think the surge came up this high, Pops." Parker points at the dry sidewalk. "We got blasted by sand, but at least it's dry."

The pavement's covered with a good two inches of sand, but Parker's right. It's dry sand, carried by wind gusts, not a storm surge.

"That's good news, right?" I say, trying to remain optimistic. Even though neither of them has admitted it, I can practically feel their anxiety. A vein's popping out on Parker's neck and Poppy's jumpy as all get out.

"Mm-hmm," Poppy murmurs, her lips pressed together.

"The sandbags are dry, too." Parker bends down, squeezing the large sack of sand blocking the door to Bungalow Three. "I'd say we didn't get any water up here."

"Whew." Poppy exhales a quick sigh of relief.

We continue on, checking each bungalow, then the villas. All of them are fine, including Villa Two closest to the beach.

"Pool and tiki bar next." Parker tips his head toward the beach.

Following the path out to the pool deck area, Parker unlocks the padlock on the gate, then cuts through the thick rope securing the iron bars with his pocket knife. The pool's filled to the tippy-top, and the bottom is thick with sand. The entire deck is white, like a Florida snowfall rolled through, and palm fronds are everywhere.

"Clean up on aisle three," I joke, my voice deadpan.

"I'll call the guys," Parker says, shaking his head. "This is gonna take a while."

"Oh no," Poppy says, groaning. "Parker! Look at the tiki bar!"

"Crap," Parker mutters, taking in the half-bare roof of the hut. The brown fronds now cover the teak bar, and a string of lights dangles down.

"We're going to have to rebuild that," Poppy says, biting her lower lip.

"It should only take a day or two, but the bar's closed for business right now."

"Good thing you know a contractor." I poke Poppy in the ribs and she shoots me a wan smile.

"Yeah. I have a feeling he's going to be really busy the next few weeks. Let's start taking notes of all the repairs we need to make. I don't want to rebook until the pool and restaurant can open, at the very least."

Parker's texting, and I wonder if he's messaging the crew—or Amber or Kimbra or the babe of the day. I feel a flush creep up my neck, all the way to my face, and my gut twists.

"Poppy, do you need me? I kinda want to go check on my house," I say, forcing conviction into my voice.

Even though I have absolutely nothing to do at the moment, and my office is closed.

"No, we're good. I'll call you later." She leans over, gives me a quick hug. "It was fun having a sleepover! Just like the old days."

Her smile's so bright, so genuine, making me feel even shittier.

I nod and fake a smile, trying to match her sincere enthusiasm. "It was. Thanks for having me."

"I hope I didn't snore too bad."

I brush her off. "You? You were fine. Quiet, even. Okay, I'm out. See ya later. Bye Parker." I wave at him and he glances up at me, shooting me a quick wave.

"Bye, Fizz. See ya later."

Even his half-hearted wave doesn't stop my stupid heart from pounding hard and fast, just because he gave me the time of day.

What was he going to do, totally ignore me?

I'm so stupid.

Picking up my pace, I race to the lot where I left the van. I want to get far, far away from Parker Montgomery at the moment. I need to regroup. Drink some ice water, read a book, go for a long, grueling jog—anything but stand by and watch him text his next hookup.

"No! No, no, no!" I cry, balling my fists at my side. "You've got to be fucking kidding me right now."

The Seaglass Celebrations van is still in the lot. Unfortunately, the windshield's shattered, a spiderweb of cracked glass radiating from the large coconut lodged in the center of the glass.

Just my luck. A coconut grenade took out my ride.

9

LIV

I CANNOT FREAKING BELIEVE THIS. I HAVE NO RIDE, AND because of the hurricane, there aren't any Ubers or cabs running at the moment.

My boss calls the insurance company and they can't come out to repair the windshield for several days. You know—due to the storm.

I skulk back to the beach to beg for a ride; it's a helluva long walk home from here and I have a suitcase. Hopefully, Poppy can break away for a few minutes and give me a lift.

Parker's talking with one of the guys from his crew when I open the gate to the pool deck.

"Hey, Fizz. Thought you were leaving."

"Yeah, me too. But my van's windshield got taken out by a flying coconut. I kinda need a ride."

He chuckles, shaking his head. "Shut up. For real?"

"Unfortunately, yes. I think the van's going to be sitting in the lot for a few days—the insurance company hinted as much."

Parker shrugs. "No biggie. C'mon, I can drop you off."

"You sure? I know you have a lot going on. Maybe I can get Poppy to take me."

He rakes his hand through his hair and shoots me a grin, knocking me off my already-precarious balance.

Damn him.

Hot pleasure rushes through me at his attention, false hope fluttering around in my belly.

"I got you. Let's go."

He gives Enrique instructions for the deck clean-up, then lopes my way. Totally unaffected by my presence, just his casual self.

Tall, lithe, hot as fuck.

I take small sips of air, cutting my eyes to gaze out at the beach. Anywhere but at his stupidly handsome face.

"You coming, Fizz?" Parker's leaning on the gate, holding it for me, one brow raised.

"Oh. Yeah. Coming." I scurry to the gate, then follow him out to his SUV, doing my best not to stare at his cute, tight ass in his work jeans.

"A flying coconut, huh?" Parker jokes, glancing over his shoulder to back out of the parking spot. "That sounds like a Jimmy Buffett song."

"Glad it's not my personal car," I say, picking at my cuticle.

Gawd, why is this so awkward? It's not like I've never hung out with Parker before.

I roll my window down, a blast of salty air hitting my heated face.

Calm down, Liv. He can't possibly know how many times you've wished you were in this exact same position.

Except in those daydreams, Parker's hand is on my thigh, inching higher with every mile we drive.

I fan myself with one hand, swallowing hard over the lump in my throat.

"Are you hot? I can turn on the AC." He cranks the air up full blast, the cool breeze blowing my hair around.

"Thanks," I murmur, although no amount of air conditioning is going to remedy this stupid crush I'm harboring.

We roll through the streets, Parker humming to the radio while I rack my brain for something—anything—to say, and come up blank.

Finally, we turn into my little neighborhood and the end of this torturous few days is near.

"You remember how to get there?" I ask, surprised as he makes all the correct turns.

"Of course. You've only been Poppy's best friend forever. Obviously I know where you live." His eyes slide from the road to my face and my cheeks burn.

Duh. It's only because of Poppy.

He makes another right turn, slowing down as we near the bright yellow duplex where I live.

"Oh no," I whisper, taking in the sad scene.

Shingles pepper the postage stamp-sized lawn, along with pieces of white soffit. Tons of leaves, pine straw, and debris cover the grass. But the real kicker?

The massive oak, uprooted and leaning at a precarious forty-five degree angle across Mr. Waycroft's roof.

I bury my face in my hands, hot panic flooding my system.

I have no house. No van. Maybe no job, if everyone cancels their events.

"Um, Fizz." Parker's voice cuts through the silence.

I lift my head and peer over at him. "What?"

"I don't think you can stay here."

10

PARKER

"Thanks, Captain Obvious," Liv snaps, tears pooling in her eyes.

"Sorry." I scrub a hand over the back of my neck.

That was a stupid-as-hell thing to say. Of course she realizes she can't live here, Parker. STFU.

She swipes at the tears, lets out a shaky breath. "I'm sorry. You and Poppy are awesome, I shouldn't have reacted like that. It's just—" her voice quivers, the muscles in her jaw clenching as she tries to rein in her emotion. "I don't have anywhere else to go."

A lone tear falls from her eyes, and it's all I can do not to gather her up in a tight hug.

Instead, I wipe the tear away with the pad of my thumb. "Hey, don't cry."

Her skin's smooth and soft, like an exotic silk. She bristles at my touch, and I jerk my hand away. I take a shaky breath and swivel my head back to the duplex.

"Think we can go inside?" Liv eyes the fallen tree, mentally gauging the risk of the situation.

"It looks like most of the tree landed on the other side of the duplex. We can make a quick sweep, get some of your stuff."

"Okay."

I jump out of the car, striding up the concrete steps two at a time. Liv follows, unlocking the door, and we step inside the dim living area.

I can tell from the smell that things inside are actually worse. A musty, damp odor assaults my nostrils. Spend enough time on construction sites and you can spot the tell-tale signs of water damage a mile away and this smell is it.

Liv's eyes dart around the living room, taking inventory of her space. "Everything looks normal." Her voice tips up, hopeful.

"Not to be a downer," I say, strolling the edge of the den, "but I'm fairly certain your soffits leaked."

"What? How?" Her eyes widen in panic as I run my hand over the walls.

"Yep, damp. The soffits flew off during the storm, and rain blew in. Soffits prevent rain from coming in through the roof eaves."

"Shit," Liv murmurs. "This is gonna be expensive, right? Like, my landlord's probably raising the rent to cover the cost?"

I shrug. "Depends on the landlord. The roof could be pricey, given the oak tree situation. But soffits aren't that big of a deal. Trouble is, more people may have damage and it could take some time to get repaired."

Liv's face falls, her brows knitting together. "What am I going to do?"

"We'll figure it out, don't worry. Right now, pack as

much stuff up as you can and let's get the hell out of here. I don't love standing around in a building with a fallen tree above my head."

"Right. Good point." Liv pulls herself together, squaring her shoulders, her full lips pressed together in a tight line. She's in command mode now and I'm kind of turned on by it, not gonna lie. She's even hotter when she's on a mission.

Blowing by me, she heads down the hall and I tag along. You know, just in case she needs help.

The smell's not so bad as we head toward the back; mostly I catch the lingering scent of Liv's shampoo. Rose petals, something floral and delicious. I want to jump on the bed and pull her down on top of me, bury my nose in her soft, warm skin.

But even if I could do that, now is definitely *not* the time.

I pause at the threshold to her bedroom, like caution tape blocks the door or something. I've never been in Liv's bedroom before—ever—and it feels intimate.

"It's okay, Parker, I don't bite. Even on my own turf." She glances over at me, and my cock stirs in my jeans.

Not the time, buddy.

I clear my throat, forcing out a strangled laugh. "Haha, I know."

I wave her off, like she hasn't just read my mind. Which I'm clearly losing.

It's another room in a house, that's all. Stop reading so much into it.

"Here." She shoves a light pink duffel at me. "Start packing. Take the drawers."

"Got it." I spin around and head over to the white

dresser, beginning at the top. Which is her bra and panty drawer, naturally.

Shit. Does she actually want me to paw through her underwear?

My mouth now dry as the motherfucking Sahara, I swallow hard before plunging into the drawer.

Let's just get this over with. And it's the closest you'll ever get to Liv's panties, so enjoy it while you have the chance.

Now I have a raging hard-on, what with all the silk and satin and lace and Liv. I'm glad to be facing her dresser because there's no way I could conceal this guy, twitching around in my pants.

I scoop every last item out of the top drawer—to be on the safe side—then move on to the next. Mercifully, this one's socks. Extremely unsexy, thank heavens. After that, it's gym clothes, then shorts and T-shirts.

"Parker, you didn't need to empty the drawers." Liv stands on tiptoe behind me, peering over my shoulder. "Unless you think I'm going to be out of this place for a long time?"

Her face creases with worry again and I stop what I'm doing to face her. "No. I'm sure it'll be fixed up soon, Liv. But better safe than sorry, right?"

She locks her eyes on mine and my heart squeezes hard in my chest. I want to hold her, comfort her, but I know I can't. Shouldn't.

Not after finding The Pact.

Liv breathes out a soft sigh, turning back to the task at hand, folding dresses and blouses and moving them into her suitcase.

"You have another suitcase or something, for shoes?" I gesture at the shoe hanger in her closet.

"Yes, definitely need to take those." She tosses me another duffel and I grab as many pairs as I can stuff into the bag.

"You good with these?" I ask, holding the bag open for her to see.

"Do you think I should bring my boots?"

"I'm hoping you'll be back here before you need boots, Liv."

A quick flash of relief crosses her face and my chest loosens up. Glad I finally said something right.

"Anything else you need? Passport, important documents, jewelry?" I tick all the "Things to Take in an Evacuation" items off on my fingers, one by one.

"Let me grab my passport and a few files. Here's my jewelry." She hands me a leather folio, and I cram it into the duffel.

Creak. The loud sound echoes through the duplex and Liv peers up at the popcorn ceiling, her eyes wide.

"It's from the wind, but yeah—let's get out of here," I say, zipping up the bag. "I don't want to be on the local news. I'm going to take this stuff out to the car."

I grab all three suitcases, leaving Liv rifling through her desk, pulling her important files.

Five minutes later, she runs out of the duplex, tossing the files into her car. "You think I should empty the fridge?"

"Damn." I eye the tree, weighing the cost-benefit of this task. The oak branches don't appear to have moved. "Probably."

I climb out of the SUV, hustling back inside. Together we toss all the perishable items into a trash bag as quickly as possible, and I tie up the black plastic bag.

"Anything else? Toiletries?" I ask.

Liv's hands fly wide. "How could I have forgotten those?"

She runs to the bathroom and I haul the garbage out to the curb, gathering palm fronds as I go. The yard's a mess, but it's gonna get trashed during reno anyway, so it's a futile effort.

Liv's locking the duplex door when I get back from the trash run. She jogs down the steps and pauses outside her car, sighing.

"It's going to be okay," I say, reaching for her hand.

So soft and small in mine, but it feels right—we're a good fit.

She stares down at our fingers for a moment, then turns to face me, biting at the corner of her lip. "You think?"

I squeeze her hand. "I know."

11

———

LIV

I FOLLOW BEHIND PARKER, ALL THE WAY BACK TO THE Seaglass Inn, my mind in a daze.

Parker held my hand.

And it felt wonderful.

Amazing.

Get your shit together, Olivia. You currently have an oak tree sprawling on your roof, therefore you're homeless, and your job may or may not be on hiatus.

Ohmygawd, what if I have to file for unemployment?

I take a deep breath. I'm getting ahead of myself.

Buzz, buzz.

I check my phone—it's my mother. I desperately want to ignore her, but she's probably worried about me.

"Hello?"

"Olivia? Are you okay? I saw the devastation on the news." My mom's shrill, pitchy voice vibrates loud in my ears.

"I'm fine, Mom," I assure her. "And 'devastation' is kind

of a stretch. Most places came through just fine, minor damages."

"Most places?" Her tone tips up an octave, and I grip the steering wheel tighter.

Shit. She caught that.

"The Seaglass Inn is fine."

"Wonderful, but what about your place? And your job? I'm assuming all your parties are cancelled."

"Events, Mom," I sigh. "And my place could be better . . ." I bite my cheek as I turn into the inn, right behind Parker.

"Olivia Drayton—spit it out already! What happened?"

"A coconut cracked the van windshield and a tree fell on my house. And there's probably water damage inside, but it's all good." The words rush out of me. I can only hope my mom's ears can't keep up.

"Oh my word, Olivia! A tree on your house? Thank God you're alright. And a coconut shattered the windshield? It's a wonder you're not dead. That's it. Sam! Sam!" My mother shouts to her husband, her voice muffled. "We need to buy Olivia a plane ticket. Yes, we do! She almost died in the storm!"

"Mom!" I cry, yelling directly into the cell, trying to get her attention. "I did not almost die! I was nowhere near my van or my house. You're overreacting."

"Now you listen here, Olivia. A mother's intuition is always right, especially when it comes to her children. You need to come to Maryland, I feel it in my bones."

"Mom, I can't. I need to stay here and help reschedule the cancelled events."

"But where will you stay?"

I suck in my breath, wondering the exact same thing. "I'm not sure yet, Mom, but I'll think of something."

"You could always stay with your aunt. I know she's a ways out of town and it'd be a bit of a drive to work, but desperate times . . ." She trails off and I sigh.

I don't particularly like hearing myself and desperate in the same sentence.

"I think I'm good for now, Mom. Thanks for the concern. Listen, I'm getting a work call. Have to take it. Say hi to everyone for me." I disconnect before she can protest, regretting answering in the first place.

Tap, tap.

Parker's staring through the window at me and I can't help but giggle. Even if the situation is a tad bit dire at the moment.

"You getting out?" he shouts through the glass.

I shoot him a thumbs-up, then climb out of the car.

"Thanks for the help, Parker."

"Sure." He stuffs his hand in his pocket, all casual. As if that hand hadn't held mine a mere twenty minutes ago.

Seems like we're back to business as usual.

"You should probably get back to your crew." I tip my head toward the beach, the sound of the waves loud and rhythmic.

"Probably." He locks his eyes on mine again and my pulse races as if I'm running a freaking 5K.

"I'm, uh . . ." I shuffle my feet, words escaping me. "Uh, I'm going to . . . go find Poppy. Yeah, that's what I'm doing." I'm not sure what's smooshier at the moment, my brain or my tongue.

"Actually, I'll come with you. I need to ask her about

reservations." He licks his bottom lip, sending my heart pounding into overdrive.

For the love, Liv. Stop.

Sure, those lips are kissable as fuck. But stop staring!

"Cool," I manage to stammer.

It's like I can't form a freaking coherent sentence right now. Probably because I'm not getting enough blood pumping to my brain.

Parker and I pivot and head to the lobby. I notice the crew's removed all of the hurricane shutters in the front, and now they're working on the back. Poppy's standing at the reservation desk, tapping away at the computer.

"Hey! I thought you went home?" Poppy glances up from the screen, her brows bunching together.

"Funny story—" I say, my expression flat. "A coconut busted my windshield and a tree fell on my house. So I'm homeless and praying I'm not on hiatus from my job."

"No!" Poppy says, her hand flying to cover her mouth. "Liv!"

"I know. And my mom tried to get Sam to buy me a ticket to Maryland."

"The worst!"

"Yeah. I'm not going, even if I have to sleep in my Camry."

"You don't have to sleep in your car," Poppy says, laughing. "You can stay here."

"I can't take up your rooms, Poppy. This is high season for y'all."

She jiggles the mouse, bringing up the reservations. "I can slot you into a vacant room. You may need to keep bouncing around though, at least for a while. Until our traffic dies down."

"What about food, Pops?" Parker points out. "She kind of needs a kitchen."

"She could eat at the restaurant," Poppy says, tipping her head toward the dining room.

"Liv might be out of her house for a while. There's water damage. That'd be a lot of meals out."

"Oh." Poppy's voice drops and she stares at the computer, thinking.

"She can stay with me," Parker says.

I freeze, my heart stuttering in my chest.

Did Parker just suggest I stay with him? At his house?

"Wait—what?" I say, shock seeping into my voice.

"Yeah. It'll be fine. I work all the time anyway, and I bet I'm going to be slammed with extra jobs after the hurricane. We'll probably hardly even see each other." He seems calm, like me being in his house—his space—will be no big deal at all.

To him.

Because it won't be, Liv. He's never even looked your way. You're practically like another sister.

"Are you sure?" I stammer, rubbing the 'O' on my initial necklace.

"Yeah." He shrugs, all cool and nonchalant.

"Um—" I gnaw on my lip, running through my other options. Of which there are zero.

"Okay, thanks. I'll take you up on that, I guess."

"Problem solved. Roomie." He punches me lightly on the shoulder, grinning, and I blanche.

What have I just agreed to?

If pining for Parker from afar has been hard, having a front-row, real-time seat to his dating life is going to be pure, unadulterated hell.

12

—————

PARKER

FOR FUCK'S SAKE. I DON'T KNOW WHAT'S WORSE—THE fact that I just invited Liv to move in with me or that I called her 'roomie.'

Out loud. To her face.

I bang my head on the steering wheel, waiting for the light to change.

I'm Parker fucking Montgomery. I have mad game. So what the hell is wrong with me when I'm around Liv? I turn into a total babbling idiot.

And back to the real fucking issue. I invited her to LIVE WITH ME.

How in the actual hell am I supposed to co-exist in the same small space with Miss Olivia-I-can-never-date-Drayton?

I just dropped myself straight into a minefield.

Killing the ignition, I stride into Seaglass Supply with a list of necessities in hand. At least I know what I'm doing in here.

"Hey Parker, how'd y'all make out in the storm?" Cal

McGillen calls out from the register. He's worked here for as long as I can remember, so basically my entire life.

"We're alright, Cal. How 'bout you?"

He bites down on the toothpick hanging from the corner of his mouth, chews it for a minute before answering. "We're alright. Got a lot of yard clean-up and need a few trees trimmed up. But other than that, we're good."

"Glad to hear it. Listen, I need a key cut."

"No problem. C'mon." He leaves the register to a young kid, motioning me to follow him to the back.

Cal fires up the key cutter, leaning back against the laminate counter while he waits for the machine to warm up.

"You been busy today?" I ask, mostly to make conversation. The store's almost empty, save for me, Cal, and the kid at the register.

"Not really. But I think most folks are taking stock. Figure business will pick up tomorrow and the next day."

"I bet you're right."

"Alrighty—where's the key that needs cutting?"

I fish through my pocket, hand him the key to my house. He places the key down, and the loud whir of metal being cut assaults my ears. Cal works quickly and carefully, and in three minutes I have a key for Liv.

"Here ya go." He drops both keys into my outstretched palm. "That for the inn? I thought y'all were changing over to that newfangled electronic system?"

"No, not yet. Poppy keeps pitching the idea, but hasn't been able to convince the rest of us. But this isn't for the inn anyway."

"No?" One of Cal's thick, grey brows raises high, his

forehead creasing even deeper as he gnaws on his toothpick.

"Liv's duplex got banged up pretty bad in the storm. Tree fell on the roof and there's water damage. I offered my extra bedroom to her."

"Did ya now? Back in my day, a man and a woman only lived together after they got married. But I know the times have changed." He rolls the toothpick to the other side of his mouth.

"No, it's not like that. We're not together or anything—I'm just helping her out." I backpedal, my face burning.

"Huh." He stares at me with muddy brown eyes, clearly not comprehending this modern-day situation.

"We're just friends," I reiterate, shoving both keys into my pocket.

"Okey-dokey. You don't have to explain anything to me." He turns and heads back to the register, and I scrub my hand over the back of my neck.

Am I going to have this same conversation with everyone in town? It's none of their damn business, but Seaglass Beach is that kind of town. Where everybody knows everybody and their cousin and one thing's for certain around here—people talk.

Do they ever talk.

I bet at least half the town will know Liv's moved in by tomorrow, now that I spilled the news to Cal.

Shit.

Grabbing the items on my list as fast as possible, I push my anxiety down. It's not like I'm doing anything wrong here. Helping a family friend is all. And my pad is the most logical place for her to stay. It makes total sense.

I pay for my supplies and wave good-bye to Cal.

"Good luck, Parker," Cal hollers out, winking at me.

I tip my head, groaning inwardly.

Why'd I have to open my big mouth in the first place? I can practically hear the rumor mill turning and Liv hasn't even unpacked yet.

After working all day at the inn, cleaning up and making what repairs we can, I'm ready to kick back and relax on my couch. The last few days have been stressful as hell with the storm, and my phone's already ringing off the hook with calls about repair estimates. I told Smith he better get his ass back to town because we're about to double our workload.

The headlights of Liv's Camry glow in my rearview and my gut clenches. *Yeah, scratch 'relaxation' off my list.* My heart's pounding so hard I may as well have just run a marathon.

I hop out, circling around to help with her bags.

Calm down, Parker.

"Let me get those for you." I snag both her suitcases, tossing her duffel over my shoulder. Every muscle in my body thrums with an electric charge and I'm the exact opposite of cool and calm.

"I can get it," Liv protests, but she lets me take all the bags, following me up the drive. We climb the three stairs up to the dark front porch and I hand her the freshly-cut key.

"Here's your key." Our palms touch as I press the metal into her hand, an electric shock sparking down my arm.

"Thanks," she says, glancing up at me from beneath lowered lashes.

I swallow hard over the lump in my throat. "Sure."

Unlocking the door, I push into the house, flicking on the nearest lamp. The den illuminates, and I'm relieved I left the place in decent shape.

"Thanks, Parker, for letting me stay here." Liv brushes dark hair out of her eyes, locking that green gaze on mine, and my entire body hums with desire.

What the fuck am I thinking, inviting her here?

"Sure, no problem." I break eye contact, dragging her suitcases through the den and down the hall toward the bedrooms. My place is an old Florida ranch, with bedrooms next to each other and a shared bath in between.

"We're going to have to work out a schedule," Liv jokes, eyeing the lone bathroom.

An image of her standing naked in my shower pops into my head and I quickly push it away, but not fast enough to escape the flush of heat roaring through me.

"I go to work pretty early, it'll be fine," I reassure her.

"So do I. And I don't want to be in your way."

Buzz, buzz. My cell vibrates in my pocket, and I ignore it, smashing my hand against the denim to silence it.

"Extra towels are in the closet. I'm a terrible host, so make yourself at home and get whatever you need. You don't have to ask."

I flip the light on in the guest bedroom and wheel her luggage in. Liv stands in the doorway, staring into the small room.

"Is this okay?" I ask, worry clawing at my gut. "I mean,

I know it's only a queen bed, and I wouldn't have picked out this wallpaper . . ."

"It's fine, Parker. This works great." Liv gives me a soft smile and some of the tension between my shoulder blades eases.

Buzz, buzz.

"Go ahead and answer it." She stares down at my pocket and a whirl of emotions runs through me—guilt, shame, regret.

And for the first time in a very long while, I don't want to be Mr. Right Now anymore.

13

LIV

I'M NOT SURE LIVING WITH PARKER'S THE SANEST decision I've ever made. For starters, his cell rings every two minutes. Honestly, he must be the number one booty call in all of Seaglass Beach.

And what am I going to do when he brings someone home? It's one thing to know intellectually he's hooking up; it's a whole other story to watch it go down, live and in person.

But I can't very well ask him not to invite women over. I'm a guest in his home. He's allowed to do whatever he damn well pleases, whether I like it or not.

"Liv? You okay?"

I snap my head up, shaking the visual of Parker kissing a busty blonde out of my mind.

"Yeah. I'm fine. You don't have to ignore all your texts and calls on my behalf." I point at his pocket, lighting up again.

"I'll call them back." He shrugs and I try to squash the fizzy feeling of hope bubbling up inside me.

Don't be stupid, Liv. He's only being courteous.

"You hungry? Because I'm starving." Parker rubs his flat stomach, changing the subject.

"Now that you mention it, yes."

"I'll see what I can scare up. Go ahead and unpack, get settled."

"You don't need help?" I arch my brow.

"I can cook, you know. I've lived on my own for a while now."

"Hey—no judgment. I'm not the world's greatest chef."

"I'm not saying it'll be gourmet, but it'll be edible." He flashes me a grin and my heart flip-flops in my chest. This is the stuff of my middle school fantasies, and all I'm managing to do is sit here and second-guess myself. I should just enjoy the moment, but I'm pretty sure I'm missing that gene.

"See you in a bit." Parker heads toward the door, his arm grazing mine as he passes, and goosebumps rise on my skin.

I need to get a freaking grip or I'm going to spontaneously combust.

Collapsing on the bed, I take a shaky breath of the Parker-infused air, the fresh smell of eucalyptus and mint tickling my nose. I want to curl up against his chest, inhale that scent until it's ingrained in my memory forever.

Because I know this won't last.

Moving in here has to be your worst idea ever, Olivia.

Shoving that thought away, I start unpacking. I hang dresses and blouses, line my shoes up in tidy rows on the closet floor, re-fold shorts and T-shirts and shove them into the dresser drawers.

Twenty minutes later, I'm all moved into the guestroom and the heady aroma of garlic tempts me to the kitchen.

Well, that and the chef himself.

Parker's standing at the stove, his back to me as he cooks. I linger in the shadows, taking him in. His broad shoulders tapering down to a narrow waist, jeans slung low on his hips. The ropey muscles in his tanned forearms from hours of physical labor out in the sun. That perfect ass swaying to the beat of the music playing on his Alexa.

He spins around, his eyes catching mine. "Hey—great timing. Dinner's almost ready. Pour yourself a drink; I even found a bottle of wine."

"It smells great," I say, forcing the words out over my dry, scratchy tongue. My heart bangs hard in my chest as I pour a glass of wine; I'm surprised Parker can't hear it, it's so damn loud.

"You working Monday?" Parker asks as he drains the pasta, steam billowing up from the sink.

"I'll log in from home, but the office is still closed. You?"

"I'm working the next month straight, probably." He shakes the colander, then snags a serving spoon from a nearby drawer. "How's the wine?"

"Good."

"Cool. Plates are behind you." He tips his head at the closest cabinet and I take two out, placing them on the granite counter. Parker scoops a heaping pile of spaghetti onto my plate, ladles out the sauce.

"Thanks for cooking, Parks."

"No problem. We can sit at the table. I usually eat on the couch, but—"

"You don't have to be fancy on my account," I tease,

bouncing my hip against his. He chuckles, and the low rumble of his laugh sends my stomach swooping, heat unfurling in my belly.

Ohmygawd, now I'm flirting with him.

"Spaghetti's pretty difficult to contain. Besides, you're worth the effort." His eyes slide up to meet mine, and warmth blooms in my chest, climbing all the way up my neck and into my face. My cheeks flame under his gaze and I'm sure I have a dopey smile on my face.

I think he's flirting back.

We stare at each other for another second, then Parker gestures at the small table in the corner. "Shall we?"

I try to sashay sexily towards the table, but it probably more closely resembles lurching.

Relax, it's not a date.

Parker dims the lights and turns the music down, the melody falling to the background.

But it feels like a date.

And even though I've been best friends with Poppy since elementary school, I've barely spent any time by myself with her brother. Well, except in my mind, alone in the dark, but that doesn't count.

Settling in at the table, Parker waits for me to take a bite before he starts eating. A small, courteous gesture that surprises me.

His mama raised him right, that's for sure.

"Well—how is it?" He leans forward, waiting for my critique, as if I'm a judge on *Top Chef* or something.

"Good," I murmur over the bite of spaghetti I'm still chewing.

"That was lukewarm. Be honest—does it suck? Needs more garlic, right?" His brows scrunch together in a frown and he's so damn cute and earnest right now, I'm falling for him even harder. Which I didn't think was possible and definitely isn't healthy.

"It's really good. Swear." I dab at my lips, then take a sip of wine and try to compose myself.

"Really? Truly? Don't lie to me, Drayton—"

I shake my head, crisscrossing my heart with my fingers in the shape of an 'X.' "Cross my heart—it's great."

He sweeps his hand over his forehead, pretending to be relieved, then takes a big bite of pasta. "Decent," he mumbles over his fork.

We eat and drink and chat, sharing horror stories from work. Parker's stories are all funny, and I have a side stitch by the end of dinner. He's every bit as charming as I dreamed he would be, and I'm surprised at the ease between us.

"You cooked, let me clean up," I say, standing and reaching for his plate.

"No, I've got it." He rests his hand on mine, and my skin burns under his touch.

"Don't be silly. You can't do everything the entire time I'm here."

"True. Tell you what—I'll let you clean the bathroom."

"Gee, thanks. But if that's what you really want—" I drag the last words out, my voice tipping up, and Parker's eyes raise to meet mine. My breath catches in my throat and my lower belly tightens at his look. I bite down hard on my lip, Parker's body angled toward mine, only inches away.

Parker swallows, his Adam's apple bobbing in his neck, and I notice the dark navy flecks in his eyes, the splash of freckles stretched across the bridge of his nose.

Neither of us says anything, the low notes of a slow country song the only sound hanging between us. Parker reaches his hand out, encircling my wrist, and I'm certain he can feel my pulse accelerate beneath the rough pad of his thumb.

Because of him.

Knock, knock. Pause. Knock, knock, knock, in a cute little pattern. The front door shakes, startling me from my deep Parker spell.

"I've got it," I say, grabbing Parker's plate and hurrying to the kitchen.

I have no idea who's at the door, but I'm one hundred percent sure the visitor will be female and I won't like her in the least.

14

______

LIV

Standing at the sink, I'm glad my back's turned away from Parker as hot embarrassment prickles beneath my skin.

I can't believe I thought he was interested in me, even for a nanosecond.

I'm so stupid. Why'd I think he'd suddenly do a one-eighty, after all this time? Because a tree fell on my house? And I'm above a pity fuck, anyway, thank you very much.

I scrub sauce off the plate with vicious force, the water scalding my knuckles, and I don't even care. Serves me right for letting my guard down around him.

Parker's low, quiet voice barely carries across the den, making it practically impossible to hear their conversation over the running water.

Which is fine. The woman du jour is none of my business anyway.

It's fine.

Totally fine.

I rinse the dish and tap the faucet, turning off the

water. Curiosity licks at me, but I know I should resist temptation. Clean up the dinner table and retreat back to my room. Fire up my laptop and concentrate on something —anything—else.

Instead, I wipe down the island, my eyes glued to Parker's back as I make large circles on the smooth granite. His arms stretch wide across the doorframe, effectively blocking my view. All I can see from here is the top of a blond head. A giggle floats on the air and my stomach clenches, hard and tight.

The conversation at the door goes on for a few minutes, and then Parker closes the door. I spin around fast, pretending I wasn't staring him down the entire time, and run straight into the corner of the open dishwasher.

"Ouch, shit!" I cry, bouncing up and down and rubbing the angry knot forming on my shin.

So much for playing it cool.

"You okay?" Parker hustles over to check on me and now I feel about two feet tall. This is what I get for spying.

"Mmm, fine," I murmur, biting my lip as pain radiates down my leg.

"Sit, let me get you some ice." He grips my shoulders with his large hands, steering me toward the couch.

"It's okay, I'm fine," I protest as he gently pushes me down onto the black leather.

"Relax, put your leg up." He pats the cushion and I do as I'm told, my face flaming.

Two minutes later, he's back with an ice pack. "Geez, Liv. That's a big one. It's probably going to bruise."

He lifts my leg and settles down next to me, pulling my calf into his lap before draping the gel pack over the large-and-still growing red bump. Really cute.

And damn it, I can't breathe again. It's like I've been on a roller coaster these last two days, and I'm not sure how long my heart's going to be able to take all of the ups and downs on the Parker ride.

"You gotta watch out for the dishwasher. The kitchen's pretty tight." He absentmindedly strokes the top of my bare foot, sending shivers straight up my leg, and I legit can't feel the knot anymore.

And I don't think it's because of the ice.

"Yeah," I murmur.

I can't think of anything better to say and I don't trust my voice anyway. I keep my eyes pinned on the shiny couch cushion because looking at Parker right now, in this moment, would be tantamount to confessing my love for him and I absolutely cannot do that.

Not now, right after last week's hook-up showed up at his door.

Not ever, let's get real.

This thing between us is all in my head, one-sided.

I should have been a creative writing major, my imagination's so vivid.

His fingertips trail over my skin, tracing a line from my foot up my shin, but staying below the injury. Totally still in the friendzone.

Goosebumps rise on my legs and I'm glad I have the ice pack as an excuse. No need to let anything on, even as my heart pounds wildly.

"Better?" he asks, glancing over at me.

I meet his gaze, his eyes dark with concern. Licking my lower lip, I only manage to nod.

Get your shit together, Olivia. You can still salvage this. Be cool. Don't let on that you're affected.

"Who was at the door?" I make my tone light, inquisitive, trying not to sound the least bit jealous.

Parker lifts his shoulders, drops them again. "Someone I met at the tiki bar. Stacy something or other."

"Oh."

Never in my wildest dreams would I have the confidence to show up at a guy's house uninvited. Gotta admire the drive. Parker must be really amazing in bed.

"Everything okay with her?" For some reason, I can't drop the damn subject. I'm like a kid, picking at a scab.

"Yeah. She was worried about me, with the storm and all." He rakes a hand through his hair, and I imagine Stacy's fingers running through those honey-colored waves. Sharp pangs of jealousy stab me in the gut and I take a shaky breath.

"You didn't have to send her away. She could have come in."

Parker's eyes lock on mine, his hand stilling on my foot. "You sure, Fizz? Because I don't want you to feel weird or anything."

The pangs amp up and now it's as if a knife's twisting and grinding into my small intestine.

I shrug, ignoring the stabbing in my colon and try to act casual. "Sure. It's not like we're together or anything. You should carry on like normal. Don't let me stop you." A hard edge creeps into my voice and I hate the wild, out-of-control feelings swirling inside me, threatening to pull me under.

I can't do this.

"Listen, I'm really tired. It's been a long day." I stretch my arms out and fake a yawn. "Thanks for dinner. And the ice pack." I lift the blue gel pack off my leg, planting my foot down on the floor.

Back on solid ground, where it belongs.

"Sure, no problem. Any time." Parker takes the ice pack from my hand, our fingertips brushing, and shockwaves pulse through me. My body clearly hasn't received the message that nothing's happening between us and we're definitely *not* going there.

Not tonight.

Not ever.

I stand, ignoring the throbbing in my leg. "Night, Parker."

"Night, Fizz. Keep elevating that leg. It'll help with bruising."

"Will do."

I'm not too concerned about my leg as I limp back to the bedroom. Mainly because the pain in my heart's a thousand times worse.

15

PARKER

Damn it.

That's not how I wanted my night with Liv to end.

Because you didn't want it to end.

True. Well, true-ish.

Honestly, I wanted it to end with Liv in bed. My bed, naked and riding my cock. Which is rock hard for her right now.

Except she's on the wrong side of this wall and I'm lying here alone in the dark, stroking my shaft and thinking of her.

Those nice, full breasts, her smooth olive skin, her sparkly green eyes fringed by long, dark lashes.

I want to feel her body under mine, press my mouth to hers and pull a soft moan from those full, pink lips.

I want her to call out my name as she quivers beneath me, because of me.

I want to have her, all of her, not just the bits and pieces she shares with Poppy and everyone else.

I want to smell her, taste her.

And then I want to make Olivia mine.

Cock in hand, I stroke my length, picturing Liv's face as I pump up and down. The tingle starts at the base and pressure builds, and I know I'm close. I can almost feel her riding me, her tits bouncing in the air.

Harder. Faster.

I come in my hand, holding in a groan as I catch my release in my T-shirt. Liv's scent wafts up from the warm cotton and my body tenses again.

So much for relaxing.

I reach behind me, my hand running over the wall separating us.

I'm not sure I'm going to be able to settle for this sorry substitute when she's only a few feet away.

Damn the Pact. And damn my sister for forbidding the one person who's perfect for me. The only girl I've ever really loved.

Why can't I have what I want?

16

———

LIV

After the disappointing end to last night, I don't bother setting an alarm. I have nowhere special to be anyway, since it's Sunday and all events are postponed at the moment. So I'm shocked when I roll over and tap my phone to find it's already nine a.m. and I have four missed calls and three voicemails—Poppy didn't bother leaving a message.

My landlord's contacting the insurance company and wants to chat later next week.

Diane needs a call back concerning the Pratt engagement party two weekends from now.

And last, but never least, my mother.

I stretch, hitting the speaker button when her voicemail passes the one-minute mark.

"I think you should consider moving to Maryland, Olivia. Plenty of job opportunities, not to mention a vibrant dating scene. Vibrant! Something you do not have at the beach, I know for a fact, because you're still single. A girl like you, in her prime and still single? A travesty.

Anyway, call me back please. Your brother even found an apartment close to him available for rent—immediately! And for a good price. Okay, honey. Talk soon! Muah!"

The message finally ends and I toss the phone on the side table, aggravated. I know my mother means well, but she can be so damn annoying about it.

No, I'm not moving to Maryland and renting an apartment next to my big brother. And maybe I'm single by choice, dammit. Maybe I'm reveling in my alone time, pursuing my own goals.

I sigh.

I'm not, but no need to fess up about that.

Coffee. Coffee will make me feel better.

I crack the door open, tiptoeing out of my room.

Complete silence, no Parker. I head to the kitchen, spotting a note on the counter.

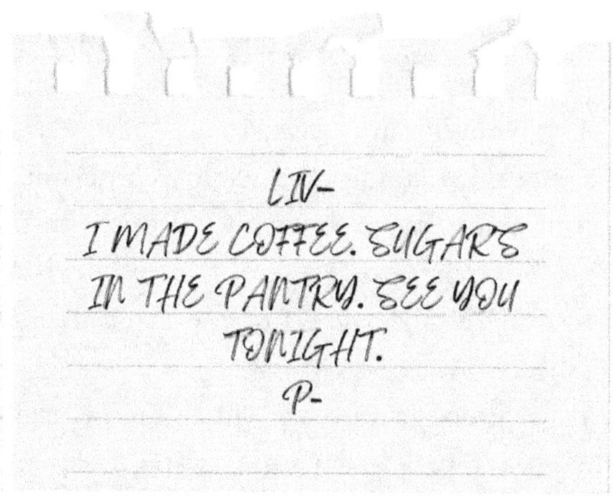

It's a note, Liv. Not a love letter. Calm the fuck down.

Still, my heart thumps a little harder in my chest and I'm lightheaded.

Because you need coffee, dummy.

Uh-huh. Keep telling yourself that.

I pour myself a cup of coffee, doctor it up with sugar, and plug in my laptop, settling in to do some work. As expected, my inbox is chock full of clients freaking out about their upcoming events.

After two hours straight at the kitchen table, my back's stiff and achy. I could use a change of venue and I'm hungry. It doesn't seem right eating all of Parker's food, either. I change clothes and head out for lunch, wondering which restaurants will be open after the storm. I turn left onto A1A, noting an increase in traffic today, although it's still much lighter than the typical summer crowds.

It seems like a lot of businesses are open. A good sign, especially for my job. We use mostly local vendors for our events; the sooner Seaglass Beach is back to normal, the better for me and my clients.

I make a sharp right turn into the parking lot of The Tipsy Taco, one of my fave places to eat, and snag a parking spot in the sandy lot.

The sun's shining, and a warm, salty breeze blows in from the ocean, making the eighty-something degree temperature much more bearable. I push through the screen door into the dim restaurant. The television above the bar streams the local news to the three people sitting within earshot.

"Hey, Liv. Sit anywhere you like. I'll be right over," Candy, the owner, calls out to me as she mixes up one of her signature margaritas.

"Thanks." I grab a booth in the corner, perusing the paper menu on the table even though I order the same trio of tacos every time.

"The usual?" Candy appears at my table, deposits a red

plastic basket of tortilla chips and a small dish of house made salsa.

"Yep. I don't like to break tradition," I say. "Looks like y'all did okay in the storm?"

"Thankfully. Stu's BBQ Joint didn't make out so great, though."

"Oh no! I hate to hear that."

"I know." Candy slides her pen behind her ear. "All the restaurants are donating our proceeds at Food Truck Friday to raise money for him. If you wouldn't mind spreading the word, that would be really helpful."

"Sure, no problem. Did you talk to Diane? She might be able to pitch in."

"Good idea. I don't think anyone called her yet—we just got the news about his generator failing this morning. Lost all his food."

"Terrible," I say. "I'll mention the event to Diane when I talk to her later."

"Sounds good, sweetie. How'd you make out? I take it Seaglass Celebrations is okay? And I heard the inn is fine, only minor damage. Happy for the Montgomerys, at least. Those folks don't need any more tragedy."

At the mention of the Montgomery name, a hot flush creeps up my neck. I take a sip of iced water, hoping to cool down.

"For sure. I'm fine, safe at least. My house—not so much. A tree fell on it."

"Oh my word! You poor dear. Where are you staying? Your folks aren't here, right?" Her questions shoot out rapid fire and I quickly debate how much to share.

I might as well be straight with her; she'll hear about it eventually.

"Parker offered me a place to stay." I fidget with the square napkin, folding it into smaller and smaller triangles.

"Did he, now? Well, that was awful nice of him." Her lips quirk up at the corner and I blush even harder.

"It was. Is. We're just friends," I clarify, tripping all over my words and waving my hands around in an effort to explain.

"Mm-hmm." She shoots me a knowing look, like she'll keep the secret I didn't actually tell her.

I clear my throat, unfold my napkin. Look everywhere but at Candy.

"Alrighty, I'll go ahead and put that order in. Let me know if Diane can do anything to help. All the money we raise is going to Stu and his family, helping them get back on their feet."

"I'll be sure to pass it on," I say, dunking a chip into the bright red salsa and avoiding eye contact.

"And you and Parker be sure to come. Two Fridays from now, y'all mark it on your calendar." She winks at me, then pivots and sashays away to the kitchen, leaving me alone with my salsa and regrets.

The entire town's going to be buzzing about me and Parker now and we're not even a thing.

17

PARKER

This living with Olivia thing is going to be tougher than I thought. I snuck out early this morning just to avoid her. Having her traipsing through my kitchen in micro shorts is only inviting complications I don't need.

Best to avoid temptation altogether.

"Parker! Is Liv with you? Did you get her settled in?" Poppy shouts at me from across the pool deck.

"No, she's not with me. And yes, she's settled in," I say, keeping my focus on the task at hand. The last thing I need is to fall off this ladder while I'm repairing the tiki bar. I wrap black metal wire around a replacement frond, securing it to the structure.

"Thought she might come by today, but I guess she's probably busy catching up with work. How bad's her house?" Poppy shades her eyes from the sun, squinting up at me.

"Bad. It's going to take a while to get that repaired. The place needs a new roof and I think she has water damage.

Can't imagine the neighbor's side is any better; his half is crushed worse."

"Ugh. Bad break. It was awful nice of you to offer her a place to stay. You're such a good brother and friend." Poppy beams up at me, and my chest squeezes hard with guilt.

Real good brother, jacking off to fantasies of her best friend riding me.

I clear my throat, trying to swallow down the burning acid in my mouth. "No big deal. Have you talked to King or Roman? They coming to town to help or are we on our own?"

"Rome's coming. I think King had some clean-up out at the ranch to deal with. Why? You need more help out here?"

"I could use it. Smith's not back until next week, and I'm getting calls like crazy for estimates on damages. And the sooner we get things repaired here, the sooner we're back open for business."

"I hear ya. I'll text Rome and let him know we need more help. Parks?"

"Yeah?" I pause, the wire cutter poised mid-air.

"Thanks for taking care of Liv. She doesn't have anyone but us to count on. I really appreciate it—and I know she does too."

I shrug, all nonchalant, even as I wonder if Liv's said anything specific to Poppy. Deep down, I know I should stay away. Honor the stupid motherfucking Pact. Leave Liv alone because I have no business touching someone as perfect as her. She's too good for me, anyway. Always has been.

I resolve—again—to keep my distance from Liv, even if

it's a monumental fucking task now that she's living with me.

Nothing good will come from that, no matter how badly I want her.

"Hey, Liv. I'm home!" I hang my tool belt up by the door, kick off my work boots, like I do every night when I come home.

But when I glance up, there's Liv standing in the kitchen looking sexy as fuck, and all the air's knocked straight out of my lungs. She's wearing a tight V-neck shirt and her dark hair's piled high on her head in some complicated topknot style. A few loose strands slip down, framing her face, her cheeks a soft shade of pink.

I shove my hand in the pocket of my jeans and casually adjust myself, hoping to conceal my instant hard-on.

"Hey. I wasn't sure what time you'd be home, so I started cooking dinner."

"You didn't have to do that."

"Seems only fair, since you cooked last night. We should probably establish some sort of system, since it's looking like I'm going to be here a while. I mean, if me staying here's still alright with you?" She tips her head, biting down on her full bottom lip, and good grief, I don't think I've ever wanted to kiss her as badly as I do right now.

"Did you change your mind, Parker?"

"No, definitely not," I murmur, tearing my eyes away from her mouth. "You're good here as long as you want."

"Great. While you were gone today, I went ahead and made up a schedule." She takes the oven mitt off, crossing to the table and picking up a stack of papers.

Of course she made a schedule. Liv is one of the most organized, type A-plus people I know.

"The first page is a calendar for the month. I color-coded it—you're blue, I'm red. I wasn't sure if you have certain days you work at the bar or work late or whatever—this is flexible and subject to change, depending on work commitments."

She hands me the calendar and I stare at the red and blue boxes, all laid-out and perfectly planned. My mouth twitches, but I don't say anything.

"Does this work? Do you hate it?" Liv asks, her voice laced with doubt.

"No. It's good. This is good. Smart system." I nod, wondering how long this took her to put together.

"The next sheet is a chore chart. I don't want to free-load, so I figure I'll take most tasks." She hands me the second paper and now a deep chuckle is bubbling up inside me.

"You know I have a cleaning lady, right? She comes every other Tuesday."

"Oh. Well, that explains it . . ." She scrunches her nose up, tapping the side of her mouth and I step in a little closer to her.

"Explains what?"

"I figured your place would be messier is all. But someone else cleans. Tell you what—I'll take the bathroom on the off Tuesdays and we can split the dishes."

"Deal," I say, stepping closer to her still.

"The next sheet is basic ground rules." She hands me the third sheet, her thumb brushing against mine, and my cock twitches in my pants. Just to remind me he's still there.

"Ground rules?"

"Yeah. I mean, I'm sure I'm cramping your style. Last night kind of proved that." She twirls a stray lock of hair, leans back a little, emphasizing her chest. Damn, that shirt's low, the swell of her breasts peeking out at me, begging me to reach out and touch. My mouth waters and I clear my throat.

"You're not. That doesn't usually happen. People are just on edge, with the hurricane."

"Either way. I don't want you to feel like I'm killing your dating life or anything. So I'm happy to leave on the weekend, or clear out anytime if you give me enough notice."

I set the stack of papers down, then meet Liv's wide-eyed gaze.

Her eyes are amazing, the clearest green I've ever seen.

I can't take it anymore.

In two quick steps, I'm pressing up against Liv, her back against the island, my arms caging her in. We're so close I smell the mint from her toothpaste, feel her warm breath on my face.

"I'm tired of rules, Liv," I murmur, my eyes locked on hers.

"We don't have to use these ones, Parker." She licks her lips and something inside me—I don't know if it's logic or common sense or morality—snaps.

"Fuck the rules, Liv. For once—let's fuck the rules."

She inhales, a soft, breathy sound, her chest rising, and I lean in and do what I swore I'd never do in my entire life.

I kiss Olivia Drayton, right there in my kitchen.

Pressing my mouth to hers, I go in soft and slow, pausing and waiting to see if she kisses me back.

"Parker," she breathes, her mouth hot and ready against my lips.

But instead of breaking away, stopping things before they can start between us, she crushes her lips to mine and I know right then I'm in deep fucking trouble.

And it tastes so, so good.

18

LIV

Holy hotness. I'm kissing Parker freaking Montgomery right now. On the lips, barefoot in his kitchen wearing a ratty T-shirt.

And oh. My. Stars.

It's hot. He's hot. I'm hot.

This entire freaking kitchen's hot.

"I think something's burning," Parker murmurs against my lips.

"Shit!" I jump, wiggling away from him and running over to the stove. Cranking the knob to the left, I shut the oven off, then grab the mitts and rescue the baked chicken.

"It's slightly crispier than normal." I eye the burnt edges, fanning the air to clear the wisps of smoke rising from the casserole dish.

"No biggie. I've had worse, I'm sure. Now can we rewind?"

I grin and saunter back over to him, swaying my hips a little more than usual, then lean back against the island in the exact same position. Parker steps forward, his beautiful face inches from mine, and I can't breathe. I can't think.

All I can do is feel.

He cups my face in his strong hands, his fingers almost hovering over my skin, like he's afraid to touch me. My back's up against the island, and the granite edge digs into me, but I don't care. I don't want to move out of this spot again and break whatever spell's come over Parker.

Dropping his lips to mine, Parker kisses me, soft and slow. I open my mouth a little, urging him on, and his tongue teases me, licking along the seam of my lower lip. A tiny moan escapes from deep in my throat, and he wraps his fingers around the nape of my neck. Pulling me in closer to him, sucking my lip in between his teeth, nipping at me. We're so close now, there's no air between us except for the air we share.

I open fully to him and he sweeps in, our tongues colliding as we taste each other for the very first time. Heat unfurls low in my belly and wetness pools in my panties. His thumb rubs up and down the back of my neck, sending a hot shiver of desire rolling down my spine.

Parker's no longer tentative. Now he's wild, ferocious, untamed, and my breathing's so shallow it's more like panting. My chest heaves as I come up for air and then we dive back down together, neither of us wanting to break the connection.

I've been waiting for this moment practically my entire life and I want it to go on for as long as possible.

In fact, I don't want to ever stop kissing Parker.

Pressing my hips to his, I feel his hardness bulging in his jeans. Heat and power. My hands find his back pockets, and I squeeze his ass, pulling him up against me.

"You feel so good," he murmurs, his hand moving from my face down the line of my neck, then dropping lower still. The pads of his fingertips skim the heated skin of my chest.

Locking my gaze on his, I grant him tacit permission to touch me. Anywhere and everywhere.

He stares at me with those deep blue eyes—so familiar, yet so different—and it's like I'm seeing him for the first time.

"Say it, Liv. Tell me it's okay to fuck the rules," he whispers, leaning his forehead to mine, his pupils wide and dark with desire.

I nod, but he shakes his head.

"I need to hear you say it's okay. Please." The low, deep rumble of his voice, the gravelly need there, shakes me. My heart pounds hard and wild in my chest, and I can't even think, only react.

"Yes, Parker. Yes."

19

———

PARKER

"Yᴇs."

That's all I need to hear to break whatever thin tether of self-control still holds me together.

I take Liv's face in my hands and kiss her like I've wanted to my entire fucking life.

Hard and desperate, I ache for her. My cock throbs in my now too-tight pants and I press up against her warm body, all softness and curves. We meld together, like we're made to fit each other perfectly, and I'm not even sure where she ends and I begin.

I rock my hips against her and she answers back, and fuck me, we're dry-humping in my kitchen.

"I want to see you," I murmur against her lips, dropping one hand down to her waist. My fingers slip under her T-shirt, trailing over her soft, smooth skin. She inhales and goosebumps rise on her stomach, her arms.

"I want to see you too," she whispers, untucking my shirt and inching it up my back. Her nails scrape along my skin and my muscles tighten beneath her touch as her fingers dance up my spine. I reach down and help her out, shedding my shirt.

Another breathy inhale, her pupils wide as she eyes me.

"You can touch, you know. I won't bite," I tease, grinning.

She gives me a shy smile, then reaches out, feathering her fingers over my pecs. So lightly I wonder if I'm imagining things. My body reacts, though, my nipples hard and my muscles flexing.

"So strong." She bites her lower lip and my cock pulses.

I want to show her just how strong I can be. But I also want to savor this moment, after all this time, these years of wanting her.

With the pad of my thumb, I caress her cheek, tracing the outline of her jaw, the bump of her chin, her mouth. Smoothing my thumb over her plump lower lip, her tongue darts out, licking, then sucking. Sending my cock into an absolute frenzy.

If she keeps this up, I'm gonna come in my pants.

She gazes up at me through her dark lashes, sucking my thumb into her mouth, and swirling around the tip and I. Fucking. Can't. Right. Now.

"You gotta stop," I rasp, gripping her by the hips and bringing her closer to me. "Or this is gonna happen way too fast."

I bend down, crushing my lips to hers and sweep my tongue into her mouth.

I'm totally out of control now. Not my typical MO at all, but I can't help myself. I'm starving for her—I've been starving for her—and now that I've broken my fast I just can't stop.

Don't want to stop . . .

My hands fist in her T-shirt and I lift it up and over her head, tossing the shirt onto the granite island. Then I drop my mouth down to her breasts, trailing kisses over her chest. Her nipples pebble, sharp points poking through the black satin of her bra.

"Gorgeous," I murmur into her warm skin, one hand already moving behind her back to unhook the lacy undergarment.

Her bra falls to the ground and I suck one pink nipple into my mouth, licking and lapping until Liv moans softly. Then I move my attention to the other side, rolling and nipping until her body relaxes into me.

"So fucking perfect," I whisper, tiny bumps rising on her skin. I palm both of her breasts, a familiar tingle starting at the base of my cock.

Her nails dig into my shoulder blades, sending tiny bites of pain shooting through me, as I pinch and roll her nipples.

"Parker," she mumbles, and I glance up at her. Her head's tipped back, revealing the long, straight line of her neck, and she's a fucking goddess in this moment. Her eyes glazed with lust, I've never seen this side of Liv—reckless, out of control.

I love it.

Even more, I love that I'm doing it to her.

I'm putting that slow smile on her face, making her chest flush, her breathing shallow.

Me.

And I want her, all of her.

Right here, right now. No more waiting.

"Liv."

Her fingers twine in my hair, her nails scraping over the nape of my neck, and shivers of pleasure roll through me. I drop to my knees, unbuttoning her shorts and sliding them down her thighs. She kicks them all the way off and I cup her ass, squeezing the firm globes in my palms.

Liv has an amazing ass. I can't even count the number of times I've wanted to reach out and touch the round peach, but never could.

Without hesitation, and before either of us can change our minds, I hook my thumbs in the sides of her panties and tease them off her. She gazes down at me, bobbing her head slightly, and I know it's a go.

It's all I can do not to rip the damn things off her with one hard yank, but I somehow manage some restraint.

Now she's naked and I'm rock fucking hard.

"You're the most edible thing I've ever had in this kitchen," I say, glancing up at her as I run my hand up the inside of her thigh.

She laughs, a light, tinkly sound, and my heart squeezes in my chest.

I want to make her laugh like that, always.

I press my lips to her skin, kissing my way up her trembling thigh until I reach the apex of her legs. Looping both my hands up between her thighs, I grab her ass and pull her to me, burying my face in her wet heat. She parts her legs for me and I lick, tasting her. She grips my shoulders hard, steadying herself as I dip my tongue into her wetness. I suck her clit, soft at first, then harder, and Liv moans, so quietly I can barely even hear it. Kneading the tight muscles of her rear, I feel her quivering and know she's close.

Rising, I wipe my mouth on my bare shoulder, then scoop Liv into my arms and carry her to my bedroom.

After waiting two decades for this moment, I plan on taking my sweet time.

20

———

LIV

*I'm naked in Parker's kitchen and his gorgeous face is
between my thighs.*

Honestly, this is the best day of my entire life.

If I had a time machine, I would one hundred percent
freeze it in this exact moment and live here forever.

The ropes of his muscles flex under my touch, every
inch of him hard and defined. I love running my hand
along the strong line of his shoulder, goosebumps rising on
his skin beneath my touch. The soft exhale of breath on
my hot skin as he sucks and licks and kisses.

Then he's standing, lifting me up into his arms, his
eucalyptus smell mixing with the musky scent of sex. I'm
lightheaded and breathless, getting swept away in a Parker-
induced euphoria.

Common sense: gone.

Reason: gone.

The rules: gone.

All that's left is lust, passion, feeling.

I know I'll regret this, but it's like I'm watching a movie and I can't shut it off before I see what happens.

Even though I know the ending, I need to see it—experience it—for myself.

Just once.

Parker lays me down on his bed and his scent envelops me. There's zero percent chance any kind of logic is coming back while I'm surrounded by him.

He unbuttons his jeans, kicking them off into an unceremonious pile on the floor, and he's naked.

Now there's no fucking way to get off this train. It's left the station and we're picking up speed quickly.

In fact, it's probably a bullet train, judging by the impressive hard-on Parker's stroking.

I lick my lips, my eyes flicking up and down his body. All hard planes and sculpted muscle. My breath hitches in my throat.

He's even more gorgeous than I expected him to be, and believe me, I've thought about it.

A lot.

"You sure you want to do this?" Parker asks, locking his deep blue eyes on me.

I nod my head 'yes.'

"Uh-uh. Not good enough. I need to hear the words, Liv." He strokes his dick, never taking his eyes off mine. Waiting for me to give him consent.

"Yes," I whisper, my heart pounding so hard in my chest I think I might actually die.

"I was praying you'd say that." He reaches into his nightstand, grabs a condom, and sheaths up. In seconds, he's next to me on the bed, pulling me up against his muscular chest. Loosening my topknot, he sends my hair cascading down my back. Brushing it away from my face, he presses his lips to mine.

And honest to goodness, time stands still. It's the most wonderful, soulful, amazing kiss, and I know I'm never having another kiss as good as this one ever again, I'm absolutely certain of it.

I've been in love with Parker Montgomery practically my entire life and now we're together in his bed, naked, kissing.

I'm either dreaming or in heaven.

I open one eye a teensy bit, peeking at him through my lashes, to verify this is really happening.

Parker's still here, his hands roaming over my body, touching me everywhere I've ever wanted to be touched. I trail my hand over the strong muscles of his back, all the way down to his firm, tight ass, and squeeze.

Yep. Real.

He's real and this is really happening.

Oh. My.

Now I'm lying on his pillows, and he's spreading my legs with his hand, dipping his fingers into me. I shiver and squeeze, my muscles tightening their grip. He gazes at me, watching my response. Then he picks up the pace, working into a rhythm, and I buck against his hand. The pressure builds, tingles of pleasure zinging through me.

"Come inside," I murmur.

Parker doesn't hesitate, pulling his hand away, aligning our hips at the exact right angle. He rubs the tip of his cock against my sensitive skin, inching in slowly, so slowly. A sharp hiss escapes his lips as he sinks into me, our bodies joined together.

"Fuck, Liv. You feel so good." His eyes flutter open and we stare at each other, the moment almost surreal.

Then he surprises me, taking both my hands in his, and lacing his fingers in mine.

It's the smallest, sweetest gesture, and in this moment, it feels like it's me and Parker against the world.

Like I can do anything with him by my side.

I smile at him and he drops his lips to mine, kissing me soft and slow. Wrapping my legs around him, I pull his body in closer to me, bringing him in deeper still.

I don't ever want to let Parker go.

21

PARKER

I'M INSIDE OLIVIA.

What the fuck am I doing right now?

I'm fucking my sister's best friend is what I'm doing.

And I'm too far gone. I can't stop.

Won't stop.

Most importantly, don't want to stop.

Locking eyes with Liv, I thrust into her. Hard, deep. Decisive.

Like I know what I'm doing.

Her eyes widen, then roll back, and I know I hit the exact right spot.

If this is happening, at least I'm going to make it count.

Even if it's a one-time thing, Olivia Drayton will never, ever forget this fuck.

I'm going to be the best fuck of her entire life, guaranteed.

I've had complaints about many things—not returning phone calls, ghosting, being generally unavailable—but sex isn't one of them. I have confidence in my skills here.

"Parker." She says my name on a sigh, almost reverently, and it's good.

Very good, but not good enough.

I want her to call out my name.

"Liv." I grind against her body, her curves hugging me, our skin slick with sweat.

Her eyes flutter to my face, her cheeks rosy, and my heart squeezes hard in my chest.

She's so damn beautiful my chest aches, and it almost hurts to look at her.

Squeezing her hands, I drive into her and she takes everything I have to give. Her back arches up to meet me and I feel her building.

"Let go, Liv," I murmur into the sweet skin of her neck. "I want to watch you come."

That's all it takes to send her crashing over the edge.

"Parker!" She screams my name, her entire body shaking with her release as she unravels beneath me. I wrap my arms around her, holding her tightly to me while she quivers, her breathing ragged. I quickly chase my own climax, exploding inside her, my vision going dark for a moment.

Then, because I might never get another chance, I breathe deeply and drink her in—the way her skin flushes a soft, dewy pink, the triangle of freckles on her nose, the roses in her shampoo mingling with my own crisp body wash.

"What?" She blinks at me, blushing a deeper shade of pink. I sweep a silky strand of hair out of her eyes.

"Nothing."

"Was that well below your usual performance standards?"

I cup her cheek, my other hand tracing up and down her arm. "Definitely not. It was great. You're great."

She smiles up at me, and my heart expands; I'm not even sure I'm going to be able to contain all of these emotions.

Liv reaches up and places a hand on my chest, right over my pounding heart, and I've never been more vulnerable in my entire life.

She has to know how I feel about her now. There's no hiding it now.

And fuck, what about my sister and the stupid-ass Pact?

The last thing I want to think about in this moment is Poppy, while I'm naked in bed with Liv.

Pushing my twin out of my head, I drop my lips onto Liv's, tasting her again. She's downright addictive and I know I'm going to want—need—more of her.

"Parker?"

"Yeah?"

"Now what?"

22

PARKER

GOOD FUCKING QUESTION.

Now what?

Per the usual, I did not think this through.

I stare up at the ceiling, Liv's soft exhales warm on my chest. I don't want this to be a one-and-done thing. Liv's amazing—we're amazing—and I shouldn't have to give that up. But I know I can't tell Poppy about us. She'll blow a freaking gasket.

Do I come clean about the Pact?

My gut knots up thinking about that convo. So—back in the sixth grade I kinda, sorta promised I'd never kiss you.

No. Not a good look, especially considering I just trampled all over that promise.

I drop a kiss onto Liv's hair. "How about dinner?"

She giggles, the sound vibrating through my chest, and I try to focus on the right here, right now. Sort of my specialty.

"I meant more globally, but okay. It's probably too late for the chicken." She rubs my calf with her foot and even though I'm stressing inside, that slight contact has me hard for her again.

Focus, Parker.

"I think I have a frozen pizza. Not fine dining or anything."

"That works." Liv lifts her chin and glances up at me, her green eyes glowing. I've never seen her this relaxed before. She's sexy as hell, her dark hair all tousled and wavy.

"You're gorgeous." I stroke her shoulder and she shivers. I love that my touch elicits that response. "Maybe we should wait on dinner, go for round two instead?" I wink and she laughs, playfully punching me in the chest.

"Later. We should eat."

"So there is going to be a later. Okay, fine then. We can eat."

She rolls out of bed, trying to cover herself up with her hands self-consciously.

"What are you doing?" I ask, raising my brow and holding in a chuckle as I watch her strategize where exactly to place her hands for maximum coverage.

"My clothes are in the kitchen." She blushes, her cheeks a deep pink.

"So? I already saw you naked. Who cares?" I kick off the cotton sheets, giving her a full view of everything I've got.

"Still. It's weird." She shuffles from foot to foot, uncomfortable.

"No, it's not. I promise you that." Rising from the bed, I wrap my arms around her waist, pulling her naked body to mine. "I love you naked. It's hot. You're hot," I murmur, brushing my lips with hers. Claiming her mouth, I swipe my tongue inside, exploring.

"Thanks," she mumbles against my lips, half-heartedly.

Breaking the kiss, I lift her chin to meet my gaze. "I mean it, Liv. Seriously. You're beautiful."

She blinks and swallows, looking away from me. "Then how come you never noticed me before?"

My chest squeezes so hard I'm pretty sure there's the bare minimum of oxygen necessary to sustain life left in my lungs. *What the hell am I supposed to say here?*

This is the moment to come clean, Parker. Do it.

I take a shaky breath, my throat dry and scratchy. "I did."

"No. I never saw you glance in my direction, not even once." Liv stands up straighter, squaring her shoulders.

"You weren't paying attention then. Because believe me —I noticed you. Everyone notices you."

She gnaws on her bottom lip, and I don't know what to do here. This is the most awkward post-sex discussion ever, and believe me, I've had a bunch.

Tell her. Tell her you've always wanted her.

"You just have to trust me, Liv. Okay?" I run my hand along her hip, stepping into her space and closing the distance between us.

Rising up on tiptoe, she laces her fingers around the back of my neck, laying a gentle kiss on my lips. "I do, Parker."

Every muscle in my body relaxes and all is right in the world, here in this moment.

Right now, I have everything I want.

I'm just not sure how to keep her.

23

———

LIV

I wake up the next day in Parker's bed, cocooned in his crisp white sheets. *Is this a dream?*

There's a warm, Parker-shaped indent next to me. Feels real.

Cocking my ear toward the door, I listen for noises. Total silence. He must be gone already. Parker has two modes: work and party, nothing in between.

Better than your one mode, Olivia. Work.

Silencing that voice (which sounds uncannily like my mother), I climb out of bed and scoop up the T-shirt Parker had on last night. I bury my nose in the soft blue fabric, inhaling his crisp, masculine scent.

I can't believe I slept with Parker Montgomery.

After all this time. And he said he always noticed me.

Not that I believe him. He was probably in the post-sex stupor guys get, when they'll say anything to make sure they get laid again.

But it didn't feel like that last night.

Shrugging into Parker's T-shirt, I decide to bask in this

delicious feeling for at least a day before I start trying to figure everything out. Because this situation is complicated.

We chatted about it a little last night and decided to hold off on saying anything to Poppy.

Not forever. Just for right now.

Because we don't want to share this—whatever this is—with all of Seaglass Beach just yet.

Maybe he'll never want to, Liv. This is Parker Montgomery we're talking about here. He's not exactly known for his long-term relationship skills.

My shoulders tense, creeping up towards my ears, and my stomach grumbles.

You're hungry is all. Stop reading so much into every little thing.

I pad to the bathroom and brush my teeth, setting my pink toothbrush at attention directly opposite Parker's blue one. So weird. Never in a million years did I think I'd share a bathroom with him.

Let alone a bed.

Effervescent giddiness bubbles up inside me and I wish I could call my best friend and talk all about last night with her.

But I definitely cannot. Because said best friend is Parker's twin sister and I'm sure she'd think it was gross. Or at least TMI. Either way, I one-thousand percent cannot tell her.

I never told anyone about my crush on Parker, not in all these years. It felt too weird admitting it out loud, so I hid it.

Because you didn't want him to be another failure, another way you don't measure up.

Shoving that cheerful thought away, I turn on the shower. Maybe I can wash away all my doubts and hang-ups, emerge as one of the confident women Parker usually pursues.

Unlikely, but maybe . . .

Poppy takes an early lunch and I meet up with her at our favorite coffee shop, Coastal Coffee. The location is great—it's right in the center of town, on Main Street, one block over from the beach—making it easy to access for both of us at all times.

Walking in, I spot Poppy ordering at the register. I smooth my hair down over my shoulder, take a quick deep breath.

Just act normal. There's no way she knows anything.

"Hey!" Poppy spins around and hugs me like I haven't seen her in a month and a half, not twelve hours. "How are you? Is it awful living with my brother?" She grips my shoulders, rearing back and staring at me with wide blue eyes.

Gawd, she has the exact same eyes as Parker.

I shake my head no, flicking my gaze to the menu I know by heart. Anything to avoid eye contact with Poppy.

"You can tell me, Liv, it's okay. I'd never breathe a word." Her voice drops to a hush, like we're in on a conspiracy or something. She reaches her hand out and squeezes my forearm, but I feel that squeeze deep in my chest and I can't breathe.

This was a terrible idea.

But I can't avoid Poppy forever. Nor do I want to, so I —we—better figure this out soon.

"No, it's fine, Pops. Honest. Parker's been great." Saying his name, heat unfurls low in my belly and my muscles contract.

Stupid muscle memory. It was one damn time, Liv, get a freaking grip.

Well, twice, if you count round two.

Mercifully, the barista calls Poppy's name and she flits off to grab her iced coffee. I place my order and pay, tapping my toes on the white linoleum floor.

"How much coffee have you already had, Liv? You seem amped," Poppy teases, linking her arm through mine and leading us to an empty table near the window. "Are you sleeping okay? I know my brother's known to have a lot of late-night company . . ." She rolls her eyes and my stomach sinks.

Because her statement's accurate and I don't want to think about.

Because I'm hiding something huge from my best friend.

Because I hardly slept at all last night since I was too busy fucking her twin brother.

"Order up for Liv!"

I spring out of my seat, happy for the distraction—and a chance to change the subject.

Iced mocha in hand, I compose myself and settle back into my seat. "How's the inn? Any idea when you want to reschedule the anniversary party?" I tap on my cell, pulling up my calendar.

Yes, get back on solid ground. Talk about something you know

—*events.*

"We're almost fully operational at the inn. Parks has the tiki bar repairs ninety percent finished and we're booked up again starting next week."

"That's great." I nod and scroll through my calendar, checking possible dates for the party.

"We might need to move the party to Labor Day. What do you think about a joint anniversary-Labor Day party? That will help us recoup some of the costs at least."

"That's a good idea." As I'm typing in the tentative date change, my cell dings with a text.

It's from Parker.

"Work text," I lie, holding up my finger. "Just a sec."

Parker: Dinner tonight? My place? Dress code is very loose. 😉

I bite my lip, stifling a giggle. After all, this is supposedly a work text and I can't remember the last time Diane made me LOL.

Liv: Haha. Sounds good. Unless you're into dining al fresco. Then we can eat at my place. Inside, yet under the stars. Kind of like a planetarium.

Parker: I'm into dining anywhere, anytime, any way, with you.

Heat flames my face, my stomach flip-flopping. I always knew Parker was a charmer, but to have his spotlight shining on me?

Heaven.

"Everything okay, Liv? You look—I don't know—flushed. Did an event get cancelled?"

I pop my head up, guilt twisting around inside me, the knots getting tighter and tighter. "What? No, everything's fine. All good." I flip my cell over on the table, just in case another text from Parker comes through. Better safe than sorry.

"You want to come over tonight? We could have movie night. I have popcorn and wine. You could sleep over, get away from my brother for a night."

The knot pulls tighter still, and I can barely swallow. "Uh, not tonight. I, uh, have a lot of work I have to catch up on. Plus, I need to talk with my landlord. Lots to do," I stammer, positive Poppy's going to find me out.

"You have a call with your landlord at night? Weird." She takes a loud slurp of her coffee, scrunching her brows together, but seems to buy my lame excuse. "Maybe tomorrow night then. Oh crap—I have to meet a potential business partner. Did I tell you about the ice cream parlor Jess Carter wants to open next to the inn?"

"No, but that sounds amazing. Love it."

"Yeah, it would be a great use of the space. Anyway, I'm late. Call me!" She bolts up, waves, and dashes out the door as I crash back against the metal chair. This whole undercover thing is harder than I thought.

There's no way I'm going to be able to keep this from Poppy for long.

No freaking way.

24

PARKER

AFTER A LONG DAY GIVING REPAIR ESTIMATES, I'M HAPPY to finally be heading home.

Even happier to be heading home to Liv.

Whistling, I swing into the Seaglass Market to pick up a few key dinner items. Namely, real food. I took stock of Liv's grocery shopping this morning and let's just say, we have some minor details to work out when it comes to menu planning. Plain almond milk, spinach, and almonds ain't dinner, babe.

I pick out a juicy T-bone, some mushrooms, potatoes, and a nice bottle of Cab, then head to the front checkout.

"Whoa, Montgomery, what's the rush?"

Coming round the corner, I run straight into Jagger Capelli and his brother, Damon, carrying two six-packs of beer each. Typical.

"Hot date, by the looks of it," Damon sneers, eyeing my shopping basket.

"Mr. Casanova," Jagger jokes, waggling his eyebrows at his brother. Dope.

"Who's the lucky girl tonight? Maybe I'll shoot her my number for tomorrow night, when you're done with her."

My right eyelid twitches, hot anger bubbling through my veins, but I tamp it down and keep my cool.

"Real fucking funny, Jagger. Not a chance I'd ever give any woman I date your number." I sidestep them and head toward the register, eager to avoid a confrontation. The Capellis are thugs and not worth my time or energy.

"You disrespecting my brothers, asshole?" Cash comes out of nowhere, hitting me in the chest and knocking me backwards.

"What the fuck? Y'all always travel together, like a pack of hyenas?" I brush Cash's fist off, like he's a swarming gnat on a humid summer day.

None of them respond to my question. I try to push past them, but now they're standing shoulder to shoulder, a wall of Capellis, and I can't move forward.

"Heard you're a real knight in shining armor, Montgomery," Cash says, thrusting out his steroid-enhanced chest.

"What are you talking about?" I ask, frowning. These guys are annoying as hell and all I want to do is get home to Liv.

"You got little Livvy Drayton all shacked up with you. Because the Big Bad Wolf Clementine huffed and puffed and blew her house down." Jagger smirks at his own joke and Damon and Cash guffaw like the stupid sidekicks they are.

I say nothing, white-knuckling my basket and trying to push past them to get to the register.

But Jagger's raring for a fight. He pushes back, not letting me pass.

"Get out of my way, Jagger," I say through gritted teeth. Now I'm pissed—and I don't love the idea that the Capellis know my business.

"What are you gonna do about it?" He scowls, the scar over his eyebrow dancing on his forehead. I'm fairly certain a Montgomery gave him that scar, I just can't remember if it was King or Roman.

"Nothing in the supermarket. Because I'm a civilized adult, unlike you cretins."

"Oh, big word from a contractor," Jagger says, his tone mocking.

I grind my teeth, my jaw flexing. *I will not take the bait. Who cares what Jagger thinks about your job?*

"Don't forget about the bartender gig," Cash chimes in, and now I've fucking had it with these buffoons.

"Both jobs are a real step up from whatever it is the three of you do. So shut the fuck up and move out of my way."

"We're entrepreneurs, Montgomery," Jagger says, thumping my shoulder. "You should appreciate that."

"So that's what we're calling it these days, huh?" I snicker.

Jagger ignores my dig. "Are you going to put Livvy's little house back together again? Because I'm sure she's not going to hang around with you for very long—no one ever does. Did you tell her she's now in your catch-and-release program?"

That's the last straw. Squaring my shoulders, I puff my chest out, standing toe-to-toe with Jagger. He's a solid five inches shorter than me, so I'm staring down at the top of his greasy weasel head.

"I don't want to hear Liv's name come out of your filthy mouth ever again, Jagger," I growl, my voice low.

"Or else what, Montgomery? What are you going to do about it?" His lips quirk up and I'm dying to punch that sneer right off his ugly mug.

"How about I make it so no words come out of your mouth for a while?"

"You hear that, boys? Montgomery's got jokes." Jagger ribs Cash and Damon, and all my muscles tense.

Jagger moves in closer to me so our faces are inches apart and whispers: "Liv."

That's when I fucking lose it. Flashes of black dance across my vision, blood pounding so loud in my ears it drowns out the easy listening seventies tunes playing over the market's loudspeaker. I throw my basket to the ground, ball up my fist, and slug Jagger Capelli square in the jaw. He staggers back into the candy on the endcap, his arms flailing. Cash rears up like a bull and makes a run at me, but I step to the side and he goes flying into a paper towel display. Lucky for him it isn't jars of spaghetti sauce or something—the paper towels cushion his fall as he slides into the tower of cotton cloths.

Damon's torn between helping Cash or taking a swing at me. In the split second it takes him to decide, I'm able to move ahead to the register, out of his direct line of fire. Now there's a lot of stuff around me and Damon wisely stands down, moving to help Cash instead.

But Jagger's not going down without a fight. He grabs me by the back of the collar, pulling me out into the open space. I whirl around, blocking his punch, gripping his arm and twisting it up behind his back.

"Not today, Jags," I say, clutching him hard and pulling

his arm up even harder. "Now leave me and Liv the fuck alone. You got me?"

Jagger's head moves up and down a fraction of an inch, so I shove him away from me, toward his stupid brothers. Picking up my basket, I ring my items up at the self-checkout and stroll out of the store, flexing my hand.

I'm gonna need some ice on my knuckles, but I'm pretty sure the Capellis got the fucking hint.

25

———

LIV

"Ohmygosh! What happened to your hand?" I eye Parker's red, swollen knuckles as he takes the gel ice pack from the freezer and gingerly places it over his hand, wincing.

"Nothing. I'm fine. Little injury on the job is all." Parker leans back against the counter, cradling his right hand in his left.

"What? How? Did you punch down a wall? I thought you used sledgehammers for that sort of thing?"

"I should have. That would have gotten the job done a lot more efficiently." He presses his lips together in a thin, tight line and now I know there's more to the story.

"Parks, did you get in a fight?" I stand directly across from him, arms crossed over my chest.

He shrugs. "Maybe a little skirmish."

"Ohmygawd, Parks. Why?" I shake my head, barely keeping my eye roll in check.

"Because Jagger Capelli's an annoying little weasel is why."

"No, not the Capellis. Parker! You know Jagger will never let this go. He'll seek revenge until he's six feet under." I huff out an aggravated breath.

Boys.

"It needed to happen, Liv. Sorry. I can't let him keep saying all the shit he's been saying and get away with it." Parker shifts his weight against the counter, crossing his feet at the ankles.

"What did he say that made you punch him?"

"Nothing," he mumbles. "Don't worry about it."

"Of course I'm worried about it! You're hurt." I move to his side, clasping his bicep.

"It's no big deal. Jagger's a freaking buffoon. And so are his brothers."

"His brothers were there too? You fought all three of them?" I ask, my voice tipping up in disbelief.

"Yeah. They suck. For thugs, they're not very tough."

Parker shrugs off the fact that he just had a street fight with the three Capellis and beat all of them single-handedly, like a damn superhero.

"Parks. You really shouldn't be getting into fights, you could get arrested." I glide my hand from his bicep over to his broad chest, rubbing my palm over his strong, defined pecs.

"I tried to resist, Liv, but he just wouldn't shut up. I couldn't let him keep disrespecting you and me."

My hand freezes over his thumping heart, a chill trickling down my spine.

"What? Jagger said something about you and me? He knows?"

"He doesn't *know* anything. Only that you moved in because your house is uninhabitable. I told him to keep your name out of his filthy mouth or I'd knock it out for him. He chose the latter." Parker flexes his hand, shifting against the granite, and my lips tip up into a tiny smile.

"You defended me?" I ask, my insides softening into a mushy, gooey, sappy pile.

"Yeah. Of course." He locks his eyes on mine and my stomach goes all swoopy, heat flooding my system.

"That's so sweet." I rise up on tiptoe, pressing my lips to his. "No one's ever defended me before."

"Not true. I decked Cash Capelli in the ninth grade when he told everyone in homeroom that he kissed you behind the bleachers at the football game."

"What? You did?"

"Yeah. I knew there was no way you'd kiss Cash Capelli, especially behind the bleachers. You weren't even in town that weekend."

My mind swirls, struggling to process all this new info. "Wait—you knew I was out of town?"

"Of course I did. I told you—I've always noticed you." Parker's deep blue gaze lands on mine, and my face flames.

"I . . . I never knew that."

"There's a lot you don't know, Liv." Parker swallows, his Adam's apple bobbing in his neck, and I wonder what exactly he means by this.

All this time, I thought I knew everything there was to know about Parker Collin Montgomery, but now I'm not so sure.

I take a shaky breath, my insides humming with an odd mix of desire and confusion. "Well, are you going to tell me?"

Parker shrugs. "Maybe. Right now, I'm gonna take a shower." He unfolds himself from the counter, puts the ice pack back into the freezer, then glances at me over his shoulder. "You coming?"

My breath catches in my throat, and once again I cannot believe this is happening. I can only nod, my heart pounding wildly in my chest as I follow Parker to the bathroom.

The small bathroom's already steamy when I join Parker, the mirrors white with fog. Shoving aside the navy-and-white striped curtain, I pause, taking in the sight of his strong, broad back. Water rolls down the long planes of tanned, rippling muscle, down over the white skin of his firm ass.

I step in, pulling the curtain closed. Humidity swirls around me and I'm lightheaded, both from the heat and my proximity to Parker.

"Hey." Parker turns to face me, pulling me up against his wet, naked body, his impressive erection bobbing between us.

"Hey," I murmur, warm water cascading over my shoulders, trickling down my breasts. My nipples harden, my lower belly clenching.

Parker's always had an effect on me, but a naked Parker? I'm surprised I'm not spontaneously orgasming, to be honest.

Heart pounding, I'm certain he knows how I feel about him. There's no holding back now.

He leans down, claiming my mouth, and a tiny moan escapes from deep in my throat.

"I missed you today," he murmurs into my open mouth, and it's a good thing his large hands are wrapped around my waist because my legs are freaking jelly.

Parker missed me?

"Me too," I whisper as he suds my back with his eucalyptus body wash, marking me with his scent.

Making me his.

And gawd, I'm here for it.

Every muscle in my body tenses and I'm wet and ready for him as his hands roam over my skin. He spins me around, soaping my breasts, my belly, then dropping lower, then lower still. His fingers find my clit, rubbing my most sensitive spot, and now I'm wetter still. I rest my head against his chest as he rains hot kisses up and down my neck, my collarbone, my shoulder.

"Parks," I moan as he dips one finger, then two inside me.

"Liv." He continues his assault up and down my neck and I can barely hold myself up, my body weak and wanting.

"I'm going to get you off now. Relax against me and let me take you, okay?" he whispers against the shell of my ear. I nod, unable to form coherent words as I press my back against his hard torso.

"You're so beautiful." He sucks on the sensitive flesh of my earlobe, sending a wave of pleasure rippling over my skin. He stretches me, another finger dipping inside, then he begins to move in a steady rhythm, in and out, hitting all the right spots.

Gawd, Parker is so fucking good.

I've never been with anyone as amazing as him. He's a musician, playing each note at exactly the right time.

Tension builds inside me, his other hand palming my breast, rolling my nipple with his thumb and forefinger. Squeezing, with just the right amount of pressure. Shock waves zing through me and I'm so close.

I tighten and clench around his fingers, pressing my thighs together to increase the friction and he picks up the pace. I'm panting now, my breathing ragged as stars dance behind my closed eyelids. My head lolls back against Parker's shoulder, and he grips my hipbone, supporting me.

"Come for me, Liv."

The vibrations of his deep voice against my skin send me over the edge, shattering on his hand, and I cry out.

"Oh. My. Parker."

"That's a good girl," he murmurs, kissing my cheek, my neck, as I shake and quiver in his arms.

He's so strong, so good, so loving.

He holds me tight against him as I come down, water streaming all around us, steam thick in the air.

I've never been happier in my entire life.

26

———

LIV

Later that night, after dinner and dishes, Parker and I head outside to the back patio. There's still a nice breeze from the hurricane and the temperature's more reasonable, although humidity's about a thousand percent. He lights tall citronella tiki torches around us, keeping the mosquitoes at bay, and I settle into an Adirondack chair.

Tucking my legs under me, I gaze up at the inky sky dotted with stars; we're lucky Seaglass Beach is small and we don't have the light pollution big cities do. Parker walks behind me, his hand absently stroking my hair before he sinks down in the chair next to me.

"Nice night." He takes a sip of his beer, his hand finding mine, his thumb smoothing over my skin.

"Mmm-hmm." Shockwaves of pleasure vibrate up my arm with every stroke of his finger and I'm warm and tingly.

"I saw Poppy this afternoon."

Parker's hand freezes on mine. "You did?"

"Yeah. We met up at Coastal Coffee."

"And? You didn't say anything, right?" Tension seeps into his voice and his brows knit together.

"No. I told you I wouldn't. But I feel bad lying to her." I bite my lip, rolling it between my teeth.

"We're not lying, exactly. Just not sharing everything."

"Well—I kinda lied. She wanted me to come over for girls' night and I told her I already had plans."

"That's not a lie—you do." Parker shoots me a devilish grin, running his hand up my arm, leaving a delicious chill in his wake.

"You know what I mean, Parks. And I'm not suggesting we blast whatever this is—" I wave my hand in the air between us—"to the entire town, but I think we should at least tell Poppy. I mean, not all the details, obviously. But something. I'm not going to be able to keep this a secret forever."

Parker leans over and presses his lips to mine, my words dying in the salty air as his tongue sweeps into my mouth. He tastes like beer and lust and I can't think straight with his mouth on mine. His fingers wrap around the back of my neck, pulling me closer to him, and heat unfurls low in my belly.

I wish we could stay like this forever. Just me and Parker, tangled up together in our safe little love bungalow. This thing between us feels so precious, so fragile, like a shimmering, glittery web lacing us together.

And I'm terrified it's going to break.

Like everything always does.

I have to set boundaries, structure, get things back under control. I've been spinning the last few days, dizzy with everything Parker, but if I'm not careful I'm going to get hurt.

Badly.

I break away, pulling back so I can see his face. Bright white moonlight highlights his high cheekbones, his eyes twinkling in the glow of the tiki torches.

"Parks, I know this isn't your usual style. I get it, I do. You keep things casual, you don't do serious." I take a shaky breath, my stomach twisting, but I dig deep, somehow finding the courage to forge ahead.

"But I'm not sure I can do that with you. And I know I should have thought of that before last night. I mean, I've had almost twenty years to think about it, but never in a million did I believe anything would actually happen—"

"Wait. Pause." Parker throws up a hand, his eyes scanning my face, and I blush under his hot stare. "Did you just say twenty years?"

I swallow, my pulse racing.

Why'd I out myself? Way to play it cool, Liv.

"Uh—maybe . . ."

"You've liked me for twenty years?" He says this slowly, as if he's digesting the words, syllable by syllable. One eyebrow arches up high on his forehead and he brushes his hair away from his eyes. "I can't believe it."

I finger my initial necklace, rubbing the smooth silver round and round. *Geez, this is embarrassing.*

"I wish I would have known sooner," he murmurs.

Leaning forward, Parker takes my face in his hands. His calloused palms rough on my cheeks, he locks his lips on mine, capturing my mouth with his. Kissing me long and soft and slow.

Like we have all the time in the world, but he'll never get enough.

He breaks the kiss, but doesn't move back into his own

space. "Maybe I'm tired of casual. And maybe I was waiting to do serious with the right girl," Parker whispers, inches away from me.

My breath catches in my throat, my heart skipping in my chest. *Did I just hear that correctly?*

"Parks. I'm being real here," I say, my pulse racing.

"So am I, Liv." His ocean-blue eyes are wide, sincere, and I want to believe him.

Need to believe him.

Parker's holding my heart in his hand. All he has to do is squeeze and I'll be crushed. And I'm not sure I can ever recover from that.

"Please don't say things you don't mean, Parker. Please," I whisper, my voice so soft it's almost carried away on the wind.

"I'm not, Liv. I promise." He laces his fingers in mine, never breaking eye contact, and I know it's too late now anyway.

I'm in too deep and I can't get out, don't want to get out.

I've been in love with Parker almost my entire life and the real him is even better than the one I dreamed up.

27

———

PARKER

Holy shit. Liv's been into me for almost twenty years.

Twenty fucking years and I never even knew.

Not that I could have done anything about it anyway.

Shitballs.

The Pact.

I should tell her.

I need to tell her.

I don't want to tell her.

"Parker?" Liv's voice rockets me back to reality.

"Yeah?"

"What are we going to do about Poppy?"

I rake my hand through my hair, feeling unsteady. *Because fuck if I know.*

There's no way she's going to be cool with this. No way. And what am I supposed to tell Liv?

Leave it to me to get into the absolute worst predicament possible.

"Let me talk to her, explain the situation. I think it'll be best coming from me."

Liv scrunches up her nose and it's so fucking adorable I have to lean over and kiss her right on that exact splash of freckles.

"Parks!" she says, giggling, as I steeple her in between my arms, standing and bending over her. I inhale deeply, the light notes of her floral scent tickling my nostrils as I rub the tips of our noses together.

"What?"

"Focus," Liv chides, smacking me on the chest.

"I am focusing. On you." I skim my lips over hers and she opens, inviting me in. Without hesitation, I sweep into her mouth, claiming her.

I want Liv to be mine.

We're so good together, everything's so easy between us, so right.

It's like we're meant to be.

I just need to make Poppy understand.

Because I promised Liv I wouldn't take things between us lightly—and I don't want to anyway.

I have a connection with her I've never felt with anyone else.

Now I need to figure out a way to not fuck it up.

Smith, my cousin and business partner, is back in town, thank goodness. Besides needing the help at work, I could also use his advice. Unlike me, he's actually good at relationships. And as an added bonus, he's discreet about shit too.

"Yo, glad you're back." I slap him on the shoulder, then go in for a bro hug. "How was Atlanta?"

"Atlanta was good, man. But I'm gonna be honest, I can't wait for Elise to move down. I'm over that drive. Traffic sucks. And it was even worse because of the evacuations. Took me twice as long to make it home."

"Dude, that blows. When's she moving?"

"Soon. The house in Atlanta's on the market. We're waiting on the building inspection here and then she and the kids can move into her beach place."

"That's awesome, man. Good for you. She's really sweet."

"She is." Smith's eyes glaze over with talk of Elise and I clear my throat to get his attention.

"So—I kind of have a predicament—" I say, dropping my voice so the crew won't overhear.

"What's up?" Smith crosses his arms over his chest, furrowing his brow.

I huff out a breath, raking a hand through my hair. "You're sworn to secrecy, got it?"

Smith tips his head, an almost imperceptible nod.

"Liv stayed with us during the hurricane. And then her house got smashed by a tree and she moved in with me. You know, temporarily. It made sense."

"Oh-kay." Smith draws the word out, narrowing his eyes.

I inch closer to him, lowering my voice to a whisper. "I kissed her."

He raises a brow, whistling. "Only kissed?"

Biting my upper lip, I tilt my head back and peer at the sky, the sun's rays blinding.

"Dude. You're so screwed."

"Gee, thanks. That's the kind of advice I'm looking for." I scrub a hand over the back of my neck, my knuckles still a little swollen from their run-in with Jagger's jaw.

"Sorry. But I'm not sure what you want me to say here. Poppy's gonna be pissed. I'm assuming you haven't told her and that's the issue?"

I shift from foot to foot, debating how much to say here. "We haven't mentioned anything to Poppy yet . . .it's kind of a thing."

"Shit, there's more?" Smith asks.

"It's a long story. But back in the day, Poppy and I made a pact where we each picked a friend of the other's and promised not to date that person. Well—Liv's that friend."

"Oh. Damn."

I grit my teeth, my back molars grinding together hard. "Yeah."

"Who's Poppy's pick?"

I shrug. "Brant somebody. He moved away after high school. So she's off the hook."

Smith claps me on the back, shaking his head. "You'd best tell Poppy about it and fast. This town is really small and you know how word travels. She's bound to find out and it's gonna be best coming from you and Liv firsthand. Secrets never keep."

Shit. Smith's one hundred percent right and it's the last thing I want to hear.

"When'd you get so wise?" I joke, ribbing him.

"I'm built like that. Thought after all this time, maybe

I'd rub off on you, but apparently not." He grins at me and I punch him in the bicep.

"Shut the fuck up, man."

"Hey, watch it. I have to install Elise's backsplash with these arms this afternoon."

"You're a simp, anyone ever tell you that?"

"Nah. That's a fucking original one, Montgomery. Never heard it before. You helping with the backsplash or are you going to go talk to your sister?"

"Let me grab my trowel."

Smith shakes his head, grinning at me. "You're hopeless, Parker. Hurry up—I'll wait for you in the truck."

28

———

LIV

I never thought I'd be happy about a hurricane blowing through Seaglass Beach, leaving a tree on my house and my office temporarily closed, but here we are.

Moving in with Parker's been surprisingly easy. The only bad part's been lying to Poppy, but Parker swore he'd talk to her today. I check my messages for the hundredth time, hoping for an update, a thumbs-up, any sign that he's communicated with his sister.

Still nothing.

I'm sure he'll talk to her. He's probably busy on a job is all.

Turning my attention back to email, I respond to the few unopened messages in my inbox, filing as I go. I do love a good clean inbox.

The Turners need to know about dessert options for a fiftieth birthday party, Diane has a client meeting set up next week, and did I remember to order the floating candles for the Seaglass Beach High reunion?

I make notes in my planner, highlighting the important dates.

Crap. I'm out of paper in my notebook. I hop up and scurry to my bedroom, wondering if I packed any extra office supplies. I'd been in such a rush, I mostly threw anything I could touch into my bags. I don't remember packing any extra notebooks, but that night's kind of a blur.

I rummage through the one duffel that's still packed and come up empty-handed. Nothing.

Now if I were Parker, where would I keep extra paper? He doesn't have an office and I know for a fact there's only a tiny Post-It cube in the kitchen drawer.

His bedroom maybe?

I tiptoe into Parker's empty bedroom. Even though I've been in his room a dozen times now, I still feel like an intruder without him here.

I'm sure he won't care, though. Parker's not the type to stress about esoteric concepts like privacy. He's an open book.

The room's dark and shadowy, the blinds shutting out the blazing afternoon sun. His clean scent lingers in the air and I breathe him in, a rush of desire zinging through me.

Focus, Liv. Paper. That's why you're in here.

I glance around, wondering where he keeps office supplies. Maybe his closet?

Opening the bifold door, I see Parker's dress shirts and polos hanging neatly in a color-coded row, from dark to light. Surprisingly organized—who would have thought? But Parker has always been particular about his wardrobe. His laundry basket sits beneath the hanging clothes and is overflowing. That's more in line with the Parker I know.

I glance overhead at the shelves, but the only thing up there is a wall of shoeboxes stacked to the ceiling.

Shutting the closet door, I spin around, thinking. I doubt he'd store office supplies in his dresser. Then I spot his nightstand and it does have two drawers. Kind of a long shot, but maybe?

The top drawer's filled with the usual things: boxers, a box of condoms, lube. Typical dude paraphernalia. Mercifully, nothing too embarrassing, but still no paper. On to the bottom drawer—T-shirts, socks, and . . . jackpot! The silver spiral of a notebook winks up at me, shiny and glistening.

All I need is a few sheets of paper, I'm sure Parker won't mind if I tear some out. Fishing the notebook out by the metal rings, I pause when I see the bright pink cover with surfing stickers stuck haphazardly all over the front.

How old is this thing? The stickers are yellowed at the edges and one flutters to the ground when I open the notebook.

POPPY'S PRIVATE DIARY. KEEP OUT.

Why does Parker have Poppy's diary?

I should probably put this back. Now I'm snooping.

No, just getting a few sheets of paper, that's all, I reason. I can't help it if I maybe, casually, read things as I flip through on my quest for blank pages.

A page scrawled in black sharpie catches my eye and I freeze, my eyes scanning the words.

Pact.

Forbidden.

*I, Parker Montgomery, promise to never go out
with Olivia Drayton.
Forever and ever.
Parker Collin Montgomery
Poppy Florence Montgomery*

I can't catch my breath as my pulse hammers double-time, a cold, hard pit lodging in my stomach, my mind racing.

Parker had a pact with Poppy forbidding him from dating me?

All this time I thought I was invisible to him, that he didn't notice me and wasn't interested.

But that's not the truth.

He wasn't *allowed* to notice me, be interested in me. My own best friend made sure of that.

Hot anger rises inside me, my insides bubbling in a rolling boil of pissed off-ness. *How dare Poppy try to control my love life? And why had Parker gone along with it?*

I've spent a good chunk of my life watching Parker hook up with every girl in Seaglass Beach, my heart breaking a little more each time. Because I wasn't good enough for him, I wasn't what he was looking for.

Or so I thought.

Turns out, my very best friend in the whole wide world was the reason Parker never so much as glanced in my direction.

How dare she? What made Poppy think she could control my life, Parker's life?

Who does she think she is?

With shaking hands, I stuff Parker's socks and T-shirts back into the drawer, then slam it shut. I have half a mind to march over to the Seaglass Inn and confront Poppy right there on the spot, but I care too much about Parker to sabotage his relationship with his sister.

This thing between me and Parker just got a lot more complicated. Before, I thought it was only the two of us wrapped up in the shimmering web.

But now I realize Poppy's been there the entire time, whether I wanted her there or not.

29

PARKER

By the time Smith and I are done tiling the backsplash, it's after five. All I want to do is go home, take a quick shower, and love on Liv. What I don't want to do is hunt down Poppy and tell her I broke our Pact.

Despite my earlier promise to Liv, I back down the driveway and head toward home. Poppy can wait another day—I want to enjoy one more night with Liv all to myself before I have to deal with the repercussions of our relationship. I know my sister's gonna be pissed and right now, I'm not up for dealing with her. I love her, but sometimes she can be a lot, and I'm betting this is gonna be one of those times. Besides, Poppy's not exactly known for her rationality, especially when she's mad.

I park behind Liv's Camry, happy to see she's home. The event business will probably crank back into full gear soon, so Liv's nights and weekends will be a lot busier. We won't get to spend much time together.

All the more reason to avoid Poppy a little while longer.

"Hey, I'm home!" I call out, crashing through the screen door. The house is quiet, and Liv's not at the kitchen table.

"Liv!"

Thinking maybe she's in the back, I head down the hall. The bathroom door's open, no sign of Liv. Same with her bedroom and mine. No lights on, no music. Where the hell is she?

Panic alarms chime in my head, but I silence them.

Stay cool, Parker. Don't freak out yet.

I walk back to the kitchen, movement catching the corner of my eye. Liv's sitting outside on the patio. Cool relief rushes through me and I exhale a shaky breath. Since my parents died, I get a little freaked when I can't locate someone, and clearly, Liv's no exception.

Grabbing a beer from the fridge, I amble out to the patio.

"Hey. I was calling you, I didn't know where you were," I say, bending down and kissing her hair. The dark, silky strands are warm, like she's been baking in the Florida sun all afternoon.

She doesn't say anything as I lower myself down into the chair next to hers, and she's swiping at her face.

"Liv? What's wrong?" I lean forward and rub her arm, but she jerks away from my touch.

"Don't, Parker," she says, her voice a low warning.

"Babe. What's the matter?"

She wipes dark smudges of mascara from below her eyes and I can tell she's been crying, wet tears staining her T-shirt.

"Don't babe me." She thrusts something in my direction, hitting me square in the chest, knocking the wind out of me due to the force.

Damn. She's definitely pissed.

Glancing down, cold dread sinks like a rock in my gut. A familiar pink notebook sits on my lap, tiny surfers taunting me as they perpetually hang ten.

Shit.

"Liv. I can explain."

"Start talking." She turns to face me, her green eyes lasers boring into my face. My palms clam up and sweat beads at the small of my back.

"It was Poppy's idea." I sound lame, even to my own ears.

"Last I checked, they did cut the umbilical cord at birth, so I'm pretty sure you're free to make your own choices, Parker."

I shift in the chair, the wood hard and uncomfortable beneath me. "I know. And it's dumb. I shouldn't have made a stupid pact with Poppy. But I was twelve, Liv." I swallow hard over the lump in my throat.

"Okay, fine, you were twelve when you signed the paper. But what about all this time? I'm a person, not a promise. You can't make a person off-limits—that's just stupid!"

Her hands shake as she waves her arms in the air, her face flushing bright pink.

"All this time I thought I was invisible, that I wasn't good enough for you." Her voice cracks and my heart squeezes hard in my chest as tears well in her eyes.

"Liv . . ."

"But even worse is Poppy! How dare she try to control my life?" Tears spill over now, glistening on her dark lashes, then rolling down her cheeks, and I'm frozen in place despite the heat.

I'm not good with tears. Or emotions. Or relationships.

I'm a one-night stand kind of guy and I'm way out of my comfort zone here.

This is the deep end and I'm used to the wading pool.

"It's not like that, Liv."

"Really? Because it seems like that from here. I loved you, Parker! All these years, all this time. And a piece of me died inside every time I saw you with another girl, flirting, dancing, kissing. I wanted that girl to be me." Her voice drops and she stares down at her hands.

I know I should say something good, pure, meaningful here.

"I wanted it to be you too, Liv." My mouth's dry, my tongue thick as the words drift out.

"So why then? Why would you sign—and then honor—a stupid pact like this?" Her eyes meet mine, and I've never seen her so raw, so vulnerable before.

"Because I'm dumb." I swallow hard, pause. "And I knew you were special and I didn't want to screw it up. And I love my sister."

"Parks . . ." Liv's face softens and I take a chance, inching closer to her.

"Liv, I love you. I always have." I grab her hands, holding them tight. "And I should have told Poppy to stuff the stupid Pact, I see that now. But she's my twin sister and I didn't want to hurt her."

"You love me?" She bites on her bottom lip, a light breeze rustling her hair.

"Yes," I say, my voice low and strained.

Because I do, but hadn't planned on admitting it yet. Not out loud, not so soon.

Liv lifts her chin, sitting up straighter in her chair. "We have to tell Poppy."

30

PARKER

"Do we?"

Liv nods, her eyes serious. "Yes. We do. I'm still super mad about this, too."

"How about we take a few days to cool off then? We don't want to go into the conversation angry," I reason. "Because that never ends well."

Liv presses her lips together tightly, thinks about it. "Maybe we can take a few days to calm down, decide what we're going to say. But that's it, Parker. I'm serious. Poppy's going to have to deal with reality—we can't keep hiding from her."

"Agreed. But can we stay locked in our own little world for a day or two? I don't want to share you." I tug at her hands, pulling her over into my lap. She giggles, her light, melodic laugh vibrating against my chest, tension melting from my muscles.

We're going to be okay.

Dropping my lips to hers, I kiss her slowly, deeply, her mouth salty with tears. I lick the salt away, trying to absolve myself of my sins and make things right between us. She opens to me and our tongues tangle, dancing. I wrap my arms around her body, hugging her to me.

I don't ever want to let her go.

"I love you, Olivia Drayton. Now can we go inside and get naked?" I murmur into the warm skin of her neck.

She giggles softly and nuzzles against me, her hands roving my chest. "I'd like that very much."

In one swift move, I stand, holding Liv cradled in my arms. The sun's dropping, a golden glow illuminating her, and she's more beautiful than ever.

"What?" she asks, cocking a dark brow.

"You're gorgeous is all."

"Parker—" she slaps my chest as I bang through the door into the house, carrying her. "You're only saying that to get me into your bed."

"No. I have full confidence I can get you into my bed without saying that. I'm just dropping truth bombs. You are stunning and I'm never going to stop telling you that."

Her cheeks blush a soft pink and my lower body tenses, my cock twitching in my pants.

I want to be like this, with Liv, every day, every night. Forever.

This terrifying thought skitters through my brain like a sandstorm blowing across the beach and I let it pass by. Not chasing after it, not grabbing for it, just letting it go.

For now.

I want—need—every ounce of my focus and attention to be on Liv in this moment. Just me and her, together.

Us.

Setting her down in the center of my bedroom, I wind my arms around her and pull her body up against me.

Where she belongs.

I cup the apples of her ass, kneading the firm flesh. Not wasting time, I strip off her shirt, then her shorts. Her nipples pebble through the satin of her nude bra and I reach around and unhook it, dropping it to the ground. Sinking to my knees, I rain kisses over the smooth skin of her abdomen, laving and sucking until a moan escapes her lips.

"So, so gorgeous," I murmur, running my palm over the cool satin of her panties. I bury my face in between her thighs, sucking her clit through the thin fabric. "Already wet for me too."

Liv's head is tipped back, her hips tilted forward as she leans in toward me.

Wanting more. Wanting me.

Hooking my fingers in the sides of her panties, I ease them down her thighs, dropping them all the way to the floor before resuming my position between her legs.

"Parker . . ." Her voice is breathy, her fingers twining in my hair.

I lap and suck, tasting her. So sweet, so incredibly Liv.

I feel her legs quaking already and I know she's close. Swirling her clit, I suck and lick until she explodes on my tongue.

"So fast. Such a good girl." I keep my hand firmly on her ass, supporting her as the orgasm rolls through her body and she comes down.

After a minute or two, she reaches her hand down. "Come here."

I stand, stripping my shirt off, and her hands roam over my bare chest, running back and forth over my pecs. Her fingers feather over my skin and ripples of pleasure roll through me.

"You're hot, Parker Montgomery. But I'm sure you know that already." She gazes up at me through lowered lashes and my heart squeezes.

"It sounds better coming from you." I claim her mouth with mine, hard and fierce. I need her to know she's mine.

And I'm hers.

She finds the button of my jeans and fumbles for a second before I help her, stepping out of my clothes and leaving them in a heap on the floor.

I grab her by the hand, leading her over to my bed and pulling back the comforter. Crawling into the cool sheets and laying on my side, I pat the space next to me. She moves in beside me and now we're face to face. Lacing my fingers around her neck, I press my lips to hers, sliding into her open mouth.

"I've been waiting to kiss you all this time," I murmur, and she wriggles her body in closer to mine, heat shimmering between us.

"Me too." She glides her foot up and down my calf, twining her legs with mine, our chests smashed together. My cock bobs against her belly, pulsing with desire. She answers my need, rubbing the tip with her thumb, spreading the drop that's already leaked out over my skin. With her hand, she encircles my cock, sliding up and down my hard shaft, and my balls tighten. My lower body coils, tingly pressure building.

I run my palm from her hipbone up to her full breast, caressing the delicate flesh with the tips of my fingers. She shivers as I trace circles, smaller and smaller, until I come to her nipple, rolling it between my thumb and index finger.

"Parker," she moans. I gently press her back against the bed, dipping my other hand down to her center. Spreading her with my fingers, I rub her hot, wet core, making her writhe with need.

"That's a good girl," I whisper, nipping at her neck and watching pleasure dance across her face.

She answers by rubbing me harder and faster and I can't wait any longer, I need to be inside Liv right now.

Breaking away, I reach inside my nightstand, tearing at the foil wrapper with my teeth. Fast and desperate, I roll the condom on and situate Liv beneath me, her dark hair cascading on the pillows.

Locking my eyes on hers, I enter her, slowly, so slowly, neither of us breathing for fear of shattering the moment. I sink all the way into her, my exhale a sharp hiss.

"You're fucking perfect." I cup her cheek with my hand, tracing her jawline with my thumb. She sucks my thumb into her mouth, the moist heat and the pressure sending sharp pulses of pleasure straight to my dick.

I drop my hand to her breast, crushing her mouth to mine, thrusting my tongue inside. She rocks her hips up and I seat myself all the way back inside her, making her moan and cry out.

We find a quick rhythm, and I piston in and out of her, the pressure building. She tightens around me, milking my cock, and I'm so fucking close.

"Come for me, Liv. Now." My command sends her over the edge and I follow right behind, erupting inside her.

"Parker," she says, half-moan, half-sigh, her nails lightly scraping along the sensitive skin of my back.

I pump into her one more time, shuddering, then pull out, dropping the condom to the floor. Wrapping Liv in my arms, I pull her onto my chest, brushing her hair from her eyes.

"You're amazing."

"You know how I feel, Parker."

"Do I?" I tease, stroking up and down her arm.

"Should I show you one more time?" she asks, rubbing her finger over the bit of scruff on my cheek.

"Yes, please. I love a good reminder."

With a smile, she straddles me, taking my face in both of her hands and kissing me hard on the lips.

"I love you, Parker Montgomery. All of you." She kisses me again and my chest swells with happiness.

Poppy better not fuck this up for me.

Because I'm not sure I can survive losing Liv.

31

___

LIV

I love living in the little cocoon Parker and I weave together.

Fun. Sexy. Easy.

Safe.

Being with Parker—his spotlight beaming brightly only on me—is magical.

And the orgasms. OMG. The man has a way with his hands. And his tongue, hips, teeth, and did I mention his cock? He's leaving every inch of me extremely well-loved and I don't mind one little bit.

In fact, I love it.

Which is how the day or two we were taking to 'calm down' turns into a few days, then an entire week, and somehow it's already Food Truck Friday. I managed to dodge Poppy all week, but it wasn't easy and now we're meeting her here. I can't avoid her forever—like I said, Seaglass Beach is really small. It feels downright microscopic when you're sneaking around, pretending not to be in love with your best friend's twin brother.

"Parker, don't!" I whisper over my shoulder, batting his hand away from my ass. "There are too many people here. Someone's bound to notice." I glance around nervously at the crowd dotting the lawn, wondering if anyone saw his fingers creeping across my backside.

"What?" he asks, peering at me with his baby blues, the picture of innocence. *As if.*

He dips down, his mouth at the shell of my ear, his breath warm on my skin. "You love that move at home."

The deep vibrations of his voice send prickles of desire shooting through me, straight to my core.

"Yeah, I do. And I'd be fine with it here, too, if we'd already come clean with your sister," I hiss.

Parker sighs, raking a hand through his hair. "I know, I know. We need to tell her. You're one hundred percent right. Absolutely."

"Right about what?" Poppy bounces up behind us and Parker and I inch away from each other. Subtly, I hope.

"About Food Truck Friday. Liv was just saying how amazing our beach community is, everyone coming together like this to support Stu and The BBQ Joint," Parker says, throwing his long arm around Poppy's slim shoulders.

"So true!" Poppy smiles, shaking her head. "I love that all the profits are going to help Stu's family. It's beyond amazing. Hey, did I tell you I met with Jess Carter about opening Seaglass Scoops next to the inn?"

Poppy hops to the next topic of conversation and I relax a bit, inhaling a deep breath of marine air. Food Truck Friday is always held in the grassy common area on Main Street, with the beach as backdrop. I tune out of Poppy and Parker's conversation for a second, enjoying the ebb and flow of the ocean waves, the light breeze coming in from the water, the low hum of reggae tunes playing on the loudspeakers. I try to focus on the beach and calm my jumpy nerves.

Everything's going to be fine.

The entire town's turned up for this event to support Stu, but also to celebrate surviving Hurricane Clementine. Kids chase one another, turning cartwheels on the grass and falling down in fits of laughter. Families catch up, talking about what's left of summer vacation, dogs on leashes bark at one another. The weather's perfect, especially now that the sun's sinking, and glancing around, I can't believe I ever even considered moving to Maryland.

"Liv? Is it true?" Poppy stares at me, wide-eyed.

"Uh . . ." I stall, my heart racing into overdrive.

"You can't move back into your house until late September at the earliest? Gawd, that's forever!" Poppy shakes her head in disbelief. "Parks, you can't do anything to speed it along? I mean, you're a contractor! Help a girl out." She links arms with me in solidarity and my pulse slows down a bit.

She still doesn't know.

"I'm sure Liv's over staying at your house by now. I've seen how messy you are."

I swallow, my chest tight with half-truths and obfuscation. "No, he's not that messy."

"Liar!" Poppy says, poking me in the ribs.

A sour taste hits me in the back of my throat and my stomach roils. I can't even make eye contact with Parker right now, instead staring hard at a dark freckle on my arm.

"I'm not that bad, Pops. Hey, anyone want a drink?"

Parker skillfully moves away from the L-word, heading toward the bright yellow Beachy Brews truck.

"Oh no, there's Cash and Damon," Poppy hisses under her breath, scowling at the two of them standing in the line.

"Let's go somewhere else," I suggest, tugging at her arm.

"What? Why? To avoid those two goons? No way. Besides, I want a Seaglass Sunset Sangria, and this is the only place that has it." Poppy marches straight up to the truck, taking her place in line directly behind the Capellis.

Parker bristles next to me, his back rigid, but he shuffles into the line behind Poppy. After a quick debate, I move to Poppy's side, figuring it'd be more awkward and noticeable if I disappear.

"Oh hey, Montgomery. And his beautiful rose of a sister." Cash leers at Poppy and Damon cackles at his brother's stupid joke.

"Ha freaking ha, Cash. Real original. I've never heard a flower joke in all my life," Poppy says, rolling her eyes.

Cash brushes past Poppy's comment, fixing his eyes on me, and I squirm under his dark stare.

"How's the love nest thing going, Livvy?" he asks, smirking.

"You're an immature asshole, Cash," I say, spitting out the words, my fists balling at my side. Parker's pinky finds mine, tapping me in a warning.

"Next?" Savannah, the bar tap at Beachy Brews, calls out and Parker thumps Damon hard on the back.

"That's you, bozo." Parker shoos Cash and Damon up in the line and they place their orders, pay, and get their drinks.

"See you losers around. Let me know when you're done feathering the nest, Montgomery." Cash leers at me, his eyes roaming up and down my body, and my skin crawls.

Parker presses his lips together so tight they turn white, but he doesn't respond.

"Hey, Parker." Savannah smiles widely at him, leaning forward and flashing a touch of cleavage, and my stomach knots. "How ya been, honey?"

Parker grins, making easy conversation with Savannah, chatting about all things construction. I try to ignore the piercing stabs of jealousy hitting me in the chest, one after the other, as the two of them share seemingly hilarious stories.

Get over it, Liv. He's flirty, always has been. You're going to have to deal with it. It's all part of his charm.

Still, the jealousy lingers and I wish Poppy knew everything already, so I could lace my hand in Parker's out here in the open.

"Liv, ignore the Capellis. They're stupid." Poppy rubs my back and guilt mingles with envy in my gut, mixing into my own personal cocktail of intense regret.

All I can do is nod, my body flushing with shame and anxiety. *How much do the Capellis know? Does the entire town know? And how's Poppy going to react when she finds out I've been lying to her all this time?*

The sooner we tell her the truth, the better.

"Poppy?" Jess Carter taps Poppy's shoulder and Poppy grins at her.

"Oh hey! So glad you came out. I was just telling my brother about Seaglass Scoops and our potential partnership." Poppy elbows Parker and he swivels around, turning his broad smile on the older woman.

"Hey, Mrs. Carter. I'm excited about the ice cream parlor—I think that'll be a great thing for the inn." Parker takes a slug of his beer, acting like everything's normal.

"Griffin!" Mrs. Carter waves across the lawn, motioning at a tall, attractive man.

"Poppy and Parker, this is my nephew, Griffin." She pats him on the chest and he nods at us, grunting a 'hey' in our direction.

"He's down here on hiatus, taking a little time off from his baseball career. He's in the major league." His aunt beams up at him proudly and Griffin swipes a large hand over the dark scruff peppering his jaw.

"It's a little more than a hiatus, Aunt Jess. I'm on the IL."

"IL?" Poppy asks, tipping her head at him, her brows scrunching together.

"The Injured List. Which means they can cut me any time and replace me with someone else. A younger, healthier player."

"Oh. That stinks. What happened?" Poppy asks, not reading the room. Griffin clearly doesn't want to discuss this, judging by his downcast eyes and his slouched shoulders.

"Tore my ACL stopping a guy from stealing third base."

"At least you stopped him, right?" Poppy says, and Griffin pauses, locking eyes with her in a cold stare.

"Yeah. At least. Surgery and six months of physical therapy, but at least he didn't steal third base."

Poppy opens her mouth, then clamps it shut again, shoving a hand in her pocket. There's an awkward silence until Parker chimes in.

"So, Griffin—how long you in town?"

Griffin exhales, scrubbing a hand over his neck. "Not sure. Depends on my team. I'm hoping to get called back for playoffs, but it's all based on my recovery. Aunt Jess suggested I come down here and enjoy the sunshine, get a change of scenery."

"I'm sure you'll love Seaglass Beach!" Poppy says, smiling at him, her tone upbeat.

Her sunny cheerfulness does nothing to melt Griffin's icy demeanor.

"Yeah, sure." He shrugs, dismissing her statement, and Poppy clucks under her breath before taking a sip of her drink.

"Well, it was nice meeting you," Parker says, trying to smooth things over. "Good luck with the rehab."

"Thanks," Griffin grumbles, folding his arms over his broad chest.

"Great to see you, Mrs. Carter." Poppy squeezes the older woman's arm and we head in the opposite direction.

"Wow—he was a jerk," Poppy mumbles, quiet so only me and Parker can hear. "Talk about a chip on his shoulder."

"Not everyone's sunshine and rainbows all the time, Poppy," Parker says, bumping her hip. "Give the guy a break—his major league career is probably over. Sounds depressing to me."

"I guess." Poppy twists a strand of hair in her fingers, her eyes fixed on Griffin's strong back. "He still could have been nicer. His aunt is lovely."

"Good thing you'll be working with her, not him," I point out. "Listen, Poppy . . ."

At my tone, Parker cuts his eyes at me, shaking his head oh-so-slightly 'no.'

"Yeah?" Poppy gnaws her bottom lip, distracted, still gazing in Griffin's direction.

Buzz, buzz.

My cell vibrates in my pocket, but I ignore it. I just want to get this over with—come clean with Poppy, and be with Parker out in the open.

No more secrets.

Buzz, buzz. Buzz, buzz.

Aggravated, I pull my cell out and read the texts.

> Parker: Not now. Bad timing.

> Parker: Trust me. I know Poppy.

> Parker: She won't take it well. One more day won't hurt.

I lift my gaze, Parker staring at me over Poppy's honey-colored head, his eyes wide and pleading.

I tap out a quick text back, Poppy paying no attention to the two of us.

> Liv: One more day, Parks. That's it.

> Liv: We have to tell her.

> Parker: I know and we will. Tomorrow.

I'm not sure I'll be able to sleep tonight, even with Parker's arms wrapped around me, holding me tight.

The burden of truth is weighing heavy on me and I just want to move on. I'm still angry at Poppy and she needs to know.

About me and Parker.
And that she isn't in control of us anymore.

32

PARKER

The Pact situation is getting stickier by the second. I know I should tell Poppy about me and Liv—it's stupid not to, she's going to find out eventually—but something's holding me back.

Probably the fear of Poppy's wrath.

She rarely gets angry, but when she does, she's a force to be reckoned with. I've seen her rage before and it ain't pretty.

One time in college she cut up every one of her ex-boyfriend's T-shirts when she found him making out with another girl. Bastard's lucky he still has his dick, to be honest.

I'm not looking forward to a similar fate.

But we don't have a choice.

She has to know.

I'm in love with Liv and there's not a damn thing she can say or do to change my mind.

"How should we tell her?" Liv asks me for the thousandth time as we lay on my couch later that evening. The television's on, season four million of some lame reality show, but all my focus is on Liv. It's hard to concentrate on anything else when her curvy body's draped over my chest, our legs tangling together, my dick rock-hard.

Plus, we've had this conversation every day this week, and I still have zero ideas.

I trail my fingers up and down her arms, watching her chest rise and fall, her nipples sharp peaks beneath the thin fabric of her sleeveless blouse.

"You're so sexy," I murmur, pressing my lips to her ear and sucking the lobe into my mouth, nipping at it with my teeth.

"Stay focused, Parker," Liv chides, batting me away, her grass-green eyes on mine.

"You're so serious all the time." I rain kisses down her neck, fondling her breast through the satiny fabric of her shirt.

"And you rarely are, which is why we still haven't told Poppy about us." She sucks in a sharp breath as I inch my hand under her shirt, palming the soft flesh of her abdomen.

"I can't concentrate when you're this close to me," I say, cupping her breast in my hand and squeezing. "You're so fucking beautiful. It's distracting. See?" Grabbing her hand, I press it to the bulge in my pants and she laughs.

"You're hopeless, Parks, you know that. If we have sex, will you be able to talk afterwards?" She purses her lips together, shimmying her body against me, and I know I'm winning.

"Yes, I think it'd make things better."

She straddles me, lifting her shirt over her head and unhooking her bra.

"Better now?" she asks, licking her bottom lip as my cock pulses beneath her.

"Heading in the right direction for sure." I cup both her breasts in my hands, rolling the pink points of her nipples with my thumbs. She inhales sharply, loosening her hair from her ponytail, the dark waves cascading over her chest as I play with her breasts.

She leans down, dropping her lips to mine, and my balls tighten, aching.

"Hang on." I sit up, shedding my shirt, then unbuttoning her denim shorts and sliding them down over her round ass. She shifts, kicking off her shorts and panties, and I drop mine as well.

"Better still?" Liv asks, straddling me again, my cock twitching against my abs.

"Much. I certainly like the view from my place." I wink and she giggles, and I fucking love that sound. I want to make her laugh as much as possible, all day, every day.

"Come here." I reach up, wrapping my fingers around her delicate neck, pulling her mouth down and claiming her lips.

She melts into me, her chest pressing up against mine so tightly I feel her heart thudding hard in her chest. I tease her with the tip of my cock, pressing up against her sensitive flesh.

"You feel so incredible, Liv. I want you. Right now, just like this. Nothing between us." I whisper into her open mouth.

She doesn't say a word, only drawing her head back a tiny bit and nodding.

I don't hesitate, easing my way into her wet heat.

"Parker," she moans, opening wider and taking me in.

"Oh fuck, you're amazing," I mumble, pressure already building low in my gut. I thrust into her, harder and deeper, and she wraps her legs around me. Trying to get as close as possible.

I've dreamed of this moment for years. Taking Liv bare, nothing at all standing between us.

"What the hell?" Poppy's shrill voice cuts through my X-rated thoughts and Liv and I both freeze.

"And ohmygawd, are y'all naked? What are you doing?" Poppy's high-pitched questions ring in my ears, Liv's face ashen as she clambers off me, reaching for her shirt.

I scrabble into my shorts, Poppy's back to us as we get decent, throwing our clothes back on as quickly as humanly possible.

"Poppy, I can explain," I stammer, my heart racing. "It's not what it looks like."

Poppy whirls around to face us. "It's not? What exactly is it then, Parker? Were you giving Liv a breast exam?" Her hands fly through the air, her face tomato red.

"No, of course not." I rake a hand through my hair, wishing I could disappear into the wood floorboards at the moment.

"I can't believe this!" Poppy rails. "How long has this been going on? I can't believe you'd do this to me, Parker." Her blue eyes fill up with tears, her lower lip quivering.

Those words send Liv right over the edge. Her shoulders square, she marches up to Poppy and clutches her shoulders.

"Do this to you, Poppy? Are you kidding me? He's— we're—" she waves her hand between us, "not doing anything *to* you. In fact, you're not involved at all. And never should have been." Liv's voice is firm, tinged with anger.

"What are you talking about?" Poppy shouts, shrugging out of Liv's grip. "Of course I'm involved. You're my best friend and he's my twin brother." Poppy pokes me hard in the chest and my insides twist, my balls aching.

This is exactly the scenario I'd hoped to avoid.

But worse. Way fucking worse.

"Pops, listen. We can talk this out." I hold my hands up and try to sound soothing, but Poppy's pacing in a tight circle, totally unhinged.

"We had a deal, Parker!" Poppy cries, pink splotches of anger mottling her chest. "You promised!"

"Haven't you heard a word I said, Poppy?" Liv asks, her eyebrows raised high. "You can't forbid us from being together. I'm a person, not a promise." She crosses her arms over her chest, her hip jutted out. Liv's definitely angry.

"You can't control our lives, Poppy. Both of us can make our own decisions, our own choices. And I choose Parker." Liv juts her chin out, resolute, and Poppy's tears finally spill over, glistening on her cheeks.

"You're picking him over me?" Poppy whispers, her voice small and full of hurt.

"This isn't about him versus you, Poppy. In fact, it's not about you at all."

Poppy and Liv stare at each other for a long moment, then Poppy grabs her keys and storms to the front door. She hesitates a second, glancing back at Liv over her shoulder.

"Don't call me when he breaks your heart."

Poppy turns and walks out, the screen door slamming behind her.

I blow out a shaky breath. "That went well."

33

LIV

"No, it did not, Parker," I say, swiping at the tears in my eyes. "That's exactly what I didn't want to happen. We should have told her." Regret wells up in me now that Poppy and her hot rage and accusations are gone.

Maybe forever.

"What are we going to do?" I sink down onto the couch, head in my hands. "She's never going to forgive us."

"She probably will," Parker says, joining me on the couch, his hand rubbing comforting circles on my back.

"Probably?" My voice tips up into the semi-hysterical range. I hadn't considered the fact that Poppy could be gone forever. Sure, I figured she'd be mad and upset about my relationship with her brother, but I didn't think she'd walk out.

She's the one in the wrong here, so why do I feel so terrible?

Because you should have been honest with your friend—your best friend—from the very beginning. Even if she did make a stupid pact and try to control your life. She's still your best friend.

Was your best friend.

"It'll be okay, Liv. She needs time to cool off is all. Then I'll talk to her, explain the situation."

"What are you going to say?" I peer over at him, taking in the slight shadow of stubble, the strong line of his jaw. He's self-assured and confident. The exact opposite of me at the moment.

Parker catches my eyes, his face serious. He tips my chin up with his thumb. "That I'm in love with her best friend."

My heart stutters in my chest and I've never felt so conflicted in my life. How can I be this happy and this miserable all at the same time?

Damn Poppy and her stupid pact.

Taking a shallow, shaky breath, I lick my bottom lip. "I'm in love with you too, Parks."

But what if Poppy's right?

Parker has my whole heart. I'm in deep with him now —and I don't have Poppy to turn to if things go south.

The cold realization of the risk I'm taking sinks in, seeping into every cell in my body. I could end up all alone —and that thought terrifies me.

THREE DAYS LATER, AND POPPY'S STILL NOT SPEAKING TO either me or Parker. I've called and texted, but she doesn't respond, leaving me unread. Same with Parker, and although he's playing it cool, I can see the toll her silent treatment's taking on him. His eyes have dark shadows under them and every time his cell vibrates, he jumps, then deflates when the caller isn't his sister.

And even though neither of us wants to admit it, Poppy's disapproval put a strain on our relationship. Things between us don't feel as fun, as easy anymore. Poppy ripped a hole in our cocoon, and the snake of self-doubt wriggled its way in. What's worse is I can't say anything about it to Parker because then he'll think I'm insecure. And insecurity is not sexy.

I wish I could talk to Poppy.

But there's no chance of that, even if she were speaking to me. The last thing Poppy wants is to hear about my feelings for her brother. She made that pretty damn clear.

"I'm working at the tiki bar tonight. You wanna come?" Parker asks, buttoning his shirt.

I kick around the idea for a hot second, then shake my head. "I don't think so, Parks. I might run into Poppy and she clearly doesn't want to talk to me."

He slides on his flip-flops, then walks over and sits down next to me on the bed. Taking my hand in his, he laces his fingers through mine. "You can't hide from her forever, Liv. She's going to have to get used to the idea of us."

"I know. But we don't need to throw it in her face either. And I'm not in the mood for another blow-out, especially in public."

Parker lifts my hand, grazing the knuckles with his lips. "You're too good. I don't deserve you. And frankly, neither does Poppy. The two of us didn't do anything wrong."

I grit my teeth, grimacing. "We sort of did. We shouldn't have lied to her."

"We didn't lie. We just didn't tell her right away."

"Yeah, that's called a sin of omission. Notably still a sin, though."

"A technicality," he says, rubbing his thumb over mine. "Poppy's the one who should be apologizing. We're not twelve anymore, so she needs to stop acting like it. We're all mature adults here."

"Are we?" I ask, jabbing Parker in the ribs.

"Hey now." He wraps his arms around me, bringing his lips to mine and kissing me deeply.

After several minutes, he pulls back to look at me. "How's that for adulting?"

"You're hopeless, Parker. Honestly. What time do you think you'll be home?"

"Not too late. Probably ten-ish. But you don't have to wait up." He stands, dropping another soft kiss on my lips. "I'll miss you."

"I'll miss you, too. See you tonight. Text me if you see Poppy."

"Will do." He shoots me his dazzling smile, runs a hand through his surfer waves, and heads out the door.

After an hour, I'm bored. The house is too quiet without Parker and I don't have any work left to keep me busy. There's nothing on TV worth watching and it's only eight o'clock. Still too early to go to bed.

Maybe I *should* go to the tiki bar like Parker suggested . . .

Poppy's avoiding us anyway. She knows he'll be there, so she probably won't go near the place.

Less than ten minutes later, I'm parked at the Seaglass Inn and strolling down the path toward the tiki bar. Upbeat dance music carries on the wind and as I get closer to the lights and noise, the butterflies zooming around my stomach fly harder and faster.

Because Parker and I hid our relationship, we haven't been out in public together as an official couple. Now that the secret's out, I'm not sure how to act around him—or how he'll act around me. Will this be weird?

I roll my shoulders, shaking my arms in an attempt to get rid of the jangly nerves.

Everything's going to be fine. We've been friends forever. It's all good.

I've been hanging around Parker too much—that's totally his voice in my head.

Slowing down, I take in the crowd. Mostly ladies, with a few couples scattered here and there, some even dancing on the beach. Parker's behind the bar, mixing up a cocktail in a silver shaker, his lopsided grin wide. Two blondes smile and chat with him, their hands waving through the air.

Clearly flirting.

And Parker's flirting back, leaning over the bar, touching a hand when he serves the cocktails. My gut twists into a tight sailor knot, black splotches dancing at the corners of my vision.

I shouldn't have come.

Maybe I'm not ready for this.

Maybe I'm not ready for Parker.

And maybe Poppy's right.

The thought claws at me, ripping at my tight gut. I turn on my heel and sprint back to my car, the sound of the waves roaring in my ears.

34

LIV

With shaking hands, I drive back to Parker's and slam my car into the driveway. Hot tears sting my eyes and I know deep down I'm being ridiculous, but I can't help it. I've watched Parker flirt with women my entire life and it's never been me. There's always been someone else, so why should now be any different? He's a perpetual flirt and I knew that going into this, but it still stings.

Like it always has.

I've felt invisible for so long, I don't know how to shut that feeling off.

Gawd, I need therapy.

Wiping my tears in my sleeve, I take a shuddery breath. For the first time since we got together, I'm not sure I can do this. I love Parker, but is that going to be enough?

I unlock the door and head to the bathroom, catching a glimpse of myself in the mirror. I look terrible—puffy eyes, black mascara tracking down my face, and my hair's wild and frizzy from all the humidity.

Why would Parker date this?

I scrub hard at my face, removing the melted make-up from my skin. Running my fingers through my hair, I smooth down the frizz and then brush my teeth. I want to crawl into bed and forget.

Forget the tiki bar, forget the fight with Poppy, forget how lame and pathetic I am right now.

Unfortunately, when I close my eyes all I can see is Parker. But he's not *my* Parker. He's the Parker I have to share with the world, the one who's never going to settle down, the one who never stays.

With a dull ache throbbing in my chest, I cry myself to sleep.

"Hey, why'd you sleep in here last night?" Parker's deep voice rouses me from sleep, his hand smoothing my hair. "I missed you in my bed."

"I don't know," I lie, my voice coming out tight and strained. Probably from crying all night.

"You okay?" He narrows his eyes at me.

"Yeah."

"I don't believe you. What's wrong?"

I swallow over the lump in my throat, debating what to say here. I decide to be radical and go with the truth.

"I went to the tiki bar last night. I saw you flirting with those women."

Parker frowns, a deep V in between his brows. "What? Who?"

"I don't know, Parks. Two blondes. I didn't stick around and get their life story."

"Liv, they're customers. That's all. I work for tips—it's kind of my job."

"You don't have to be so touchy-feely all the time. It's not like you need the money."

Jealousy leaks into my voice and I hate myself a little bit right now.

Worse, I hate feeling like this—small, insecure. Like a little mouse hunting for a morsel of cheese, taking any scrap I can get.

Fuck this.

"I don't know if this is going to work for me, Parker." I hold my breath, the tick-tick-tick of Parker's clock in the next room almost deafening in the quiet.

"Liv. Don't say that." He rakes his hand through his hair, a honey wave flopping down over his eyes.

"Here." Parker holds his phone out to me. "You can go through it, read my texts, delete every number in there. I don't care."

"No."

"Do it. Take it." He thrusts the cell at me, forcing the cool metal into my hands.

The screen flashes to life, a selfie of the two of us kissing on the beach popping up. We look happy. Carefree. In love.

My heart squeezes as I tap the glass. "What's your code?"

"0-4-2-7."

I freeze, my eyes flying to his. "My birthday?"

He nods. "Yeah. It's a number I know I'll never forget."

Now I really feel like an asshole and my insides are a mushy, gooey mess. He uses my birthday as his passcode?

I suck.

"Go ahead. Scroll through it. Read everything. I don't care."

Sitting up, I hand his phone back to him. "I don't need to, Parker. I trust you. I'm not that girl. I'm sorry I doubted you."

He cups my cheek, his thumb trailing over my jaw. "I'm sorry I gave you reason to doubt me. I'll do better. Be better. Promise."

We lock eyes for a full minute before I lean over and kiss him gently on the lips. "Me too, Parks. Me too."

35

PARKER

"I don't know what she expects from me, man. I'm out at the tiki bar doing my job and she freaks. Didn't even tell me either. I had to drag it out of her. I'm not a fucking psychic." I rip a large piece of drywall from the studs, chucking it down to the ground in a heap.

"She expects you to not flirt with everything that moves," Smith says, smashing into the wall with his sledgehammer.

"I don't do that."

He peers at me through the lenses of his safety goggles. "Really? You can say that with a straight face?"

"I'm friendly is all. When did that become a bad thing?"

"When you got a girlfriend, dude. Have you ever had one of those before?" He cocks a brow at me and I flip him off.

"Haha. Very funny. Yes, I have."

"When?"

More drywall clatters to the floor. "Let me think here . .

. okay, it's been a while. But like, two years ago? I dated that gal from Tifton, remember?"

Smith shakes his head. "No. Not ringing a bell. Was it dating or texting?"

"You're an asshole, you know that? Anyway—forget my past love life and let's focus on the present. So now what do I do? I think she's over last night, but how do I not fuck this up? You're good at relationships . . ."

"I never said that. Not sure I qualify as expert enough to give any dating advice." His hammer flies through the air again, making a hole in the wall big enough to see clear through to the next room.

"But you are. You and Elise have a good thing going, right?"

Smith's eyes glaze over. "Yeah. We do."

"And that shit's complicated. She's got an ex, kids. What's your secret?"

"Don't be a dick."

"I'm not a dick! Never was a dick." I shake my head, wiping sweat from my brow.

"Fine. Be yourself, but be extra amazing. I know this is something you may not be used to, but you have to put in the work."

I frown. Putting in work seems more like a job than a love life. "What do you mean?"

"Effort, bro. More than just texting and sex. Take her flowers. Buy her gifts. Cook dinner, plan something special for the two of you. Be thoughtful."

"Geez. I already got the girl."

"Yeah. And now you have to keep her. That's the hard part."

Well, shit. What did I get myself into?

"Don't worry, Parker. You can do this. I have faith in you." Smith smacks me hard on the shoulder and we get back to the reno, my mind whirring over all the ways I can impress Liv. Or at least be slightly more amazing.

THAT NIGHT ON THE WAY HOME, I STOP AT THE MARKET and grab flowers, a bottle of wine. Nothing fancy, but a good start. Then I hustle out of there because I want to try to make it to the beach for sunset.

When I pull up to the house, though, Liv's car isn't there. Instead, the van's parked in the driveway, sans coconut.

Shit, did Liv say she has an event tonight? I don't recall her mentioning it, but maybe I wasn't listening.

"Babe, I'm home!" I bang through the screen door with my groceries. Liv's standing at the kitchen table surrounded by mason jars. Cardboard boxes of white roses litter the den, and the room smells like burnt rubber from the glue gun she's holding.

"Hey. How was work?" She barely glances up from the glass jar she's bending over, attaching string lights with hot glue.

"Good." I sidle over to the table, wrapping my arms around her narrow waist. Pressing up against her, I nuzzle in and sprinkle kisses across the nape of her neck.

"Parks, hang on a sec. I don't want to mess this up. There's no time for mistakes."

I stiffen, hands frozen on her hips while she wields the

glue gun around the rim of the jar, winding the lights in a circle.

"Now?" I murmur, nipping at her soft skin.

She sets the gun down, turning and kissing me on the lips. "Yes."

I answer with a long, deep kiss, urging her mouth open, my tongue sweeping in. "I missed you today."

"Me too."

My hand creeps up to her chest, fondling her full breast.

"Let's not get carried away here," she murmurs, lacing her fingers in mine and easing my hand back down. "You see how many jars I have to decorate tonight?"

"Tonight?" I ask, glancing at the rows of jars, all standing in line awaiting their turn. "I had plans for us."

"Aww, that's so sweet, Parks, but I have to finish these up. Diane needs them by nine tomorrow morning."

Disappointment settles inside me, but I hide it. "Let me take a quick shower, then I'll come help. Together we'll get this knocked out in no time."

"Really?" Her voice tips up, her grassy green eyes sparkling under the kitchen light.

"Yeah." I press my lips to hers one more time, then head to the shower. "Oh—almost forgot. I brought you these."

I grab the bouquet of sunflowers off the counter, handing them to her.

"Parker. They're beautiful. And my favorite." She gazes up at me, smiling, her cheeks flushing a soft pink. I gotta remember to thank Smith—he's definitely on to something here.

"They're only half as beautiful as you." I wink and head

to the bathroom, pleased with how this is going. In fact, I think I might totally have this relationship thing down.

Two hours later, we're still fucking with the jars. I'm beyond bored and the only reason I've made it this long is Liv. No way in hell would I hold twinkle lights for anyone but her.

"I think Diane needs to hire an assistant," I say, my finger narrowly dodging the metal tip of the glue gun.

"I am her assistant," Liv says, deep furrows of concentration lining her brow. "Last one here. Then will you help me load all this into the van?"

"Sure." The sooner I get the mason jars out of here, the closer I am to getting Liv into my bed.

"Last one." Liv clicks the glue gun off, smiling in triumph. "We make a good team, Parker. Thanks for your help." She bends across the table, careful to bridge over the boxes of jars, and brushes her lips across mine.

"You're welcome." Our eyes meet and my chest swells; I've honestly never felt this way before about anyone.

And that's saying a lot, having just assembled two hundred-something damn mason jar centerpieces.

"Not to ruin the moment," Liv bites her lip, "but have you talked to your sister?"

Dammit. I spent my whole night doing a nice thing and we have to talk about Poppy—again?

"No. You?"

Liv shakes her head, her shoulders slumping. "Nope."

"It'll be fine, Liv." I squeeze her arm, trying to reassure her. Trying to reassure myself.

I've never gone this long without talking to my sister before. She's really taking this Silent Treatment thing to the next level.

"Tell you what—I'll stop by the inn tomorrow and catch her at work. Make her listen and hear me out."

"Think you should loop Roman or King into it?"

"Nah. Let's keep the casualties to a minimum."

She nods, and I hope and pray I can get Poppy to come around because no matter what Liv says, Poppy's still up in our relationship and it's time for her to see her way out.

Because three really is a fucking crowd.

36

LIV

"Olivia, the centerpieces are perfection—nice work." Diane lifts a mason jar to the light, rotating the glass slowly, examining it for flaws.

Of which there are none, thank you very much.

"Thank you. That took some time." I set the last box of jars down on the table in the office Diane jokingly calls 'The Boardroom.'

"Good thing you're single." Diane flips through the calendar in her leather planner, marking the task off the never-ending To-Do list.

"Actually, I'm technically not anymore."

Her pen pauses over the page and she glances up at me. "Oh. Do tell."

"Well . . ." I hesitate, wondering how much to say here. Diane's my boss, and even though we're friendly, I wouldn't say we're friends. We don't have a let's-grab-a-drink type of relationship; more like a mentor/mentee thing going on.

"Please tell me you didn't meet him on that bumblebee

app," Diane chides, staring at me over the rim of her tortoiseshell glasses.

"No. Definitely not."

"Do I know him? Is he local?"

I lick my lower lip, my throat dry. *Why am I so nervous to say this out loud?*

"You do know him, I'm sure. I'm kinda, sorta seeing Parker Montgomery." I say his name quickly, then hold my breath.

"Parker? Isn't he—"

I cut her off. "Yes. Poppy's twin brother."

"Oh." Her mouth forms a perfect red 'O' and something inside me breaks. Maybe because I have no one else to talk to, maybe because I feel like Diane can help, maybe out of sheer desperation. But I can't help myself and the words come tumbling out in a rush.

"A tree fell on my house and I had nowhere to go. Parker offered to let me stay at his place and one thing led to another and now we're together and Poppy's so mad she's not speaking to us. She won't even take my calls." I stare down at the dark wood floor, my pulse thudding hard in my neck, wishing I didn't just have verbal diarrhea all over the office.

"That is a predicament. Dating your best friend's brother is a sticky situation for sure. But y'all are grown. As long as everyone treads lightly, it should all work out."

I exhale, the tightness in my chest easing a little. "I hope so. Because right now, everything is good between me and Parker. But I miss my best friend." My voice quivers and I need to get my shit together. I can't afford to lose my job, too.

"You should talk to her, Olivia."

"I've tried! She sends me to voicemail and doesn't reply to my texts."

"Go find her, sit down, and have a chat. Figure out why she's so upset about it."

I swallow hard, my breathing shallow. I know why she's upset, but no way am I telling Diane about the Pact.

"Thanks for the advice. I'll do that."

"One other thing—take it or leave it, depends on how you feel about small-town gossip. But maybe go slow with Parker as well?"

Anxiety rolls through me, knots bunching up in the muscles of my shoulders. "Oh-kay. Any particular reason?"

Diane fiddles with her gigantic diamond ring. "I've heard he's quite popular. A nice guy, but more of the look, don't touch variety. Not exactly husband material."

Smoothing my blouse, I mentally imagine doing the same to my emotions. *Stay calm, it's only small-town hearsay. You know Parker better than everyone in this town, except for his own family.*

"Thanks for passing that on. Duly noted."

"Just something to keep in mind. I don't listen to all the town gossip, but when you've heard the same thing from multiple sources . . ." Her voice trails off and I seriously regret bringing any of this up with her.

"Got it. I'll keep that in mind. What's on the agenda for the remainder of the week?"

The packed calendar is enough to distract Diane from my love life, but not me. I can't stop thinking about her words the rest of the day.

And my day keeps going downhill. After the super fun chat with Diane, I deal with a bride having an absolute meltdown over the seating chart—and her wedding's six months out. Then the mother of the groom decides to come by the office to rail on the bride's family and how they have all the prime seating at the reception. I round out the afternoon with a stop at Everything's Coming Up Roses, the local florist, thinking it'll be a quick pop-in. But the order is jacked and I end up spending an hour on the phone, working with the client and adjusting her selections to get the delivery on time.

Hanging up the phone, I'm officially done with this workday. Normally, I'd text Poppy and we'd head over to The Tipsy Taco for Taco Tuesday, but I'm sure that's not in the cards at the moment. And Parker's supposed to be talking to her right about now, so he's out. Maybe he can meet me after the chat with Poppy. Maybe everything will go great and they'll both come . . .

I text Parker:

> Liv: Good luck with Poppy. Meet me at Tipsy Taco when you're done?

> Parker: Thanks, babe. I'm sure I can bring her around. Heading to inn now. Tacos sound good.

> Liv: Invite Poppy too

> Parker:

With that settled, I drive over to Tipsy Taco alone, cranking the radio up to drown out my obsessive thoughts playing on loop. I need to trust Parker to work this thing out with his sister and then things will go back to normal. We'll be the three of us again, except even better because now I can finally be with Parker. Out in the open, where our relationship can breathe and grow.

I snag one of the last open parking spots and wander inside. The place is packed with both locals and tourists, the five-dollar Tuesday margarita special being a big draw. Loud music blares through the spicy air and every booth is taken. I spy two empty seats at the end of the bar and weave my way through the tables. Hopping up onto the red pleather stool, I claim my seat and set my bag down on the empty stool to save it for Parker.

"Hey, Liv. What's up?" Candy slides a plastic menu across the bar. "Margarita?"

"Please. I could use one after today."

"What about Poppy? She want one too?" Candy points at the empty stool and a wave of sadness washes over me.

I stare hard at the menu, the taco descriptions and combinations swimming together. "Not tonight. I'm not sure she's going to make it. Parker's coming, though, but it might be a while."

"Okay, hun. I'll have that drink up in a sec." She slides down the bar to take another order and I slump in my seat, chin in hand.

This totally sucks. I get that Poppy might be mad at Parker for breaking the stupid pact, but why me? I didn't even know about it and last time I checked, we didn't have some sort of sis code going between us. Should I have told Poppy about dating Parker sooner? Probably. But now it's time for her to get over herself. I deserve to be happy and so does Parker.

"One margarita on the rocks with salt." Candy sets the drink down on a white paper napkin and I shoot her a wan smile.

"Thanks."

"Sure thing. You want the usual? Taco trio, extra avocado?"

I nod. "Sounds great."

"It'll be ready in a few."

She sidles away and I take a long sip of the drink, licking salt from the rim. I pull out my phone and scroll through Instagram more out of habit than desire or interest, shutting out the crowd in the restaurant. I've had enough peopling for today, honestly.

The stool beside me scrapes the floor and I snap my head up to see Jagger Capelli's sneer.

Super.

I never want to talk to Jagger, but even less so at the moment.

"That seat's taken." I wrap my hand around the back of the chair, dragging it up against the bar.

"By who? The invisible man?" Jagger eyes my lone margarita. "It looks like little Livvy is all alone tonight. What happened, lover boy already found someone new?" He leers at me, his thin lips twisted into a crooked smile.

A hot flash of anger rips through me. "No, Jagger, Parker and I are still together. Sorry to disappoint. And not that it's any of your business, but he's on his way. So you better scram before he gets here. He won't be too happy to see you—and you and I both know how that turned out last time." I glare at him and he snickers.

"Yeah, it ended with precious Parker running away. Real tough guy."

"Uh-huh." I roll my eyes and turn away, take another sip of my drink. Anything to break eye contact; out of all the Capellis, Jagger's the one who's always given me the creeps.

Seconds later, meaty fingers tickle my skin, sending a chill racing down my arm. I swivel in my seat.

"What are you doing? Get your hands off me." I brush Jagger's hand away, but he grips my bicep tighter.

"C'mon, Livvy. We could have some fun, make your precious Parker jealous. Maybe that would get him back."

I try to wriggle out of his grip, but his fingers clamp down harder and now he's hurting me.

"I said get the fuck away from me, Jagger. Now." I grit my teeth against the pain, trying to make my voice as menacing as possible. He doesn't even flinch. Instead, he steps in closer, his neck so near I watch the faint throb of his pulse in his thick vein.

"You've always been fucking uptight. Besides the nice tits, I have no idea what that fuckboy sees in you."

Now my arm's aching under his fingers and I try to scoot away, but he's holding me so tight I'm more like a worm wriggling around on a hook.

"Get the fuck away from her, Capelli." A deep, familiar voice rumbles behind me.

Jagger drops my arm like a hot iron, backing away from me, and I rub my bicep, trying to get blood flow to return.

"Relax, Roman. I was just getting ready to tell little Livvy here the good news." Jagger straightens up, puffing out his chest, but does move back.

"I don't give a shit if you were about to tell her you're the new President of the United States of America. Get the fuck away from her." Roman spits out the words, sharp and low, trying not to make a scene.

"Y'all swagger around here like you own everything—

and everyone." Jagger cuts his eyes at me, but his gaze doesn't linger. "But guess what? You don't. Meet your new landlord, Livvy."

My stomach curdles, margarita washing back up my throat. *What the fuck? The Capellis bought my place?*

"What are you talking about, Jagger?" Roman asks, stepping between us, blocking me from him.

"We bought your duplex. Your landlord's worried about the cost of repairs, so we got a sick deal too. Rent's still due the first of the month, by the way." Jagger cocks his chin at me and sweat beads at my back.

No way do I want a Capelli as a landlord. And he probably has a key to my place now. Ugh.

"Consider this my one month's notice then, Jagger. I'll be moving out as soon as I can get in there and pack my stuff." I work to keep my voice flat and monotone, even though my insides are shaking.

"I'll need that in writing, sweets. You know—for legal purposes. See ya around, Rome." Jagger salutes Roman, then struts out of the restaurant like he's the king of Seaglass Beach.

"I fucking hate that guy," Roman mutters, sliding into the seat next to me. "You okay?" He turns to face me, his eyes full of concern.

"Yeah." I blow out a breath I didn't realize I was holding. "I'll be fine. Thanks for the assist."

"No problem." He signals at Candy for another round of margaritas. "It's always my pleasure to ruin a Capelli's day. How come Poppy's not here?"

I rub my initial necklace, debating. "We're kind of going through a thing."

Roman raises a dark brow, but waits for me to give more details.

"Have you talked to Parker?" I ask, then take a sip of my drink, the tequila burning my throat.

"Nah. I've been busy helping King out at the ranch. What's going on?"

Candy returns with fresh drinks and Roman takes a long swallow as I stall, searching for the perfect words.

"It's complicated. You know I moved in with Parker, right? Temporarily?"

Roman nods and my cheeks heat under his gaze.

Gawd, this is embarrassing. Worse than telling Diane.

"Parker and I are together. Like together-together." I bite my lip and wait for Roman's reaction. He shrugs.

"So? I'm surprised y'all never hooked up before, to be honest. Anyone could see you like him and it's pretty obvious he's always had a hard-on for you."

Ohmygawd. Am I that transparent? My face flames as his words sink in.

Surprised.

Always.

"Anyway," I stammer, "Poppy's pretty pissed about the whole thing. Apparently, she and Parker had some secret pact back in the day and now we've broken her trust."

"Geez, Poppy's so dramatic. Love her to death, but this isn't Lit class. She needs to get the hell over herself. Y'all can date, have a good time, fuck—it's none of her damn business."

He slugs down the rest of his drink as I sit there, stunned, and let his words sink in. Poppy does need to let this go. But I should apologize for not being honest with her from the beginning.

Suddenly, I need to get out of here.

"Thanks, Rome." I give him an awkward side hug because Roman's never been a big hugger, then throw some cash down on the bar. "I've gotta run. Tell Candy you can have my tacos—I appreciate your help with Jagger."

"Anytime. And Liv?"

"Yeah?" I glance back at him over my shoulder.

"If anyone can get Parker to settle down—it's you."

37

PARKER

Despite what I told Liv, I've been putting off this conversation.

Because I hate that I let my sister down.

Because I hate that I lied to her.

And because no matter what, I know Poppy's not going to believe me anyway, so why bother? She doesn't think I can be serious, so why should I work to convince her?

But Liv wants me to try to make things right with Poppy, so here I am at the inn. The dutiful brother, trying to mend fences.

I'd love for Poppy to come around, don't get me wrong. But every once in a while she digs in, and this feels like one of those times.

I stroll into the inn, standing tall and giving off more confident vibes than I feel. My gut's churning, palms are clammy, and I desperately need something to drink, my mouth's so fucking dry.

Poppy's standing behind the front desk with that new

guy, Griffin, talking to her. I sidle up, shoving a hand in my pocket.

Poppy ignores me.

Real fucking mature.

"Hey, Pops. Can I talk to you a sec?" I'm shuffling my feet, so I lean against the desk to keep myself still.

"What?" She trains her eyes on the keyboard, avoiding my gaze.

"Maybe in private?"

"I'm busy. With Griffin. So anything you need to say, say in front of him."

Fanfuckingtastic.

"It's okay. Give me the key to the building and I'll get out of your hair. You two can talk," Griffin says, holding his hand out for the key.

"No, that's okay. You were here first. And that counts for something." Poppy lifts her head, glaring at me, her eyes narrow.

"It's really fine. I don't mind." Griffin runs a hand through his hair, inching away from the two of us.

"No. Stay." Poppy grabs his arm and Griffin stops backing away.

"Fine. You want to air our dirty laundry in front of him, whatever. Listen—I'm sorry you're upset."

Poppy's right eye twitches. "Not an apology, Parks. You're not admitting anything."

I shove my hand deeper into my pocket, agitated.

"I'm sorry we snuck around behind your back, Pops."

Griffin's brow raises slightly, but Poppy stands perfectly still. Waiting for more.

"We should have told you about us." I let out a shaky breath, a weight lifting from my chest with the admission.

"And?" Poppy asks, her pink lips a tight, thin line. Like a mother scolding a child, waiting for me to admit everything I've done.

"And that's it. We shouldn't have hidden the relationship. But that's all. I don't apologize for being with Liv."

"Um—any chance I can get that key now?" Griffin scrubs his face and Poppy turns her vicious glare on him.

"Just hang on . . ." Poppy says, holding a finger up to Griffin, motioning for him to wait. "What about the Pact, Parker?" Her foot taps double-time behind the desk, and Griffin huffs out a deep breath, fully understanding he's in the middle of a family drama and wishing he wasn't.

"The Pact is dumb, Poppy. I signed that when I was twelve fucking years old. We're lifetimes away from that now."

Poppy's cheeks flush a bright pink and I know I'm in for it now.

"Promises matter, Parker! Right, Griffin? A deal's a deal!"

Griffin clears his throat. "Well . . ."

"Well, what?" Poppy practically shouts, turning her anger onto him.

"Well, holding someone to a promise they made at twelve years old is kinda crazy. I mean, dude probably hadn't even hit puberty yet."

Poppy huffs out a breath, shaking her head. "You don't understand. He promised he wouldn't date my best friend. And next thing I know, I walk in on them naked!" Poppy's hands fly through the air, almost smacking Griffin in the face. He dodges her wild palms and she keeps on.

"Naked!" she hisses. "Having s-e-x on the couch. Can you believe it?"

Griffin arches a brow, his lips quirking up at the sides, but Poppy is so pissed she doesn't notice.

"That was last week, Poppy. Hardly 'next thing you know.' It's been like two decades," I point out, wishing she wasn't telling everyone about my sex life right now.

"See, Parker? That's just like you. You don't take anything seriously—ever." Poppy's voice is high, almost hysterical.

"That's not true, Poppy. I do take things seriously. But no one notices. I'm the get-along guy and I'm sick of it! I run my own business, work two jobs, have a house. So what if I never have a serious girlfriend? It doesn't mean I'm incapable."

"What does it mean, then?" Poppy asks, folding her arms across her chest.

"Do you really want to hear me say it, Poppy?"

She juts her chin out and I take a deep breath, swallowing hard over the lump in my throat.

"It means all this time I was waiting for Liv." The ocean breeze blows in through the open patio doors, the sound of the crashing waves echoing on the tile. "I love her, Poppy. I've always loved her, but I held off because I love you too and we had a deal."

Poppy blinks, but doesn't say anything.

"I honored that deal for two decades. But I deserve to be happy, Pops, and so does Liv. If you love us—really love us—you'll get over it and be happy for us too."

Poppy's deep blue eyes fill with tears, and my heart twists in my chest, but I'm done.

I'm done with the stupid Pact.

I'm done with the lies.

Most of all, I'm done with the charade of who I am.

I've always wanted Liv. And now that I have her, I don't plan on letting her go for anyone.

Not even Poppy.

Without another word, I turn and walk out of the lobby, leaving my sister behind at the front desk.

For all of our sakes, I hope she'll come around, but I've said my part. The rest is on her.

38

LIV

I'm buzzy as I pace the living room, waiting for Parker to come home, and it's not from the half of a margarita I drank at The Tipsy Taco.

For starters, I'm homeless. Because there's no way in hell Jagger Capelli's gonna be my landlord. I'll sleep in my Camry if I have to.

And Roman's words keep echoing in my head: *If there's anyone who can get him to settle down—it's you.*

So Roman knew all along? What about King? And if the two of them knew, surely Poppy had to have some kind of clue. Which makes all of this even worse. Does she not care about me at all?

All this time, I thought I hid my true feelings, but obviously not that well.

Good thing I'm not a spy or something. I'd probably be dead.

Gravel crunches outside, headlights shining through the window. Parker's home.

I perch on the couch, folding my hands in my lap and trying to seem calm.

Ha freaking ha.

Parker lopes through the door, his hair tousled, worry lines etched across his forehead. Not good.

"Hey, sorry I didn't make it to The Tipsy Taco," he says in a dull tone. He sounds defeated and my heart sinks. Things definitely did not go well with Poppy.

"Do I even need to ask?" I pick at my cuticle, hope seeping out of me like a deflated balloon.

Parker shakes his head, collapsing on the couch next to me and kicking off his shoes. He leans back and stretches his arm out, winding it around my shoulders.

"No. Be glad you weren't there." His fingers trace the warm skin of my shoulder and I wince when he touches the spot where Jagger gripped me.

"Babe, what happened?" Parker's eyes widen as he studies my face.

"Nothing. It's fine." I shrug it off, wanting to hear more about Poppy rather than recount my ugly encounter with Jagger.

Parker sits up and examines my arm. Stupid Jagger actually bruised my bicep, leaving a nasty black and blue mark blooming on my skin.

"That's not nothing. How'd that happen?" Parker's holding my arm out, gently stroking beneath the bruise.

"It's no big deal, Parks. I went to The Tipsy Taco and sat at the bar to wait for you. Jagger came in and tried to sit next to me. I told him I was saving the seat and he grabbed my arm."

"That motherfucker touched you! I'm gonna kill him." Redness creeps up Parker's neck all the way to his cheeks. He jumps off the couch, but I grab him by the hand.

"Don't. We don't need any more problems. Roman came in and told Jagger to beat it."

"Rome was there?" Parker pauses.

"Yeah."

"Thank goodness. If that asshole ever touches you again though, babe, I swear I'm going to knock that stupid grin off his face permanently."

"I appreciate it, I do. But let's try to stay out of jail, 'kay?" I pull him back down onto the couch next to me, smoothing my hand over his strong chest, his heart thumping hard against his ribs.

"That guy. I'm glad Rome was there."

"Me too. Um—listen. I did hear something tonight . . ."

"What?" Parker settles back against the couch, gathering me up into his lap. I snuggle into him, his shirt smelling like freshly cut wood and coconuts, a signature blend of him and Poppy.

"I'm going to be officially homeless at the end of the month."

"What? I thought your landlord's making repairs?"

"Me too." I sigh, long and heavy. Ever since Hurricane Clementine ripped through Seaglass Beach, my life's been topsy-turvy.

"Jagger said he bought the property. He's the new landlord. No way in hell am I paying the Capellis rent."

Parker smooths my hair, his thumb tracing over my cheekbone. "Absolutely not."

"I guess I'll start looking for a new place tomorrow. And I have to move my stuff out ASAP. I don't want the Capellis going in there and rummaging through my things. The idea of him having a key to my place creeps me out." A cold shiver races through me and I tremble.

"Babe." Parker lifts my chin, locking his ocean-blue eyes on mine. "Stay with me."

My heart skips in my chest. "What?"

"Just stay here. Don't look for a rental—move in with me."

"Parks—it's kinda fast, don't you think?"

He tucks a stray lock of hair behind my ear, licks his bottom lip. "Liv, I've known you most of my life and loved you for just as long. No. It's not fast."

I'm speechless and can barely catch my breath. Parker seals his lips to mine, kissing me so softly I think I'm dreaming.

"Stay."

"Okay," I murmur into his warm mouth. "Thank you."

"Anything for you."

39

PARKER

Now that I've had Liv, I need more. I don't think I'll ever get enough of her. Her luscious body, her sweet smile, that tinkly little laugh.

I want her wrapped around me. I want to bury myself in her, so deep I don't know where she ends and I begin.

I want her—need her—to be mine.

Taking both her hands in mine, I stretch them above her head, rain kisses down the long lines of her neck. Her pulse flutters beneath my lips and I lick at her delicate skin, nipping softly until she moans a breathy exhale into my hair. Snaking my hand up her shirt, her flesh is warm as I cup her breast. Her nipple pebbles through the thin satin fabric of her bra and I pinch and roll the sharp point. She wraps her legs around my hips, squeezing me closer to her, and my cock swells and hardens.

Capturing her lips, I sweep into her mouth, our tongues intertwining. She tastes sweet and salty, and I know I'll never get enough of her.

"I want you. Right now," I murmur, releasing her hands

to strip out of my clothes. I don't care that I haven't eaten dinner, the lights are on, we're still on the couch. Nothing matters in this moment except taking Liv, claiming her, making her mine.

Liv smiles, watching me drop the rest of my clothes in a heap on the floor. "What's the rush? Looks like I'm going to be here for a long while."

"I'll never have enough time with you. And last time we tried this, we got interrupted. I like to finish what I start."

"Well, then, by all means." She sits up, lifting her shirt off in one fluid motion, unhooking her bra and letting it fall to the floor. Then she shimmies out of her shorts and panties until she's naked on the couch, her bare ass on the leather.

"Beautiful," I say, watching as her hair tumbles over her shoulders. She gazes up at me through lowered lashes and I'm the luckiest guy on the entire fucking planet.

She crooks her finger at me and I join her on the couch, spreading her legs open and dipping my head down to taste her. Her back arches and she moves slightly away from me, but I grip her hips and spread her legs open wider. I flatten my tongue, licking and tasting her sweetness, and she quivers beneath me.

"Parker," she moans, and I bury my face even deeper in her wet heat. She bucks as I circle her clit with my tongue, sucking the sensitive flesh into my mouth.

"You're so fucking wet for me," I whisper, the vibrations of my voice causing goosebumps to rise on her thighs.

She grips my shoulders, her nails digging into the flexed muscle, a sharp sting that hurts so good.

"Oh. My." She shudders beneath me, a wave of release coursing through her. "Parks."

I lift my head, wiping my mouth on my shoulder, pleased. "That was only round one, baby."

Shifting my weight, I climb her body until we're chest to chest, her round breasts against my hard pecs. She grazes her lips with mine, a soft, gentle kiss that I deepen. I nip her bottom lip, sucking it between my teeth and her breath catches. Her nipples harden and my cock pulses against her hot center.

"Take me, Parker." She locks her eyes on mine, her pupils dark with desire, as she encircles my cock with her hand. Stroking the shaft until it hardens and lengthens, ready for her. My balls tingle, my lower body coiling, and I know I'm not going to last long like this.

I drag the tip of my cock through her wetness, nudging at her swollen clit, and she arches up to meet me. I ease into her, inch by inch, slowly filling her up.

"You feel so good, Liv. So fucking tight." I thrust into her, and her muscles clench around my cock, milking me. She's gorgeous as her body melts into mine, her eyes glassy with lust.

We find the perfect rhythm, rocking together as I thrust in and out of her. Pulse racing, I watch as Liv's skin flushes pink and we rocket toward our release.

"Come for me, Liv," I whisper into her ear.

That's all it takes to send her tumbling over the edge, trembling and breathless.

"Parker!" she cries out, her thighs squeezing and gripping me.

I follow her lead, plunging into her harder, sinking myself in deeper until I explode.

"Fuck," I rasp, shuddering as I convulse, emptying myself inside her.

She wraps her arms and legs around me, pulling me tighter against her body, our skin sticky and clammy with sweat. Our breathing syncs, the thumping of Liv's heart vibrating against my chest. I lace my hand in hers, rubbing her thumb with mine.

"I love you," I whisper into the air.

"I love you, too, Parks. And I'm sorry about Poppy."

"Me too." I hold in my sigh even as my chest aches at the thought of losing my sister. I don't need to pile more onto Liv. This is my mess and I need to deal with it.

40

LIV

LATER THAT NIGHT, AFTER WE SHOWER AND SCROUNGE for dinner, I'm cuddling beside Parker in his bed in the dark. My hand tiptoes up and down his abdominals, my nails scratching lightly over his skin.

"Want to talk about it?"

Parker inhales, his chest rising, then falling. He runs his hand over my hair, his fingertips brushing my forehead.

"What do you want to know?"

"What happened? What'd she say?"

"Nothing good. Or productive. I apologized for sneaking around behind her back and not being truthful. But that wasn't good enough for her." His hand stills on my head and I feel his heartbeat picking up.

"And?"

"And I told her the Pact was dumb. She can't declare a person off-limits."

"I bet she didn't take that very well."

"No. The funny thing is, that guy we met at Food Truck

Friday? Griffin? He was there and he sided with me. Told Poppy it was the dumbest thing ever, in fact."

"He did?" I ask, raising my head to glance at Parker.

He nods, grinning. "Yeah. It was kind of awesome, actually. I really like that guy. Not many people have the balls to say anything negative to Poppy."

I laugh. "You know, you're right. Most people take her side, no matter what."

"Exactly. But this dude straight up told her she was in the wrong. I think his exact quote was 'Holding someone to a promise they made when they were twelve is kinda crazy.'"

"He said that?" I ask, my voice tipping up. Parker's right—no one ever stands up to Poppy. Mostly because she's usually right, but also because she has this presence that exudes confidence. A real 'don't fuck with me' attitude.

Unlike me. I'm the people pleaser, the one always bending over backwards to make everyone happy.

Well, not anymore.

"Yeah. He's cool. I should probably invite him out for a drink. He can't have many friends here."

"I'm sure Poppy will be thrilled about that."

Parker shrugs, his entire body shifting. "At this point, we have to live our lives. I told her I'm done trying to make everyone happy. We deserve to be happy, Liv."

The clock tick-ticks in the darkness as I mull over this statement. Deep down, I know Parker's right. We do deserve to be happy.

But I can't help worrying about Poppy. And I miss her.

"I'll try to talk to her, Parks. Maybe I can smooth things over."

"Good luck. She's still pretty pissed."

"She can't be as mad at me. I didn't even know about the pact."

"True. If anyone can get through to her, it's you."

Parker presses his lips to my hair, enfolding me in his arms, and I snuggle into his warmth. Even though I don't have my own place and my best friend's not talking to me, I'm still wildly, blissfully happy.

Happier than I ever thought I could be.

And not even Poppy's tantrum can ruin this moment for me.

THE NEXT MORNING, I SEND POPPY A TEXT:

> Liv: We need to talk

I wait a few seconds, staring down at the screen, but per the usual I get no response. Then something surprising happens. Three blue dots pop up, disappear.

Poppy's writing to me.

> Poppy: Fine

Wow, poetic.

> Liv: I have a meeting at four PM. Want to meet for drinks afterwards? Seaglass Sips around 5:30?

Poppy: Sure

Damn, she's on fire today. You'd almost think she's getting charged by the letter.

Liv: See you then

No response. But it's fine. At least she agreed to meet me. I immediately text Parker.

Liv: I'm meeting Poppy tonight at 5:30 for drinks. Wish me luck.

Parker: Want me to come? For back-up?

Liv: Don't think so. Let me try to talk to her 1:1 this time

Parker: Okay. Good luck, babe. Love you

My heart flip-flops in my chest, seeing those words pop up on the screen. I don't think I'll ever get tired of Parker saying he loves me.

Liv: Love you too. Have a good day

Parker: You too babe. See you tonight

Throwing my phone in my bag, I head to work. Sure to be a welcome distraction from my real-life issues.

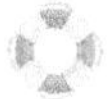

At 5:15, I power down my laptop, tuck my planner into my bag, and lock up the office. Seaglass Sips is also on Main Street, near Coastal Coffee, so less than a ten-minute drive from the office.

I make it there in seven, including finding a parking spot. Sometimes small-town beach living has its perks, and lack of traffic is definitely one of them. I stroll up to the wine bar, a tight ball of nerves winding and knotting in my stomach. Taking a deep breath of the salty air, I try to focus on the warm breeze from the ocean, the sound of the waves in the distance. Normally, I love meeting Poppy here after work, having a glass of wine and sharing stories about our day.

Normally.

But not tonight.

Pushing into the bar, I don't see Poppy at any of the black bistro tables or at the corner booth. She's not at the long walnut bar, either, so I assume I beat her here. I wave to Daphne, the owner, and motion at the outdoor tables. She nods and I saunter outside, claiming one of the small round tables. I take a seat, tipping my head back and letting the sun warm my cheeks. Today was stressful—tons of to-dos checked off the list, but the hurricane really messed up my work flow. Now we have double the work in half the time because of all the event reschedules. Hopefully by September, we'll be all caught up and life will get a little less frantic.

"Hey, Liv. What can I get you?" Daphne's voice interrupts my thoughts. "You waiting on someone?"

I nod. "Yes, Poppy should be here any minute. I'll take a glass of rosé, thanks."

"Okay. I'll bring two waters as well. Be right back."

She bustles off and I check my phone. 5:30 on the dot, no missed calls or texts.

Relax, Liv. I'm sure she'll be here soon.

I scroll through Pinterest, checking out venues and floral arrangements. Daphne brings me the wine and two waters, but still no Poppy. I sip my rosé, trying to take the edge off my anxiety.

Buzz, buzz.

> Poppy: Sorry I'm late. Guest lost his key.
> Waiting on locksmith. Raincheck?

Ohmygawd. After all this, Poppy's going to cancel?

No. Just no. I have to talk to her, straighten this out. Things aren't going to be right between me and Parker without her blessing, I feel it deep down in my bones. Parker can act all tough and pretend he doesn't care what Poppy thinks, but it's written all over his face.

He cares. A lot.

And honestly, so do I.

I want my best friend back.

> Liv: I can wait. Or come to the inn.
> Whichever

Poppy leaves me hanging for a solid five minutes, my

palms sweaty and my heart racing. So much for taking the edge off.

Finally, she texts back.

> Poppy: Locksmith here. I should be there in fifteen.

I sip the rest of my wine, chasing it with the water, refill my glass and drink more water. Poppy and I have been friends since elementary school. There's no reason I should be this nervous to talk to my best friend.

Except now I'm sleeping with her brother. Slight plot twist, but she should get over it.

Ring, ring.

I grab my cell, answering automatically. "Hello?"

"Hi, Olivia. How are you?" my mom trills down the line.

Shit. I should have checked caller ID, but I thought for sure it'd be Poppy.

"Hi, Mom. I'm good. I'm actually meeting Poppy for drinks, so I can't talk long. What's up?"

"Just checking in. Wanted to see if you got the wedding invitation to your cousin Lola's wedding and if you RSVP'd."

"No, but I haven't checked my mail in a few days. I'll have to swing over and collect it." I drum the menu with my fingers, eager to hang up. I want to be in the right headspace for my discussion with Poppy and chatting with my mother definitely isn't it.

"You're still not back in your place?" she asks, and I can envision her worry lines so deep and tight they actually touch.

"Uh, no. And I won't be going back, either. Turns out, my landlord sold my place."

"What? Oh my word, Olivia. What are you doing? Where are you staying? At the inn with Poppy?"

"No . . ." I drag the word out, stalling, as I debate how to break the news of my current living arrangement to my mother.

"Well, are you at your cousin's? Because the least your Aunt April could do is give me a call and let me know where my only daughter is living."

I love that my mother is affronted at a situation that's not actually happening. Classic.

"Mom, stop. Don't go getting all mad at Aunt April. After the hurricane, Parker invited me over to his house. And now that my place is sold, he asked me to stay. So I'm moving in with Parker."

"What?" Two screechy voices shout at me in tandem, one over the phone, the other coming from directly behind me.

Oh shit.

"Mom, I gotta go. Talk soon." I hang up on my mother and whirl around to face an ashen Poppy.

"You're moving in together?" Poppy asks, her voice tipping up in disbelief. "You've gotta be kidding me."

"Wait, Poppy, I can explain." I jump up, pushing my seat out so hard it clatters backwards, tipping and hitting the sidewalk.

"This is fucking unbelievable," Poppy mutters, almost to herself. Her cheeks go from white to splotchy pink, and she runs a shaky hand through her hair. "When was anyone going to tell me about this?" She levels her gaze on mine, her deep blue eyes icy.

"Today. I've been trying to talk to you for weeks now, but you're not taking my calls," I point out, keeping my voice even although I'm freaking out on the inside. But this is not the time for hysteria—one of us needs to stay calm.

"Have you thought this through, Liv? Like, at all? How many women have you seen my brother with? Ten, twenty? Three dozen?"

She does have a point and I hate it, but I know Parker's changed.

"He's different with me, Poppy."

"Uh-huh. I'm sure that's what every other girl thought too. I love Parker, I do, but I don't think you know what you're getting yourself into."

"I do know, Poppy. And I know you probably don't want to hear it, but your brother is amazing. He's kind and thoughtful and sweet. And I love him." My voice trails off and Poppy stares at me, unblinking. She scrunches her perfect pink bow mouth to the side and shakes her head.

"I think you love the idea of loving him. Getting the playboy of Seaglass Beach to settle down. But he's playing house, Liv. Parker's never going to stick around, even for you. That's why I made the Pact with him. I didn't want to lose my best friend when he broke your heart."

A sharp pain hits me in the gut as her words sink in. Poppy knew what she was doing all along. She wanted to keep me away from Parker, and I can't help but wonder if she had a selfish ulterior motive.

"Are you sure you weren't protecting yourself, Poppy? Because you think that if me and Parker are together we'll cut you out?"

Poppy's eyes flash and darken and she takes a few steps

towards me. My hands are shaking, so I shove one into my back pocket, rubbing my necklace with the other.

"No, Liv. I'm sure I'll be just fine. I was looking out for you, but if you want to be on your own, that's your prerogative. Like I said before, don't call me when he gets bored and moves on to his next fling."

Hot tears prick at the corner of my eyes, but I will myself not to cry. I won't cry in front of Poppy about this.

Not now, not ever.

Somehow, I dig deep and try to move past her sharp words. "I want to stay friends, Poppy. Even more, I want things to be good between you and Parker. He'd kill me for saying this, but I know he misses you. I miss you. Can't we forget all this and move on?"

"Forget you lied to me? Forget you snuck around behind my back? Forget that you picked Parker over me?"

I hold my breath as anger rolls off Poppy, her hands ticking off each transgression. She shakes her head, her honey blond bangs falling over her eyes. Just like Parker's.

"No, Liv. I don't think I can forget those things. I'll always love you, but I can't forget what you and Parker did. How can I ever trust you again?"

"Poppy, you're overreacting. We were going to tell you."

"Don't, Liv. Don't condescend to me and tell me I'm overreacting."

Her harsh tone triggers something inside me and I finally snap.

"You know what, Poppy? I'm tired of being a pawn in your game. Like I said before, I'm a person. You can't mark a person off limits, this isn't some schoolyard game of keep away. For fuck sakes, we're all grown-ass adults. I, for one, think it's time you start acting like one!"

Poppy's nostrils flare and I know she's good and pissed off, but I keep going. "I'm sorry we lied. I'm even more sorry you walked in on us, but I'm not sorry—and never will be sorry—about my feelings for your brother. I love him. He loves me. We're moving in together. I want you to be happy for me—for us—but if you can't do that, then stay the hell away from me."

I bend down and pick up the chair, find my wallet in my purse, and throw a twenty-dollar bill on the table to pay for my drink. Then I turn and walk away, leaving my best friend standing on the sidewalk, speechless.

I've never stood up to Poppy in my entire life. I guess a lot of things are changing, whether Poppy likes it or not.

41

———

LIV

#fail

I wanted Seaglass Sips to work its magic, for it to be like old times between me and Poppy. Nope. Definitely did not happen.

Ironically, now I think things are even worse between us. I hadn't intended for her to find out about me moving in with Parker like that, but here we are.

But I meant what I said—she's just going to have to deal with it.

It doesn't make me any less sad, though, as I swipe the tears from my face, running my fingers under my lash line to clean up any mascara smudges. Parker's already home and he doesn't need to see me like this. He's going to have to deal with Poppy a lot more than me; the least I can do is try to be calm about the situation.

"How'd it go with my sister?" The first words out of his mouth as I walk in the door, his brow raised.

"Um—" I flounder for the right words, my voice shaky.

"Shit. That bad, huh?"

Cheeks puffing, I huff out a huge, heavy sigh, running my fingers through the slight waves in my hair. "Yeah. Sorry, Parks. She walked up on me right when I was telling my mom about my change of address."

"Oh, shitballs." Parker scrubs a hand across the back of his neck.

"Yeah." I collapse onto the couch, kicking off my sandals and tucking my legs up underneath me. "Less than ideal. She did not take that well."

Parker grabs two glasses of water, brings them over to the couch and hands me one. Then he sits next to me, unfolding his long, lean body next to mine, draping an arm around my shoulder. I breathe him in, the masculine scent of wood and spicy cologne tickling my nose. Everything's great when it's just the two of us, but I'd be lying if I said I'm not worried about the rest of it. Poppy, my mom, Parker's past history and reputation.

What if Poppy's right?

I push that thought away, gnawing at my bottom lip.

"What else happened? You're shaking." Parker's fingertips caress the bare skin of my arms and I close my eyes, resting my head on his shoulder.

"It was kinda awful, Parks."

"Tell me."

More tears sting my eyes as I remember all the horrible things Poppy and I said to each other.

"The highlight reel? Poppy doesn't think we're going to last. I'm making a huge mistake. You'll never settle down. She's pissed we lied to her. And she planned the entire pact to keep me and you away from each other so she didn't get cut out. That last bit she didn't admit to—it's my sneaking suspicion. She didn't deny it, though, so there's that."

"Whoa." Parker sits perfectly still, digesting all this. "That's pretty shitty. I mean, I can kind of see her point—"

My head swivels, my gaze flying to his. "What? Really?"

He slides his thumb along his jawline. "Yeah. With me and you together, Poppy doesn't have anyone to hang out with. Now as an adult, it's lame. But as a twelve-year-old—I get it."

"But we're not twelve," I point out. "We're just acting like it right now."

"True. So she needs to drop this shit."

"Okay, so we agree. Poppy's in the wrong."

"For sure."

"Why do I still feel so bad then?" I ask, tucking my head up against his broad shoulder. I love how his body's so hard and strong beneath me, supporting me.

He runs his hand over my hair, the tips of his fingers rough as they brush over my forehead.

"Because you're a good friend, Liv."

Despite my best efforts, a hot tear slips out, plopping on Parker's T-shirt and blooming into a dark wet spot on the grey cotton. My breathing's jagged as I hold in my sobs. I'm tired of feeling like this, but I don't know how to make things better anymore.

"I don't want to come between you and your sister, Parks. Y'all have already lost so much, what with your parents—" My voice breaks and now I'm really crying. Parker's body tenses beneath me and I bury my face in his chest.

He wraps his warm, strong arms around me, murmuring

shushing sounds in my ear like I'm a baby. Which, honestly, I feel like at the moment.

A big crybaby.

I don't want to lose Parker, but who am I to ruin his relationship with his twin, to come between family?

I need to let Parker go.

The very thought cracks my chest wide open and I'm in actual, physical pain. But I know in my heart it's the right thing to do.

For Parker.

For Poppy.

For everyone but me.

"I think we need to break up." I whisper the words and squeeze my eyes shut, trying to block out the pain.

A metaphysically impossible task I'm going to be doing the rest of my life. Because I know I'll never be over Parker Montgomery.

42

———

LIV

"WHAT? NO WAY." DISBELIEF AND AGGRAVATION MINGLE in his voice as he rubs my back. "No, Liv. Fuck that. Poppy can either get over herself or be alone—her choice. But I'm not losing you."

He's firm, resolute, his voice strong and unwavering.

"Parks, you have to think about the long-term consequences of this." I sit up, dabbing my eyes with my shirt. "What about work? How awkward is it gonna be when you're at the inn bartending? Won't that be weird? And what about holidays? I can hardly come sit at the family dinner table—Poppy hates me now."

"Work will be fine, I hardly ever even see Pops anyway. She doesn't walk out to the tiki bar that often. Besides, I'm trying to hire a guy to cover my shift. The contracting business is picking up—and I want to have more nights and weekends free to spend with you."

He takes my hand in his, lacing our fingers together, and I can't even right now. I love Parker with my whole heart, my entire being—how can I walk away from him?

"I want that too, Parks," I whisper as he tucks a stray lock of hair behind my ear. So tender, so gentle, I can't imagine ever loving anyone half as much as I love him.

"And holidays will be fine. We'll stick Rome in between you and Poppy. He's a great bodyguard."

"Stop." I punch him in the bicep. "Be serious."

"What? I am being serious. He protected you from Jagger and I've seen him take more than one dude in a bar fight. He's got some serious street cred." Parker shoots me his lopsided grin and my heart melts.

"So please don't leave, Liv. Stay." We lock eyes and my breath catches in my throat, the decision looming heavy in the air.

I should leave. 100%. Definitely.

"I'll stay, Parker. And I'm really sorry I couldn't change Poppy's mind."

"Babe. The only person who can change Poppy's mind is Poppy." He glides his thumb across my cheek, his light touch electric.

I know he's right. Poppy is stubborn, but I thought our friendship meant more to her than holding on to her anger.

Guess not.

"You okay?" he asks, faint worry lines crinkling at the edges of his eyes.

I nod. "I guess. I want things to go back to how they were before. Well—between me and Poppy, not you and I. I'm pretty happy with our new relationship status." I smile up at him and he grins back.

"Same, babe. Hurricane Clementine was the best storm of my life."

He leans in, pressing his lips to mine, and I surrender.

My lips, my heart, everything in this moment. Because we feel right together and I've never been more alive.

Parker cups my cheeks with his large hands, his touch comforting. "Are you okay? Are we okay?"

He searches my face, trying to read my expression.

I nod. "I'm fine. Sad about Poppy, but you're right. She's making her choice and we're making ours."

"Will you be okay here alone for like an hour?"

I lick my lower lip, twisting the hem of my shirt. "Yes, I'm fine."

"You'll still be here when I get back, right? I don't have to worry about you packing all your stuff and taking off to Maryland or something?" One brow arches high as he strokes my thigh.

I shake my head, forcing a laugh. "No, I won't stalk off in the night. I'll at least wait until the morning," I tease.

"Not funny, babe. I need you here." He squeezes my leg and I lean forward, brushing my lips against his.

"I won't leave, Parks. Promise. Where are you going?"

His lips in a tight line, he stands, grabbing his keys. "I'm going to talk to Poppy and set things straight with her. I'm over her bullshit. She made you cry—that's the last straw."

"Don't you think we should give her some space to cool off?"

"No. She's had her time, she's had her say. The thing she hasn't done? Listen. To our side of the story. I'm going to tell her the truth and she's just going to have to accept it. I love you and that's that. Period. End of story. So she can get with the program or butt out—her choice."

"Tread lightly, Parks. She's in a mood."

"I'll try. Don't worry—I have a lot of experience with

Poppy. I can finesse her with the best of them." He winks at me and I know this to be the absolute truth.

Parker's nothing if not charming.

"Okay. I'll be here when you get back. Either way."

"This ends tonight." His tone is final, his jaw square.

Shoving one hand in his pocket, Parker strides out the screen door on a mission. Anxiety churns in my stomach, along with the rosé.

I hope he can get Poppy to come around. But I'm not sure she's ready to accept this new reality yet—or if she ever will.

43

———

PARKER

Seeing Liv cry over the bullshit with my sister triggers me and my protective instinct kicks in hard. I love Poppy, but she's being fucking selfish at this point.

Did I screw up? Yeah. Of course.

Should I have been honest from the beginning? Also yes.

Do I regret breaking the Pact and sleeping with Liv? Hell no.

Best decision I ever made. Probably shouldn't lead with that, but it's the truth.

And Poppy needs to accept it. I hate watching Liv beat herself up over this thing between me and Poppy. And I know she's sad to have lost her best friend, even if it's only temporary.

So this ends tonight. I'm going to get Poppy to come around, no matter what.

I slam my SUV into a parking spot in front of Poppy's apartment at the inn. Good, her car's here and the lights are on—I'm certain she's home. I didn't call or text on the way over. Better to surprise her. Plus, she might not have agreed to see me. This way, she doesn't have a fucking choice. She's listening to what I have to say, whether she likes it or not.

Knock, knock, knock.

I bang on the door and wait, shuffling nervously.

Relax. This is fucking stupid and you know it. All you have to do is convince Poppy to forgive you and Liv.

Poppy cracks the door open, peeping out at me with one eye. "What do you want? Thought for sure you'd be busy with Liv." Her tone's sharp, biting, and pain flits across her face.

"We need to talk."

"Pass."

"It isn't a request, Poppy." I shove the door open, forcing my way in. She huffs, but moves out of the way and allows me entry.

"This is bullshit, Pops, and you know it."

"Great opening line, Parker. Did you work on that on the way over here?" Her face twists into a scowl.

Damn. Already not going well.

"This isn't some rehearsed fucking speech. I'm telling you how I feel, how Liv feels."

"I think I saw how the two of you feel the other night when I walked in on you banging my best friend on your couch."

Ouch.

I shove a hand in my pocket, scrubbing a hand over the back of my neck, the skin flaming.

"Yeah, sorry about that. We didn't know you were coming. Obviously." I glance up, my eyes flicking to hers.

"That was super awkward, Parks. A horrible scene for

me to witness—you with any girl—but with my best friend? Too much." She shakes her head, her ponytail flopping across her shoulder.

"I regret that." I swallow hard, choking on the words I know I need to say.

"Look—" I take a deep, shuddery breath. "I'm gonna lead with something I should have said before. I'm sorry. I really, truly am. I didn't mean to hurt you, Pops. I know this is an awkward situation—and trust me, I've had many years to think about it—but I deserve to be happy, Poppy. And so does Liv."

Poppy throws her hands out wide. "What about me, Parker? Y'all don't care about me anymore? I don't deserve to be happy? Now that you and Liv have a love shack together, I'm on my own?"

"Whoa—pause. No, obviously not. First, please don't ever refer to my house as a love shack. It's *The Love Shack,* get it straight."

Despite her obvious anger, the corner of her lip twitches as she suppresses at least a glimmer of a smile.

"Shut up, Parks. Be serious for once."

"Fine," I say, holding my palms up. "And no, Poppy—we obviously want you to be happy and care about you. Very much. That's why I'm here. Liv's so upset she was crying after she talked to you. She said she's moving to Maryland and breaking up with me, over the fight you two had."

"What?" Poppy's smooth brow furrows, her eyebrows scrunching together. "She can't move to Maryland. She hates Sam and his cats. Do you know their entire guest room is a cat play yard? Where will she stay? And what about her job?"

"I see you skipped over the part where she was crying." I level my gaze at her and her cheeks flush pink.

"I'm upset too, Parks. Y'all lied to me. You *know* I hate lying and sneaking around."

"That's on me, Poppy. Because of the Pact. Liv wanted to talk to you a bunch of times, but I kept asking her to wait. Because I knew this would happen—I knew how you'd react."

"But you made it worse by lying," Poppy points out, channeling our mother during one of her many honesty lectures.

I sigh, running a hand through my hair. "I know. I blew it. I fucked up, I admit it. But don't hold that against Liv—that was all me."

"Fine. But you should have heard the things she said to me today, Parks. She was downright mean at Seaglass Sips."

"And what did you say to her?" I tip my head to the side, staring straight into her wide eyes. Acting all innocent, even though we both know she isn't.

"Nothing. Same things I've said to you. I'm pissed y'all lied. I'm pissed y'all got together behind my back. I'm pissed you broke your promise to me." She balls her fists at her sides, a vein popping out in her neck.

"Again—mainly my fault. I made the move on Liv, I asked her to wait to tell you, and I made the Pact back with you in middle school. Liv didn't even know about it."

"Fine. But don't act like she's blameless. She had to know getting together with you would piss me off."

"Why, Pops?" I honestly don't know the answer to my question.

"Because—" She breaks away from my gaze, her bottom lip quivering. "Now I feel like I'm third wheeling all the time. The two of you are my best friends. Now that you're together, where does that leave me? Alone, that's where."

I pause, letting her words sink in.

"That's fucking selfish of you, Poppy."

Her lips smash together, turning white. "See? And this is why this isn't going to be okay!"

"No, Poppy. *You're* the reason this isn't okay. Things don't have to change between you and Liv. Y'all have been friends forever. She's still your friend. Even if she's with me. You're the one cutting her out. She wants to be close to you. She's trying, but you're pushing her away. Don't do that, Poppy." I reach out, touching her arm, and she freezes, her eyes on my hand. I can't see her face, but her sniffles echo off the white tile and her shoulders shake.

"I know, Parks. It's just—I'm so sad. I feel like everything's changing and I can't keep up, ever since Mom and Dad died. Like I'm running on the beach, but the sand's slipping beneath my feet and I'm digging a hole, deeper and deeper. Until eventually I'm going to be swallowed up."

"Pops." I step forward, wrapping my sister in my arms, dwarfing her tiny body with mine. Sobs rack her chest and I absorb the vibrations, like I've done my entire life. I'm big enough, strong enough, tough enough, for the both of us.

Palming her head, I stroke her hair. "No one's leaving you behind. And things aren't all that different. You and Liv still have something special, something I'll never have with her. She can tell you stuff she'd never tell me. But you have to let this go. You have to let Liv be happy, Poppy. Let me be happy. That doesn't mean you can't be happy. Be happy for us. With us. We want you to be. I don't know if Liv can be happy without you, not really."

Poppy pauses, sniffling. Tipping her head up at me, she asks, "Really? She seemed pretty fucking happy at the wine bar."

"She hyped herself up to talk to you. She was so nervous about it. Trust me—she's faking it. Only your blessing can assuage her guilt."

Poppy sighs. "Fine. I can do it. On one condition."

I narrow my eyes. "What?"

"Promise me I'm never going to walk in on the two of you again. Seriously, my retinas are burned."

I chuckle. "I'll do my best. Call first. And for the love— do not just walk in. If you do, all bets are off."

She scrunches up her nose. "Gross."

"So, do you forgive me? Forgive Liv?"

"I guess."

"I'll take it. Can I ask you to do one thing?"

Now it's Poppy's turn to narrow her eyes at me. "Maybe . . ."

"Talk to Liv. Please. It's not the same coming from me. She needs to hear the words from you."

Poppy bites at her upper lip, her bare heel tapping the tile double-time. "Deal. As long as you promise not to be naked, I can talk to Liv."

I hold out my hand to her. "Secret handshake on it."

Poppy smiles, clutching my hand and pumping three times, then sliding her fingers away and slapping first the front, then the back of my palm.

"I love you, Pops," I say, bringing her body into mine and hugging her tight, the weight I'd been carrying for weeks lifting off my chest.

"I love you too, Parker."

44

LIV

Buzz, buzz.

I check my phone while waiting at the stoplight, my fingers drumming the steering wheel. I'm on my way to the inn to scope out the best layout for the upcoming Labor Day / Anniversary party make-up. Even though Parker told me everything went fine with Poppy last night, I'm still nervous as hell to see her in person after our blowout at the wine bar. I can't remember the last time we had a fight like that—probably in the tenth grade when Poppy thought I wasn't going to ride to school with her after I started dating Jeremy Britton.

> Poppy: I need to talk to you

My heart pounds double-time, hammering hard against my ribs. I hurry to text her back before the light turns.

> Liv: Ok. I have all the plans for the Labor
> Day party, so don't worry about that

> Poppy: Not about the party

> Liv: Oh. I'll be there in 5. Was heading your way

> Poppy: I'll meet you in the storage room. We can check the table & chair situation

> Liv: Ok

Nerves humming, I drive the rest of the way to the Seaglass Inn trying to tamp down a brewing panic attack. My clammy hands slide over the steering wheel as I park behind the main building, close to the storage room where they keep all the extra tables, chairs, linens, and decorations. I've coordinated the anniversary party the last four years, ever since I started working at Seaglass Celebrations. The first time I ran the party, Mrs. Montgomery was at the helm. This party was her baby, and now it's Poppy's.

I take a deep breath, then grab my bag, stuffing my cell into the side pocket.

Here goes nothing.

The white shell gravel crunches beneath my feet as I cross to the back door, entering the bright fluorescently lit storage room. Poppy's standing in the back corner, tabulating RSVPs.

"What's it looking like? Are most people able to make the new date?" My voice bounces off the bare white cinderblock walls, loud in the otherwise quiet room.

Poppy's honey blond head swivels around to face me, her expression neutral. "More people are attending now, actually. Because we have some Labor Day peeps too."

"Wow. Okay. We can make it work. I need the final count today to pass on to the vendors."

"Alright."

I cross the room and stand next to Poppy, peering over her shoulder at the RSVP list. It's a veritable Who's Who of Seaglass Beach. Minus the Capellis, of course. The only time they venture down to this part of the beach is to scavenge for real estate deals. Of which there are none because Montgomerys and Capellis mix like oil and water and nobody wants to stir up the turf war.

Both Poppy and I stare at the list, neither of us saying anything.

#awkward.

Blood rushes in my ears and I'm overly warm, even though the room felt chilly a few seconds ago.

"Listen, Liv . . ." Poppy's voice trails off and she turns to face me. "I forgive you."

She probably means this in a good way, but her words are still a sharp sucker punch to my gut. Anger courses through me and I breathe deeply through my nose, trying to stay calm. I lick my lips, choosing my words carefully.

"*You* forgive *me?*" I point at her, then myself, one brow rising. Taking another deep breath, I imagine a cool blue wave of calmness washing over me.

Unfortunately, my visualization exercise doesn't work and acid rises up the back of my throat instead, burning my tongue.

"Yes. For lying and sneaking around with my brother."

Fine. She does have a point.

I could say a lot of bitchy things here, but it's not worth it. I want to put all this behind me—behind us—and move on.

"Okay, thanks. I am sorry about that. I wanted to tell you, but . . ." I stop myself before I spill the tea and blame Parker. No need to throw fuel on the fire.

"I know—Parker told me last night. I should have known that was all him. Sneaking around's not really your style."

A smile tugs at the corner of my lips, but I'm not quite there yet. We still have some making up to do before I can relax.

We stare at each other for a second, Poppy flicking the corner of the RSVP list, me rubbing my necklace. I hope we can find our way back to each other because this strain between us is too much. Extremely uncomfortable and I don't like it.

"Liv—"

I stand still, meeting Poppy's deep blue gaze.

"I'm sorry I said those things to you yesterday. Especially the stuff about you and my brother being a fling. When I saw him last night, he was different. He is different with you."

My heart hammers at her words.

"Thanks, Poppy. That means a lot to me."

"In fact, I need to change my thinking on your relationship—don't break my brother's heart." She presses her lips together, a perfect pink bow shape, and my chest squeezes tight.

Me break Parker's heart? The thought is so ludicrous, so outlandish, I almost laugh. But if anyone knows Parker, it's his twin sister.

"I won't, Poppy. You know that."

"He really is in love with you. Who am I to stand in the

way of that?" Her voice wavers and tears shimmer in her eyes.

"Pops—you know I still love you. So does Parker. We never meant to hurt you. Ever. This rift is killing me, and I know it's killing your brother too. Can we move on and go back to the way things were?"

Poppy shakes her head. "No, Liv. I don't think we can."

A rush of sadness floods me and my knees almost buckle. I did not expect that answer. I reach out, steady myself on the laminate counter.

"I'm sorry to hear you say that."

Poppy touches my arm. "Things won't be the same, Liv. But that doesn't mean they can't be good. Great, even."

A tiny flicker of hope lights up inside me. "Really?"

"Really. As long as Parker promises not to hog my best friend. I don't want to be constantly third wheeling. We still need girls' night, and Parker can't come with us to the spa. That's a hard stop."

I laugh. "Truth. I don't need anyone seeing me get a mud facial."

Now it's Poppy's turn to laugh. "Right? It's really not a great look. But afterwards—" She kisses the tips of her fingers, a chef's kiss. "Absolute perfection. The dewiness— so gorge."

"I love you, Pops." I step forward, hugging her and she hugs me back, so tightly I can feel her heart thudding against mine.

"I love you too, Liv. Always."

After a second, I drop my arms and pick up my bag. "Okay, now that that's out of the way—let's finish planning this party. It's going to be the biggest, best, most epic

Labor Day/Anniversary party Seaglass Beach has ever seen."

A huge smile spreads over Poppy's face. "One thousand percent. Because I have the absolute best event planner in the world helping me. Let's do it."

45

LIV

"Well, how'd the meeting go with my sister?" Parker asks as soon as I walk through the front door. He's standing in the kitchen, munching potato chips straight from the bag. He's still in his work clothes, his jeans slung low on his hips, emphasizing the way his waist narrows and tapers down to that sexy V-thingy.

I love that spot on a guy, especially Parker.

"Good. Everything's squared away for this weekend."

"How was Poppy?" Worry lines march across his suntanned brow.

"I'm happy to report we made up."

"You did? Like, really did? Not just a short-term truce for the sake of the party?"

I shake my head. "Nope. Real apologies, then we hugged it out. But bad news . . ."

Parker's face falls. "Oh."

"You're not invited to Spa Day."

He throws his head back, laughing. "Good. I'm not a

spa guy, unless it's a couples massage. That, I can get behind."

"Mmm," I murmur, tossing my bag on a stool near the counter. "I like the sound of that. Hey, Poppy wanted me to check—you have your suit back from the cleaners, right?"

"Ugh. I have to wear a suit?" Parker moans through his mouthful of chips, a crumb falling to the counter.

"Yeah, Parks. You do. You and your family are the hosts. You definitely need the suit."

"I hate dressing up."

"But you look so handsome when you do." I cross to the counter, feathering his hair with my fingers. He grabs my hand and grazes my knuckles with his hot, salty lips.

"You know how I like you best, but I doubt you'll show up like that," Parker teases, pulling me to him and wrapping his arms around my waist.

"Parker Montgomery! No, I'm not going to the Labor Day party naked."

"Oh good, you caught my drift." He dips his head down, trailing kisses down my neck, all the way down to my chest.

"Not to be a prude, but try not to get grease stains on this shirt, okay? It's silk and it stains super easily."

"We can solve that problem." He quickly washes his hands in the sink, drying them off, then spins and lifts my shirt over my head.

"How's that?" he asks, grinning.

"Super." I take my shirt, tossing it onto a kitchen chair. Out of the line of fire.

"You know what? I hear bras stain really easily too." He

snakes his arm around my back and unhooks the black fabric in one easy movement.

The benefits of dating a reformed player, I suppose.

He tosses the bra over to the chair with my shirt and I start to unzip my skirt.

"Nah. Leave that on. That's sexy."

His hand dips down to the hem of the skirt, easing it up over my thighs until it bunches around my hips. "But the panties need to go."

Looping his thumbs into the sides, he eases the small scrap of satin fabric down my thighs until they drop to the floor. I step out of them and start taking off my heels.

"No. I like those too. Very hot." He tips his head to mine, licking my bottom lip and urging me to open to him.

He nips and sucks for a second, then I let his tongue plunge inside, the saltiness of his mouth sharp and tingly.

"You taste good," I murmur and he grins.

"So do you. Always."

His hands grip the apples of my bare ass, kneading the flesh, and a ripple of desire shimmers through me. Heat unfurls low in my belly and I'm already wet for him.

"This is kind of a one-sided situation. Seems unfair," I pout, tugging his shirt out of his jeans.

"We can fix that, babe. No problem at all."

Within seconds, Parker's naked in the kitchen, his muscular frame pressing up against mine. I run my hands over his smooth, broad chest, circling his nipples until they peak. He flexes beneath me and I breathe him in. His hard work, his sweat, the last few lingering notes of his body wash from this morning.

"You're gorgeous, Parks," I whisper, raking my eyes over his tanned body. "Ten out of ten."

"You're not even on the scale, Liv. Honest to goodness. Come here." He places his hands on my hips and easily lifts me up onto the counter, the granite cold on my bare cheeks. "That's better. Easier access."

He crushes his lips to mine as I wind my legs around his back, careful not to dig my heels into his skin.

"So fucking sexy. Best thing I've ever had on my counter." He works his tongue around my mouth, tangling with mine, and I'm pretty sure I'm leaving a puddle on his counter. His hands trace up and down my back, sending a shiver of pleasure shooting down my spine, and my nipples harden against his flexed pecs.

One hand drops down to my hip, then lower still. He eases me to the edge of the counter, spreading my legs wider. Slipping one finger, then two into me, he crooks his finger and finds my G-spot, sending sharp pulses of pleasure straight to my core. My head lolls back and stars dance at the corners of my eyes.

This man is the King of Sex, I swear. Definitely worth the wait.

"Parks," I moan, and he claims my mouth, fast and hard. He slides his fingers in and out of me, stretching me in all the right ways, and I'm so, so close to crashing over the edge.

"Parks, wait."

"Why?" he whispers. "You okay?"

"Yeah. I want you inside me. Now."

"Oh. Well, you don't have to ask me twice." He lifts me easily in his arms, my skirt still gathered at my hips, and eases me down onto his hard cock. I take him in, inch by inch, until he's all the way inside me.

"Liv, you feel so fucking good on my cock," he

murmurs, as I squeeze my muscles, milking him. I rock my hips against him and we find a good pace, our bodies pressed together so tightly I can't see where Parker ends and I begin. I ride him, his strong arms supporting me as he thrusts deeper and deeper inside. My breasts bounce against his chest, the friction pebbling my nipples to sharp, pink points.

"You're beautiful," he says, squeezing my ass cheek. "Especially like this. You know how many times I fantasized about fucking you?"

I shake my head 'no,' tingly pressure building in my core as I undulate on Parker.

"Probably thousands. But reality is so much better."

Blushing, I smile at him, kissing him gently on the lips. "I love you, Parker."

"I love you too, baby. Now be a good girl and come for me because I can't hold out much longer."

That's all I need to push me over the edge, my body shuddering as I come. Parker follows my lead, plunging harder and deeper, chasing his release. He explodes inside me, his muscles tensing, then uncoiling.

Pressing me tight to his chest, our bodies absorb the aftershocks, our breathing ragged.

"You're fucking amazing, Liv." He lifts me back onto the cool granite, smoothing my hair from my flushed face, my skin dewy with a light sheen of sweat.

"You're more than amazing, Parks." I trace my fingers over his jaw, his light stubble prickly on my skin. "I never thought I'd be here, like this, with you."

"Me neither. I'm the luckiest guy in the entire world." He grins, pressing his forehead to mine. "I love you, Olivia Drayton."

"And I love you, Parker Montgomery."

46

PARKER

LABOR DAY WEEKEND IS HERE. THE OFFICIAL END TO the summer, and what a summer it's been.

Hurricane Clementine rocked my world, in the best possible way. Now that things are cool between me, Poppy, and Liv, everything's been great. And things will only get better once this weekend is over. Liv's been working twelve-hour days getting ready for the weekend's festivities—I can't wait to have her back to myself. I even picked up an extra shift at the tiki bar just so I could see her this week.

Buzz, buzz.

I check my text.

> Liv: Meet me at the bonfire. Still setting up here

> Parker: I'll head up soon

> Liv: xoxo

> Parker: always

Geez. I'm a total sap now.

But it's cool. It's between me and Liv, no one else's business.

Buzz, buzz.

> Smith: Hey Loverboy. You headed up to the bonfire yet?

> Parker: Shut the hell up. And yes. You?

> Smith: Leaving now.

> Parker: See you soon

I grab my keys and head to the inn. Every parking spot near the lobby's taken, so I circle around back and park near the loading zone. The Seaglass Celebrations van is here, too, and I spot Liv's perfect ass peeking out from the back. I slide my SUV up next to the van and kill the ignition.

"Hey, babe," I murmur, stepping up behind her and wrapping my arms around her waist. She's wearing a short, gauzy sundress and my fingers tiptoe beneath her skirt, skimming the silky fabric of her panties.

"Hey." She nuzzles back into me, but pulls her skirt down lower, covering herself.

I take one last swipe across her panties, then desist—I suppose she is on the clock.

"Can I at least get a raincheck on that?" I ask, my lips brushing the shell of her ear. Goosebumps rise on her skin and I press a soft kiss into the warm, golden skin of her neck.

"Definitely. Want to help me carry the last few centerpieces over to the ballroom?"

"Sure."

Together we empty the back of the van, lugging the oversized arrangements of seashells, sea glass, and hydrangeas over to the side door of the main building.

"Wow, Liv—this place looks great." I glance around at the ballroom, transformed for the anniversary dinner tomorrow. White linens cover large round tables, with teak high-tops scattered around the room artfully. The centerpieces dot each table, surrounded by floating candles and more blue and green sea glass. White twinkly lights drape the walls and the ceiling, creating an indoor canopy. Makeshift bars sit in opposite corners, ready for drink service tomorrow night.

"Thanks. Poppy helped a lot. We've been really busy, but I think it all came together nicely."

"Absolutely." I press my lips to her dark hair, breathing in her floral scent and her goodness. I don't know how I got so lucky.

"Have you seen Poppy?" Liv checks her watch. "The bonfire's about to start."

"Nope. Just you."

"Hmmm. I don't know what happened to her." Liv gnaws at her bottom lip, worrying.

I reach over, lacing my fingers through hers. "She'll meet up with us. Let's head out to the beach. I don't want to miss sunset."

We shut the lights off in the ballroom and head out through the lobby, blending in with the other hotel guests here for the long weekend. The family ahead of us chatters about the barbeque dinner after the bonfire, the kids more excited for the s'mores than the ribs.

Making our way down the path, we all head toward the beach. The tiki bar's pumping reggae tunes and I wave at the bartender, my new hire, Julio. I'm happy he came aboard, otherwise it'd be me slinging drinks right now instead of going to the bonfire with Liv. I drape my arm across her delicate shoulder, pulling her in close to me as we traipse through the sand, down towards the water. She leans into me and my heart flip-flops in my chest.

I can't believe this is my life.

The evening's perfect for a bonfire, not too windy and not too warm. Multiple firepits are already blazing, the red and orange flames bright against the dusky sky. The last few rays of the setting sun streak pink across the horizon, the waves lapping at the white sandy shore.

"There's Smith." Liv waves at my cousin and we head in his direction. Elise is with him, and I spot Roman standing beside Smith as well.

"Hey, y'all," I say, patting Smith and Rome on the back, then giving Elise a quick hug. Liv gives hugs all around and we settle down in the Adirondack chairs around the fire, the strong smell of burning wood thick in the air.

"Hey. Everything ready for tomorrow night?" Roman asks, taking a sip of his beer.

"We're good. All set up. You all need to be here for the photos around four p.m. I sent an email about it earlier this week." She flips her hair back over her bare shoulder, smoothing the dark waves down.

"Got it. We'll be here," Roman says, nodding.

"All four of you, plus Smith in some of the shots.

Poppy's making a big deal about needing the photos for her display."

"Did somebody mention me?" Poppy sneaks up behind us, squeezing Liv's shoulders before plopping down in the empty seat next to mine.

"Just relaying the message that everyone needs to show up for the photo shoot. Wearing their suits."

Rome rolls his eyes, conveying exactly how I feel about the suit thing.

"C'mon, Rome. It's one night. You can do it," Poppy says, tapping his knee. "Right?"

He shrugs, takes another swig of beer. "I 'spose. Rather not, though. It's so tight and uncomfortable."

"Hopefully the Capellis won't show up. It'd be hard to throw a punch wearing a suit jacket," I joke, catching Rome's eyes across the firepit.

He smirks, and Smith shakes his head. "You guys. Let's try to keep it civil, okay? I'm sure Liv put a lot of effort into the decorations."

"And we have a huge cake. If that thing gets knocked over, I'm going to kill someone," Poppy says, glancing pointedly at me and Roman.

I salute her. "Got it, Boss. No fucking up the centerpieces, no toppling of the cake. Check and check."

She groans, shaking her head. A server walks by with a silver tray lined with wooden skewers strung with fluffy white marshmallows, stacks of golden graham crackers, and thick squares of chocolate. He offers them to us and we each take a skewer and the ingredients for our s'mores.

I stand, ready to toast my marshmallow, and Poppy taps me on the shoulder. She leans in close to me.

"Hey, can we talk for a sec? Alone?"

I nod, balancing my skewer on the edge of my chair, then trail behind her down the beach. She walks quickly and I lengthen my stride to keep up, trudging through the sand. We walk all the way to the edge, finding a vacant firepit, the flames dancing against the now-inky sky.

"What's up?" I ask, sinking down into a chair. A tiny hint of worry pulls at my gut.

"I wanted to talk to you."

"Okay," I say, rubbing a hand across my jaw, the tugging stronger now. "What's up?"

Poppy leans forward in her chair, grabbing something out of the back pocket of her jeans. Something I recognize and my heart sinks.

"Seriously, Poppy? We're gonna talk about this again?"

"Nope. We're going to put it to rest. Once and for all."

She hands me the pink notebook decorated with the tiny surfers catching waves.

"What am I supposed to do with this?" I ask, glancing down at the shiny cover.

"Find the Pact."

I flip through the white lined pages, searching for the black Sharpie-scrawled pact.

"Here it is." I stare down at our middle school handwriting, the words we swore to so long ago.

"Tear it out," Poppy's firm voice instructs.

"Are you sure? You don't want to frame it or something?"

Poppy shakes her head, her bangs feathering down over her forehead. "Nope. Quite the opposite. Tear it out."

I do as I'm told, ripping the page from the metal binding, the edges of the paper fraying.

"Now what?" My eyes flick to her face, the orange glow from the fire reflecting in her wide blue eyes.

She doesn't answer, only holds her hand out to me, her palm open. I give her the paper and she stands, inching closer to the firepit. Then she tips the corner of the paper down into the blaze, the edge flaring, then kindling. Dropping it quickly down into the bonfire, we watch as our pact goes up in flames, the edges of the paper curling, smoking, turning to black ash.

"Take good care of Liv, Parker," Poppy whispers as the last bit of paper disintegrates into the firepit.

Poppy reaches over and squeezes my shoulder, then heads back toward the group, leaving me standing alone in front of the dancing fire.

47

LIV

I HARDLY GET ANY SLEEP THE NIGHT BEFORE THE anniversary party, I'm so nervous. I don't know why, I've thrown tons of events by this point, but this one feels different. Special.

Maybe because the Montgomery family means so much to me, and always has.

Maybe because this party means so much to them, and our beach community.

Or maybe because I'm truly, madly, and deeply in love with Parker Montgomery, and want this night to be perfect.

For him.

For his family.

For us.

Us.

Never in a million years did I think I would use the word 'us' in a sentence with me and Parker, but here we are.

And the best part is Poppy's okay with it.

Being with Parker—living with him—feels so right. I slid into his house, his life, and neither of us ever looked back.

I feel like I'm finally home.

"Liv, you ready?" Parker swings out of the bedroom and my heart stutters in my chest, my breath catching in my throat.

"What? It's too tight, right? I think the damn cleaner shrunk it." Parker stretches out his arms, eyeing the dark blue fabric.

"No, Parks. It's perfect. You look handsome." I step in, straightening his striped tie before rising on tiptoe and kissing him on the lips. He tastes minty as he opens his mouth to mine, his tongue slipping in as his hand winds around my back and grabs my ass.

"Don't wrinkle the dress," I murmur, and he chuckles.

"I could lift it up and we could have a little quickie before we go, take the edge off. I promise the dress won't wrinkle." His ocean-blue eyes twinkle as he gazes down at me.

"Later. I have to get to the inn. And the photographer's going to show up in about twenty minutes. I have to help him set up."

"Fine. You're such a workaholic," he teases, slapping me playfully on the rear.

"I give my all for my clients," I sing-song, winking at him.

"Let's get going then. The sooner we take these photos, the sooner I can relax. Maybe lose the suit jacket at least." He wriggles in the fabric, even though it stretches across his broad back perfectly as we walk out the door.

Ten minutes later, we pull into the drive of the Seaglass

Inn. If anything, the inn's even more crowded tonight. Parker drops me off in front of the lobby, then goes to park in the back.

I glide into the lobby, careful not to slip on the tile in my strappy heels. The navy blue banner announcing the anniversary party's strung across the back wall, above the glass double doors leading outside. A table's set up for check-in near the ballroom, sea glass decorating the crisp white linen.

Poppy waves at me from the front desk. "Liv! The photographer's here, setting up by the pool. He said we'll start in the lobby, then move to the pool, then from there we'll hit the beach for sunset. My brothers are gonna freak —that's a lot of pictures for those guys." She smiles her sunshiny Poppy smile and I know we're all good.

"They are, but I don't care. This is a special night for y'all. And I know you want to display the photos. You're going to get some great shots."

"Where are we doing this thing?" Roman strolls in through the glass doors, shrugging into his jacket.

"Rome! You're so handsome." Poppy runs over to her brother, throwing her arms around him. Roman scowls at his sister, but lets her fuss over him as he runs his fingers through his short dark hair.

"Yeah, yeah, yeah. I even shaved for this."

"Nice. I like the scruff, though."

"Rome!" Parker lopes in, slapping his brother's shoulder. "You clean up nice, bro."

"Thanks. You too."

The photographer comes in through the back doors and he scopes out the room, searching for the best light.

"Are we all here? I think the natural light coming in

through the back's going to be the best." He motions to the wall of glass and we all make our way over.

"King should be here any minute. Let's start with the individual shots, then we can do the group ones," Poppy says, following behind the photographer. She fluffs her hair, smoothing it down over her shoulders as he turns her this way and that, finding the perfect angle. He starts snapping photos, Poppy smiling at the camera while her brothers shuffle awkwardly nearby.

I scroll through the event checklist on my cell, keeping close track of the time. We need to be done with the photo session by five-thirty at the latest in order to make cocktail hour.

"Next!" The photographer waves at Parker and he steps forward, taking Poppy's place.

He's so damn handsome, I can hardly peel my eyes from him. Parker grins at the camera, and the photographer snaps several shots in a row.

"Gawd, Liv, you're so obvious." Poppy elbows me in the ribs, shaking me from my Parker-induced haze.

A hot blush creeps up my neck and I can't stop smiling. "What? I'm not obvious."

"Please. Y'all are both obvious. And so stinking cute, I can't even." She flings her arm around me, squeezing me tight, and happiness blooms in my chest. I'm so glad to have the old Poppy back.

"Y'all started without me? Good. The quicker we wrap this up, the better." King strolls in, his deep voice rumbling through the lobby.

Unlike his brothers in their navy suits, he's wearing dark wash jeans, a button down, and a blazer, no tie. The outfit's completed with his deep brown cowboy boots.

"Hey! How come he's not wearing a suit?" Parker whines, pointing at King.

"Because I'm the oldest and can do what I want, that's why. You done?" King tips his chin at the photographer, who nods. Parker rolls his eyes, stepping away from the windows so King can take his shots.

Unsmiling, of course.

The new patriarch sure is a lot grumpier than the old one. Even though they weren't my parents, I still miss Mr. and Mrs. Montgomery as if they were. I practically lived at Poppy's house when we were younger, and being here today, in their space, makes my heart physically ache despite my happiness with Parker.

"Next!" The photographer ushers Roman over and King gladly steps aside.

"We good here?" he asks me, shoving off his blazer.

"Um—no. We have two more photo spots. Plus, the cocktail hour and the dinner. Maybe you can lose the blazer after the salad course is served. Until then, I think you need to keep it on. Besides, you look handsome."

He scowls, even as his cheeks flush a light shade of pink.

"Y'all and all this formal shit," he mutters, but he keeps the jacket on.

"Okay, everyone out to the pool!" The photographer rounds us up and we all trail down the path to the pool, Poppy and Parker greeting guests in friendly voices as we walk. Roman keeps to himself, and King's grouch game face stays strong.

"Smitty!" Parker waves to Smith, who's leaning casually on the tiki bar, waiting for us. He's also wearing a navy suit with a light blue shirt and a bright pink tie. Elise stands at his side, wearing a chic little black dress and strappy heels. Not very Florida, but she'll get the hang of it eventually.

"Family photos now, with the pool in the background. Men in the back, ladies in the front." The photographer gestures with his camera, urging us to line up.

"There's only one lady," I say, pointing at Poppy.

"No. There are two." She grabs my arm, pulling me into the shot.

King, Roman, Parker, and Smith stand in the back, while Poppy and I pose in front. Poppy puts me directly in front of Parker and the photographer arranges our hands just so. After a few shots, we wave Elise in as well, standing in front of Smith. The sun's setting now and there's a slight breeze coming in off the ocean.

"We better hurry if we're going to get any decent beach shots," Poppy says. We all trudge out to the beach, kicking off our shoes. Well, everyone except King, who leaves on his boots.

"What? They're all-purpose," he mutters when Poppy shoots a sidewise glance at the leather boots.

"Classy, King. Real classy."

"I want the photos to represent our personalities. This is mine, take it or leave it."

"Fine. As long as you'll at least attempt a smile," Poppy says.

"His face'll crack," Roman jokes and Parker chuckles.

"Stop, guys. Leave King alone," I say, defending the eldest Montgomery. He shoots me a look of gratitude as we all line up again.

"Y'all look great. Perfect. Now smile!" The photographer snaps a bunch more shots as the sun sets, the waves crashing behind us.

Finally, the photo session's finished. "Okay, y'all. We need to hustle to make it back to the cocktail hour. Everyone try to be friendly and mingle. After that's a brief speech from Poppy, followed by dinner, then everyone heads out to the beach for dancing under the stars." I recite the itinerary by heart, having gone over every last detail roughly three thousand times.

"Sounds good," Poppy says, nodding.

Parker loops his arm around my shoulder as we walk back to the inn and pure happiness courses through my veins.

The next hour flies by as I assist at check-in, making sure every guest is ticked off the list and accounted for. I do manage to snag a glass of champagne, the bubbles going straight to my head.

I venture into the ballroom and find Poppy. "Speech time. You ready?"

She nods and I squeeze her hand. Together, we walk to the podium set up at the front of the room. I grab the microphone, adjusting it down to my hcight.

"Welcome everyone to the Seaglass Inn Anniversary party!" Applause sounds through the ballroom and then a hush falls over the crowd. "I'm so glad all of y'all could make it tonight. As you know, this is a very special event for the Montgomery family and the historic Seaglass Inn. Tonight wc celebrate the history of this great town, and this great family. Please welcome your hostess, Poppy Montgomery!" I throw my arm out, waving Poppy to the stage as the crowd applauds.

Poppy gives me a quick hug, then takes the micro-phone, lowering it farther still.

"Good evening, everyone. First, I want to say thank you

for coming. This is the capstone event for the Seaglass Inn each and every year and I appreciate y'all making time in your busy schedules to come out and help us celebrate." She pauses and there's another polite smattering of applause.

"As y'all know, this party was my mom's favorite day of the entire year." Poppy swallows, tears shimmering in her eyes. "It's my great honor to keep the tradition alive. We, as Montgomerys, believe in giving back to this town and this community. Giving back to you all, our family—if not by blood, by time and shared experiences. We hope y'all have an amazing time tonight."

"I also want to say a special thank you to my friend and the best event planner in the world, Liv Drayton." She gestures at me and my cheeks heat as I smile and wave at the crowd.

"She's not only fantastic at her job, she's an all-around awesome person and I couldn't be happier to have her in my life. So thank you, Liv. For the wonderful party—and the love you bring to our lives."

Poppy smiles at me and now I have hot tears welling in my eyes.

Well, damn it. I promised myself I wouldn't cry tonight, but Poppy's pushing me over the edge. Parker wraps his hand around my waist, pulling me up against his chest and I relax into his strong warmth, contentment flooding my body.

I love this man. I love this family. And I love this town.

"Alright, enough about me. Let's eat, drink, and be merry, y'all!" Poppy beams her dazzling smile at the audience and cheers erupt as the lights go up just a touch in order for people to find their seats.

"I love you, Liv," Parker whispers into my ear, guiding me to the head table with the rest of the Montgomery family.

"Me too, Parks."

The salad course comes out first, right on cue, the servers circulating quickly to make sure everyone gets their food on time. Keeping with tradition, the Montgomery family's served last, as the hosts of the party. Roman and King sit quietly, sipping their beers, while Poppy chats with Elise. Parker and I hold hands under the table and I supervise from my seat.

Finally, our salads arrive, the ladies served first, then the men.

"What the?" King stares at the server. "Juliet? What are you doing here?"

Oh shit. How did Juliet Capelli end up on the catering staff?

Major fail. But how would I know to check the caterers list of contractors? I need to make a note for next time, though.

"Hello."

One word, her voice flat, even a little cold.

She places the salad down, then the next and the next, moving around the table. Everyone is silent as Juliet circles the table, finally placing King's salad down last.

"Bon appétit." She hustles off without so much as a smile. King's eyes follow her, his face pale, like he's seen a ghost.

"How the hell did a Capelli get in here?" Roman growls, stabbing an innocent leaf of lettuce.

"I'm really sorry. I checked the guest list and the

vendors, but the caterers sub out for independent contractors. I didn't even know she was back in town."

"It's fine," King says, his voice gruff. He knocks down the rest of his beer, then stands. "Anyone need anything from the bar?"

Parker throws his hand up. "I'll take another beer, thanks. Liv?"

"Wine would be great. But I can get it. You sit and eat." I motion at King to sit back down, but he shakes his head.

"No. I got it. Anyone else?"

Everyone declines and King skulks off to the bar, obviously pissed off at the Capelli situation.

"Sorry," I murmur under my breath to Parker. "I honestly had no idea. Do you want me to get rid of her?"

Parker shrugs. "Nah. She's fine. We don't have any real beef with her anyway. Other than the fact she was born a Capelli. Real unfortunate for her, to be honest." His hand rubs my upper thigh and I feel a tad bit better.

"Okay. If y'all change your mind, say the word and she's gone."

Parker nods, then tucks into his salad, unaffected. I try to eat, even though my mind swirls. That was an odd exchange between King and Juliet and I wonder if anyone else noticed. I'm sure Poppy did, but I can't chat with her about it now.

King returns with the drinks and I sip my wine, trying not to drink too fast. I need to stay focused through the rest of dinner and dessert, then I'm off the clock. I notice Juliet's not our server for the rest of the courses, although King's gaze follows her around the room the entire dinner service. I wonder what the story is there, but now's definitely not the time to inquire.

"The food's wonderful, Liv. Great pick on the caterer," Poppy says, and I'm glad for the distraction. That shatters the weird vibe at the table, and Smith and Parker chat about a hurricane repair-turned-reno they're working on, while Poppy quizzes Elise about her upcoming move.

"We're all moved in. Your brother and cousin did an amazing job on the house and we couldn't be happier." Elise beams at Smith and he blushes. I've never seen Smith flustered over a woman and it's kinda cute.

"It was an easy enough reno," he says, acting all suave and confident. "Nothing major."

"Still. So fast and smooth," Elise purrs, and Parker grins over at Smith, knocking his elbow.

"That's Smitty for you. Fast and smooth."

Apparently, you can't take the sex jokes out of a player, even if he's reformed.

Dessert is served, a chocolate ganache cake with vanilla bean ice cream, and then plates are cleared and everyone moves outside to the beach.

"This has been great, Liv," Parker says, pulling me into his arms on the beach and kissing me softly on the lips. "You slayed."

"Thanks. Sorry about Juliet. I had no idea she was back." I pause, hesitating, but I can't help myself.

"What's up with her and King?" I ask, lifting a brow as I stare at Parker's older brother, leaning on the tiki bar and sipping a bourbon on the rocks.

Parker shrugs. "I dunno. Why?"

"It just felt strange between them, you know?"

Parker glances at his brother and shrugs again. "I didn't notice. King's grumpy. Always has been. I'm sure it's just the Capelli feud."

"Okay," I say, unconvinced. It felt like more to me, bigger than an old family feud.

"C'mon, let's dance." Parker grabs my hand, twirling me around, and I giggle, lightness filling my chest.

Tonight's really been incredible, outside of the Juliet thing. I decide to let it slide and enjoy dancing under the stars with Parker.

Tonight, I'm living in the moment.

And this moment is absolutely perfect.

48

PARKER

I had mixed feelings coming into tonight, but being here with Liv makes everything better.

Mom would have been tickled pink to see us together, I know it. She always loved Liv like one of her own.

A sharp pang hits me in the chest, but the pain dulls when Liv's gaze lights on mine. I've never felt so calm, so confident, so complete, in my entire life.

It's like a piece of me was missing and now I've found it.

And I don't intend to ever let her go.

She nuzzles into my chest as we spin around on the sand, the band playing "You Look Wonderful Tonight" behind us.

I could dance with her all night long, if that's what she wanted.

I love this woman with all my heart and I'll do anything to make her happy.

The song ends and several people leave the beach. The

party's winding down, although the tiki bar's packed. I hope the new guy knows what he's doing.

"You thirsty? I want to go check on the new hire, see how he's holding up," I say, my palm resting on Liv's lower back.

"Sure, let's do it."

We head over to the bar and join Poppy, Roman, and King at the far end, closest to the water. Poppy scootches over on her stool, making room for Liv, and she hops up next to my sister.

"What do you want?" I ask Liv.

"Wine. Whatever's open is fine."

Sliding behind the bar, I check on Julio first thing. "Hey, dude. How's it going? You hanging in?"

He tips his chin at me, nodding. "It's good. Busy, but I've got it. Looks like a good turnout." He measures out a shot of tequila, shaking up another margarita, then strains it into a glass.

"It is. I think it's our biggest party yet. You need any help?"

"Nah, man. You enjoy the night."

"Cool. I'll grab my own drink, though." I duck down, grabbing a bottle of beer, then pour Liv a glass of rosé. "Thanks for helping out tonight. We appreciate it."

"Sure thing, man." Julio salutes me, then turns back to the ladies he's serving.

I dive back out from under the bar, heading toward the family. King's sipping his bourbon, his eyes glazed as he stares directly in front of him, frowning. Don't know what's going on with him, but figure now's not the time to ask. Roman's chatting with Smith and Elise, his tie gone and his shirt unbuttoned, the sleeves rolled up to his fore-arms. Liv's checking her cell, probably making sure she hit all the to-dos on her list. And Poppy's talking to Mrs. Carter and the new guy, Griffin. He's leaning against the bar, swirling a glass of tequila on the rocks, looking like he would rather be anywhere but here.

"Here you go." I hand Liv the glass of wine, our finger-tips grazing, sending electric shocks down my arm straight to my dick. I quickly shove my hand in my pocket to distract from the situation below the belt, then lean over the bar.

"Hey, it's Griffin, right?" I startle him, his head jerking up at his name.

"Yeah. You're Parker?"

"The one and only. You know how much longer you're gonna be in town?"

Griffin huffs out a heavy sigh. "Too long. My aunt needs my help setting up the ice cream shop, and I'm still doing rehab anyway."

"Bummer. Sorry about that."

Griffin shrugs. "Is what it is."

Liv chimes in. "When's the opening? Seaglass Celebrations can help plan a kick-off if y'all want."

"Oh, great idea!" Poppy claps her hands together, joining the conversation Griffin seems like he doesn't want to have.

"I love that, Liv," Mrs. Carter says, and Griffin takes a long slug of his drink, clearly unimpressed.

Liv starts rattling off grand opening ideas to Mrs. Carter and Poppy turns her attention on Griffin.

"Why don't you like it here?" She pops out her bottom

lip, pouting and acting like someone not liking Seaglass Beach is a personal affront.

Griffin scrubs a hand over the back of his neck, his shoulders slumping. "It's alright. For a small town."

"What's that supposed to mean?" Poppy asks, her hand on her hip. "What's wrong with small towns?"

Griffin takes another drink, then turns to face Poppy. "They're kinda boring. Lots of gossip about people I never heard of. Everybody's up in everybody's business. It's the same old thing every damn day."

"Huh. Kinda like baseball?" Poppy asks.

"No. Nothing like baseball. But you don't strike me as a baseball fan." His eyes rake over her body and Poppy's cheeks turn bright pink.

"Maybe I am."

"No way. You're not the type."

"What type? There's not a baseball type."

"Wrong. There absolutely is. Mathematical, patient, loyal to their team."

"Dude," I breathe under my breath. This guy just totally insulted my sister.

"And how do you know I'm not those things? You don't even know me." Poppy crosses her arms over her chest, her nostrils flaring.

"I've seen you talking to people. You're sociable, chatty. Flitting from group to group, making small talk. That's not patient. You also switched from wine to whiskey, so not particularly loyal. I can't really speak to your mathematical abilities."

Poppy squares her shoulders, stretching to her full five foot-nothing height. "You don't know me from Eve, Griffin

Carter. So how about you stop making assumptions? Because you know what they say about people who assume."

The corner of Griffin's mouth quirks, a hint of a smile, but he manages to turn it into a scowl.

"I never said I wasn't an ass." He breaks eye contact, then knocks back the rest of his drink and sets the empty glass on the bar.

"Nice party. See y'all around." He shoots us a half-wave, then strides off toward the inn.

"He's right about that," Poppy grumbles, huffing out a breath. "What a jerk."

"Sorry about my nephew, Poppy," Mrs. Carter says, tapping Poppy on the arm. "He's in a bad place right now. He'll come around eventually. No one can stay that grumpy forever."

"I don't know, have you met King?" Poppy cocks her head at King, who's still staring straight ahead, as if he's in shock. "He's pretty damn grumpy."

"We'll ply Griffin with ice cream. He'll cheer up." Mrs. Carter smiles at Poppy and Poppy relaxes.

"It's fine. I have a way with people," Poppy says, puffing out her chest with confidence. "I'll change his mind about Seaglass Beach."

I chuckle. "If anyone has a chance at that, it's Poppy." I elbow my sister and she grins.

"Exactly."

"I'd say the party was a success," Liv says, glancing around. Only a handful of people remain, the clean-up crew starting to collect empty glasses and cans.

"Let's all chip in so we can go home and get some rest,"

Poppy suggests, gathering empties from the bar and handing them to Julio.

The rest of us follow her lead, including Smith, Elise, and Mrs. Carter, and the beach and tiki bar are cleared in no time. The band packs up and I dim the lights on the bar, only the string lights illuminated.

Winding my arm around Liv's waist, I pull her body close to mine, burying my face in her dark hair. Breathing in her goodness, grateful everything's working out.

"Can we stay out here a second longer?" I whisper in her ear and she nods, smiling.

"Sure."

The rest of the family disappears up the walkway, leaving me and Liv alone on the beach, standing under the stars. A light breeze ruffles her hair, her dress fluttering around her knees, and she's so damn beautiful it almost hurts to look at her.

But I know deep down I never want to stop.

"Listen—" I clear my throat, my heart hammering hard against my ribs. I have no plan, no scripted speech.

Gripping her hands, I lace my fingers through hers, step in so close her breath tickles my cheeks.

"I love you. These last few weeks have been the best of my life, even with all the drama. And I know that this might feel kinda quick, and I didn't plan this out, so I'm sort of unprepared . . ."

I sink down onto my knee in the sand, gripping her left hand. "Liv, I've liked you from the first moment I met you and loved you almost as long. We work perfectly together and I've never been happier in my entire life. I can't imagine spending one more second without you. Will you marry me?"

Her full pink lips form a round 'O,' then her other hand flies to her mouth. "Parker—" she says, her eyes wide. "I—"

She hesitates and my chest tightens, my heart stuttering, beads of sweat breaking out on the small of my back.

"Yes, Parker, yes," she half-laughs, half-cries, tears swimming in her eyes. "I love you, too."

She dips her head down, and I cup her face, claiming her lips. She's warm and soft and sweet and I can't believe I'm going to get to spend the rest of my life with this woman.

"I love you, Liv."

"And I love you, Parker." She grabs my hands, pulling me to standing, and I wrap my arms around her, bringing her in close to me. The ocean waves lap the shore, moonlight bathing the beach in soft white light.

We kiss under the stars for what feels like an eternity and a moment all at the same time and my heart is full. Fuller than it's ever been.

And in a strange, roundabout way, I have my sister to thank.

Without that stupid pact, I probably would have screwed things up with Liv a long time ago. Thanks to Poppy's enforced waiting period, I was Mr. Right Now a few dozen times—all of which led me to finally being Mr. Right with the right woman.

Not that I'll ever tell Poppy.

That will always be my little secret.

THE END

Want to see Parker pick out a ring and formally propose to Liv? Subscribe to my mailing list and you'll get instant access to an exclusive bonus scene!

Want more in the Seaglass Beach series? Keep reading for a sneak peek at Poppy and Griffin's book, UNSTOPPABLE!

UNSTOPPABLE SNEAK PEEK
POPPY

True-confession time: I've always wanted to be an ice-cream flavorologist. I know it sounds made-up, but it's a real thing—the dream job of developing new ice-cream flavors. So fun, right?

Which is why I'm living my best life with Jess Carter, who runs Seaglass Scoops right next door to the Seaglass Inn. She lets me help with the menu and be as wild and creative as I want to be, testing out all the unique flavor combos I can think of. Blueberry lavender ice cream? Sure. Buttered popcorn? Could be tasty. Pear and blue cheese? Let's give it a whirl. She'll try anything once, and I freaking love that about her.

"What do you think about a margarita sorbet?" I ask, scrolling through the notes app on my phone. I've been jotting down ideas when they come to me, day or night—I have more than one hundred of them stored at the moment.

"You have a recipe?" Jess glances up from her inventory

binder, where we've been keeping track of flavor hits and misses.

"Yep. Not that many ingredients—lime, triple sec, and tequila. Garnish with sea salt."

"Sounds good. Let's whip up a batch, see how it tastes. I'll add limes to the grocery list."

"Perfect. Oh, and I want to make the double-espresso chocolate recipe I found last week. That looked yummy."

"All right, adding that to the lineup. Poppy, honey, do you ever sleep?" She squints over at me, seemingly assessing my overall health and well-being.

"Mm-hmm. Seven hours every night, like clockwork. Why?"

"Between running the inn and helping out here, you can't have any free time."

"Free time's overrated. I love being here, helping you come up with new flavors."

"Don't you want to go out? Hang with your friends?"

Underlying subtext: Get a life.

"I do hang out. I meet Liv at the Tipsy Taco every Tuesday." I twirl a loose strand of hair around my finger, shuffling from foot to foot.

It's true—I have been spending a lot of time with Jess at Seaglass Scoops. Mainly because my best friend's now engaged to my twin brother, making me a clunky third wheel, despite their protests.

I'm happy for them, I am, but they're firmly in the honeymoon phase, and I'm a single pringle. Totally harshing their couple vibe.

"Plus, things are slow at the inn. Fall's a down time. I'll be busier again come the holidays. Oh—speaking of holidays. Seasonal flavors. I have a special folder for that. Hang on."

I pop a finger in the air as I flip through my notes, changing the subject. "Pumpkin everything. Also, apple spice, caramel apple crunch, oh—and here's a fig one I want to try."

Jess laughs, her face crinkling into a wide smile. "I love you, Poppy. But there's not enough time in the world to try all these recipes."

"Pshaw. Scoops is going to be here forever. Tons of time."

She shakes her head, gray hair falling across her brow. "I don't want you missing out on things because you're hiding away here, helping run the ice-cream parlor. What about dating? A cute young girl like you should be out there having a good time."

I wrinkle my nose in distaste. "Jess, Seaglass Beach is tiny, and I'm related to practically every man in town. Who, exactly, am I going to date?"

Her dark eyes twinkle under the bright fluorescent lights. "I happen to have a very handsome nephew staying in town for a while."

Somehow I manage to hold my eye roll in check. I don't want to hurt Jess's feelings, but her nephew is the last man on Earth I want to date.

Griffin Carter. Pro baseball star and the grumpiest person I've ever met. Sure, he's tall, dark, and handsome. Broad shoulders, just the right amount of scruff peppering his square jaw, rocks for biceps.

He's also a grade A asshole. Like, the worst. I don't even know if he has dimples, because I've never seen the man crack a smile, let alone laugh. His signature look is a scowl. He probably drinks sour milk for breakfast. Since he moved to town a couple of months ago—temporarily, thank goodness —every interaction we have seems to end up in an argument.

"He's single . . ." Jess dangles the idea out there one more time, just in case I wasn't picking up what she's laying down.

"Sorry, but no. Griffin pretty much hates me."

"Nonsense." Jess waves her hand through the sweet, chilly air, dismissing the notion. "He's in a bad place is all. Worried about his baseball career. Once that's sorted, he'll be back to his old self."

I seriously doubt Griffin's old self is any better than his current self, but I don't share my thoughts on account of Jess's feelings.

"Besides, I'm too busy to date. Between running the inn and helping out here, my calendar's jam packed. In the best way." I squeeze Jess's arm, reassuring her.

Jingle, jingle.

I glance over at the door as a rowdy group of teenagers spills into the shop, chattering loudly.

"Welcome to Seaglass Scoops!" Jess sings out, waving. The girls move toward the freezer, perusing the tubs of brightly colored ice cream.

"Ooh, salted caramel swirl sounds good. Can I try?" a curly-haired brunette asks, pointing at the creamy tan-and-white ice cream.

"Absolutely." I dip a tiny pink tasting spoon into the tub and hand it over to her.

She pops the spoon into her mouth. "Delish. Can I get a cone of that?"

"You bet. Sugar or waffle?" I gesture at the cone display perched atop the freezer.

"Hmm." She screws her mouth up, debating. "Waffle."

"Good choice." I grab a cone and scoop out a large, round ball of salted caramel, then another. "Here ya go." I hand the cone over to the girl, then help her friend, then another friend after that.

"Do y'all have a dog out there?" Jess cranes her neck, trying to see over the girl gang's heads.

"Yes, ma'am. Nathan got a puppy, and his mom asked us to walk him," the blonde teenager says.

"Oh, cute! What kind of puppy?" I scoop two round balls of vanilla ice cream into a cup and hand it to her.

Honestly, I can't believe anyone chooses vanilla when there are so many fun flavors to try, but to each their own.

"A goldendoodle. He's really adorable. Want to come see?" the blonde girl asks, plunking her credit card down on the marble countertop.

"I definitely would." Jess rings up the ice-cream orders. "Can he have a treat?"

"Sure."

Jess reaches into the glass jar next to the register and pulls out one of the heart-shaped dog biscuits she keeps for our furry visitors.

"Be right back, Poppy." She hustles from behind the counter, leaving me behind to listen to the chattering of the girl gang.

Apparently the brunette has a huge crush on Nathan, hence the accompaniment on the dog-walking errand. The blonde approves, but the other friend isn't so keen on the relationship. I lean in, fully engrossed in the middle-school drama.

Seriously, I have no life.

"He's into gaming, though. That's, like, really annoying. He's always playing with the boys," the dissenting girl protests.

"It's cool he has hobbies," the blonde points out.

The brunette bobs her head up and down. "Yeah. And he has lots of friends. That's a good sign, right?"

A shrill howl cuts through the girls' chatter, and I grip the counter, startled. Cold dread shoots down my spine as I stare out the window. I don't see Jess out there anywhere, and Nathan and his friend are hunched over, staring at the ground.

The friend pushes through the door, panic etched on his adolescent face. "Come quick! Ms. Carter hurt herself."

"Oh no!" I fly around the counter, my sneakers squeaking on the black-and-white-tile floor.

"Jess! What happened?" I crouch down on the sidewalk next to Jess. The kid who must be Nathan clutches a squirmy puppy to his chest, a long, red leash dangling down to the ground.

Jess's brows squish together, her eyes welling with tears, as she cradles her wrist. Her hand dangles at a geometrically funky angle—I'm no doctor, but that does not look good.

"The puppy got excited, running circles around me. I got wrapped up in the leash. Then he saw something across the street and started to sprint away. Took me straight down. I know I shouldn't have used my hands to break my fall, but it's reflex, you know? I think I might have broken my wrist." Her voice is reedy, threaded with pain.

"Oh no," I groan, stroking her shoulder. "I'll call 911. You need to go to the hospital."

"No, don't call. I can drive."

"What? You can't drive. Your wrist might be broken. I'll close down the shop and take you."

"No. You stay here and manage the shop. Call Griffin."

"Oh, I know!" I snap my fingers. "I'll call my brother. Parker's probably off work by now. He can take you." I slide my cell out of my apron pocket, my finger hovering over his icon.

"Don't bother Parker. Call Griffin."

I press my lips together, not thrilled at the idea of calling King Asshole.

"How about Roman? He's good in emergencies."

"Poppy! For the love—don't bother your brothers. Call Griffin." Jess's body trembles beneath my hand, and I know I should get her to the hospital quickly. Still, I can't force myself to make the call.

"I don't have his number," I say weakly.

"Use my cell. It's in my pocket." She tips her head down at her apron, and I hold in my protest, fishing her cell out while the teenagers huddle at a nearby table, petting the fluffball of a puppy.

"Can't make the call. Your phone's locked."

"The code's 1-2-1-2."

I punch in the numbers, and Jess's phone flashes to life —a cute pic of her hugging Griffin at one of his baseball games pops onto the screen. He's even smiling.

"He's pinned at the top. 'Greatest nephew ever.'"

Of course Jess would have him labeled that way. Probably the only person in America who likes the guy.

I dial his number, holding my breath, my heart pounding.

"Hello?" Griffin's deep voice rumbles down the line, and

my stomach flip-flops. Why, I have no freaking idea. I'm probably in shock.

"Uh, hey, Griffin. It's Poppy. You know, from the inn," I stammer, my usual confidence gone.

"Why do you have my aunt's phone?"

"There's been an incident."

"What do you mean? Is she okay?" To his credit, he sounds worried.

"Probably," I say, drawing out the word.

"What's that mean—she either is or isn't okay. What the hell?" he growls.

Such an asshole. And this is exactly why I hadn't wanted to call him.

"I don't know, Griffin. I mean, she's alive."

"Fuck. What happened? She's breathing, right? Did she have a heart attack?"

"No, not a heart attack. And yes, she's breathing. Calm down. She tripped. Over a dog. May have broken her wrist. I wanted to call 911, but she insisted I call you instead. So here we are."

"I'm on my way. Don't move."

He disconnects without so much as a goodbye, leaving me fuming on the sidewalk.

Jess peers up at me expectantly. "He's coming, right?"

"Yes. He said don't move."

"Ridiculous. Of course I'm moving." Jess tries to stand, pain dancing across her face as she struggles to get up.

"Let me help." I grip her elbow on the uninjured side, supporting almost all her bodyweight as she slowly rises.

Maneuvering Jess into a chair at one of the café tables set up outside Scoops, I peer over at the teens. "Hey, can you sit with her for a second?" I wave the brunette over. "I'm going to grab some ice."

The girl nods and I dash inside. I search for a bag, then dispense ice from the drink machine into the plastic bag and tie it shut. I grab a few paper towels and jet back out to the patio.

"I got some ice. Here." I try to hand the ice to Jess, then realize she can't hold it with her injury. Setting the bag on the table, I gently lay Jess's hand across the ice, and she winces and bites her lip.

Shit. This is bad. Very bad.

"You need anything else, Ms. Poppy?" the brunette asks.

"No, thank you for your help. Be careful with that dog. He's a wild one."

Nathan nods and the teens take off. I turn my attention back to Jess.

"Is anything else hurt?" I do a quick scan, taking inventory of the patient. Both palms scraped and bloody, but her face is fine, and she still has all her teeth. Some might even consider this a win.

"Did you hit your head at all?" I ask, dabbing at her left palm with a paper towel.

Jess shakes her head. "No. I caught myself with my hands. For better or for worse."

"How are your knees?"

"Sore." She lifts her right leg, then her left, kicking them out and grimacing. "But at least I'm wearing jeans. I'll be all right."

"Oh, Jess." I rub her back, trying to comfort her—and myself.

"Aunt Jess!" Griffin's gruff voice rumbles behind me, and

I jump, my entire body stiffening. Even his voice has me on edge.

"Are you okay?" He rushes to her side, his navy eyes filled with worry. "Did you hit your head?"

Jess shakes her head gingerly, pressing her lips together in a tight line. Her face is pale, her breathing shallow.

"Her arm should be elevated." Griffin shoots me a death stare, and I stand taller, puffing my chest out.

"She's icing," I say, spitting out the words.

"I know. You can ice and elevate at the same time. Ever heard of RICE?"

I swallow hard over the lump in my throat, annoyance gripping me. "Yeah, I have, Mr. Pro Athlete. But her arm hurts and the wrist is all dangly. So I had her rest it on the table."

"That's terrible for swelling." Griffin shakes his head in disgust, and a hot swirl of irritation rolls through my stomach.

This guy.

"I did the best I could. I'm not a freaking EMT. Plus, there was a puppy, and teenagers, and your aunt's in pain . . ." I list off all the complicating circumstances as Griffin scowls at me.

"Uh-huh."

Clearly he thinks I'm useless.

"Kids? Think someone could drive me to the hospital now? Or are y'all gonna stand around and debate best emergency practices all day?" Jess glances from me to Griffin, her jaw tight.

Griffin shoots me one last look of disgust, then helps his aunt to her feet. She clutches her wrist against her chest, and Griffin wraps his muscled arm around his aunt's tiny waist, supporting her. Together they slowly limp out to the parking lot, and Griffin eases his aunt into the leather seat of his black Range Rover.

"I'll mind the shop, Jess," I say, waving at her. "Don't worry about a thing."

"Thanks, Poppy," Jess whispers, closing her eyes against the pain.

Griffin says nothing as he pushes past me, the bare skin of our arms brushing. To my chagrin, a hot flash of something shoots through me.

Probably aggravation.

He climbs into the car and glowers at me through the windshield, shaking his head in disgust. The vehicle roars to life, and Griffin peels out of the parking lot, leaving behind a swirl of dust.

My heart sinks as worry sets in. I don't think Jess is going to be scooping ice cream anytime soon. And as much as I love the place, there's no way I can take on a second full-time job.

Which leaves one person.

King Asshole, Griffin Carter. The world's grumpiest human.

UNSTOPPABLE IS AVAILABLE NOW!

ALSO BY KARA KENDRICK

SEAGLASS BEACH SERIES

Unmistakable

Unstoppable

Unrivaled

Undone

PEACHTREE GROVE SERIES

Rushing Into Love

Turning Up the Heat

Chasing After Forever

MAN OF THE MONTH CLUB: STARLIGHT BAY

New Year's Renovations

Love in Bloom

Stars & Sparks Forever

MAN OF THE MONTH CLUB: SYCAMORE MT.

Snowbody But You

MAN OF THE MONTH CLUB: CANDY CANE KEY

Reeling Him In

Lights, Camera, Christmas

HOLIDAY NOVELLAS

Christmas in Cayman

Mr. Right Under the Mistletoe

My Charming Holidate

Snowed In With the Scrooge

BILLIONAIRE SERIES

Charming the CEO

Flirt Like a (Fake) Groom

HEART OF A WOUNDED HERO SERIES

Soldier On: Heart of a Wounded Hero

WILD BROTHERS SERIES

Forever Wild

Find them all at www.karakendrick.com

Kara Kendrick writes fun and flirty small-town romance destined to give you all the feels. A reformed English major, she also has a master's in counseling and was an elementary school counselor in her pre-mom life.

She loves the beach, wine, and rock-hard abs, not necessarily in that order. When she's not dreaming up Happily Ever After's, you can find her chasing after her boy-girl twins, working out semi-hardish, or walking her adorable Shiba pups with her husband, who's not too bad himself.

Let's be friends! Sign up for the VIP newsletter and be the first to hear about upcoming releases, promos, and giveaways.

Find her at www.karakendrick.com

ACKNOWLEDGMENTS

Deepest gratitude to all the people involved in helping me put this book out into the world:

My alpha readers, my sisters and mom; Valentine Grinstead and the entire Valentine PR team; Nancy Smay at Evident Ink; Yvette D'Eon, proofreader; Sarah Sentz at Enchanting Romance Designs; and my ARC team and all the bookstagrammers and bloggers who took a chance on me.

Last, but never least, thank you to my home team—Lance, Luke, and Kinsey. I love you all and am so grateful for the opportunity to pursue my passion. Xoxo.